SLANTING TOWARDS THE SEA

A Novel

LIDIJA HILJE

SIMON & SCHUSTER
New York Amsterdam/Antwerp London
Toronto Sydney/Melbourne New Delhi

Simon & Schuster
1230 Avenue of the Americas
New York, NY 10020

First Simon & Schuster hardcover edition July 2025

Interior design by Wendy Blum

Manufactured in the United States of America

10 9 8 7 6 5 4 3 2 1

Library of Congress Cataloging-in-Publication Data
Names: Hilje, Lidija, author.
Title: Slanting towards the sea / a novel by Lidija Hilje.
Description: First Simon & Schuster hardcover edition. | New York : Simon & Schuster, 2025. | Identifiers: LCCN 2024041676 | ISBN 9781668078679 (hardcover) |
ISBN 9781668078686 (trade paperback) | ISBN 9781668078693 (ebook)
Subjects: LCGFT: Bildungsromans. | Romance fiction. | Novels.
Classification: LCC PR9170.C873 H55 2025 | DDC [Fic]--dc23
LC record available at https://lccn.loc.gov/2024041676

ISBN 978-1-6680-7867-9
ISBN 978-1-6680-7869-3 (ebook)

To Juraj, Jasna, and Iris.
You believed in me, and after a while, so did I.

PART ONE

VLAHO

ONE

SOMETIMES I STALK MY ex-husband.

I open his socials and sift through his photos. I know their sequence like I know the palm of my hand. Better even, because I can never memorize what my palm looks like, how the life line twirls into the love line, how it begins tight and uniform, but then turns ropey. It scares me to look at it, to trace the lines, to see where they might lead me in years to come. But I know Vlaho's photos by heart. They start with the most recent ones, his son, who turns six in a week, frowning at a drawing of imaginary monsters; and his daughter, an angelic creature just short of four, with the kind of wispy hair that slips through your hands like corn silk. His lovely wife, a blonde with an oversized nose but gorgeously high cheekbones, laughing into the air on their sailboat.

Once upon a time, he told me he didn't like blondes. He whispered it in my ear, brushing his fingers through my then long, lush hair. We'd been together for maybe a few months, and I'd asked him what would happen when we broke up. If he would find someone like me, or someone exactly the opposite. "That will never happen," he said. "Besides, I don't like blondes."

Lie.

Lie.

I always get stuck on a single photo. It's not a photo of their wedding day, or the birth of their first child. In fact, it's probably the least spectacular photo in the album. They're not even the main subject—whoever took it aimed for their daughter, in focus in the foreground. But behind, her mother is looking up as my ex-husband is passing her a glass of juice, and they share *the look*. The one I used to be on the receiving end of. The one that had long ago made me feel like I was a pink diamond carved straight out of a rock. And it's for her.

I remind myself that this was my decision. I let him go, willingly. But despite reason, the image spreads through me like ink in cold water.

—

The first thing I hear in the morning is the clanks of a spoon hitting the side of the džezva, the same coffeepot that's been in our family since I can remember, and then some. Always the same six clanks, in even succession, as my father prepares his Turkish coffee. The sound invades my sleep, and I want to scream, *Could we not do this for one fucking day?*

Six clanks, and then it takes a couple of minutes for the smell of coffee to crawl under my bedroom door. Despite my earlier grumbling, when the aroma reaches me, I'm grateful for it.

Lying sideways, I stare at the shelves and dressers lining the opposite wall. Every morning I tell myself I'll pack the rag dolls, the snow globe, the bright red-and-yellow babuška, and other knickknacks, and store them in the attic. They have no business cluttering a grown woman's room. But they've been there since my childhood, and on some level, I'm afraid that if I remove them something bad will happen. As if more bad things could happen to me. I'm thirty-eight, single, barely employed, and living with my dad. Sleeping in the same room I've been sleeping in since the day I was born, save for the ten years I shared a room with the love of my life.

Vlaho.

Of course I think of him, imagine where he is, what he's doing. It's a compulsion, like being unable to look away from a car wreck. If I still had a therapist, which I probably should, I'm sure she'd tell me I'm slightly obsessed, but I can't help it, filling my days with thoughts of him the same way I used to fill them with his presence. It's a source of pain that's somehow become pleasurable. The kind that reminds me I'm still alive.

I see him lying on his back, in his boxer shorts because he never wears pajamas, Marina's hand resting on his chest, caressing the place over the heart that once beat for me. Then Tena and Maro jump onto the covers like a baby avalanche, their chubby arms and legs flying every which way until they land in their parents' embrace, the smell of family rising as they lift the covers to tuck themselves in.

In that moment, despite everything, I'm happy for Vlaho. I am.

I focus on the babuška that my grandmother gave me a long time ago, its plump wooden figure, its bright reds and yellows, the typical Slavic ornamentations. In the eighties, before the Homeland War, almost every household in Croatia had one. Now, it's just a relic of old times, a forgotten little figurine on a shelf. It's just a doll, within a doll, within a doll, but there should be two more dolls inside her. I lost them, somewhere, sometime. Now, it's as hollow as I am, and we stare at each other in mutual understanding.

When I make my way into the living room, Dad is already watching the news. "You won't believe this, Ivona. Our finance minister wants to raise taxes again. The parasite."

"Good morning, Dad." I reach for the džezva and pour coffee into my cup, then add a few drops of almond milk. *Bogus milk*, my father calls it.

"Seriously, how much do they think we can take? We're the country with the highest tax rates in the world by now."

I sit at the dining room table instead of next to him on the couch. His ability to get worked up over events he has no control over can be strangling. Mom was different. She couldn't care less about politics. Instead, she obsessed over things on a smaller scale. A tear in the couch upholstery, a mark on the hardwood floor. She and Dad canceled each other out beautifully. She couldn't understand his fuming over state affairs any more than he could understand her boiling over household ones, their respective fires eventually dwindling to embers. Now that she's gone, there's nothing to stop him from rambling.

Dad turns the TV off, throws the remote on the couch. "Screw the lot of them. They're ruining this country, one tax at a time."

I focus on the garden outside, the bare branches of the hibiscus, and the always green, leafy top of an olive tree swaying in the salty bura wind.

Dad limps around the kitchen counter and pours himself another cup of coffee. It must be his third by now. Per his neurologist, he shouldn't be drinking more than two cups after his stroke, but I've stopped warning him. It falls on deaf ears.

"Where are you off to this morning?" he asks, taking stock of my outfit.

"The bank."

"Because of Lovorun?"

"Yeah, Lovorun." Funny how the taste of a word can change with circumstances. Lovorun used to melt on my tongue like honey, a magical place from my childhood where I spent school holidays with Baba—my maternal grandmother—eating grapes and blackberries straight from vines and brambles. A place where things grew, beautiful and strong. For a while after, it turned salty, like grief. Now it tastes like curdled milk.

A few years after Mom died, Dad made a unilateral decision to turn Baba's old estate into a heritage hotel. "This place has a soul. Tradition and history seep from it," he said, "and tourists will eat that right up." Never mind that the renovation ended up chipping away at the very soul of the place, no matter how careful Dad was to preserve it. Turning a humble peasant abode into a luxurious villa will do that to a place.

"I have a meeting with the personal banker. I'll try to get another extension on our loan," I say, even though I know the effort will be futile. Vlaho told me as much when we talked the other day, and he should know. He works at the bank and knows its policies inside and out.

Dad nods, his right hand trembling as he raises the cup to his mouth. He steadies it with his left. I avert my gaze, because I know it bothers him when I see all the ways his body is failing him.

Dad used to be a presence one couldn't ignore. One of those people who would change the energy in the room as soon as they entered. It wasn't his physical appearance that made people take notice of him, though he is tall. It was his confidence, the way he took up space, claimed it as his own. When he spoke, people listened with gazes of hypnotized cobras.

I didn't like that aspect of him, the attention he garnered, the opinions he bestowed with little consideration for those opposing ones, but there's always a subtle pang when I notice the absence of that power in him, when I see how his illness has reduced him to a man who can't even control his own shaking.

"Did I ever tell you how rampant insolvency was back in the nineties?" he asks.

Of course, he's told me, not once but so many times we could recite the story in unison. It's such an old people's trait, regurgitating past events to the same unfortunate listener over and over again, and he's not *that* old.

He launches into the familiar tale of how *those banking leeches* asked him to declare bankruptcy when he himself was owed money, how they had a bureaucratic, backward way of looking at business because Croatia had just emerged from communism, and many people and companies were struggling with switching to free market. Not Dad, though. He'd been made for capitalism, and when it finally came to Croatia, he took to it like a lung to breath.

Outside, a single ray of sunlight cuts through a cloud and falls on my hands, folded around the cup in front of me. My father's words blur into the background, and that distinct sense overcomes me, when I'm both inside my body and not there at all, like my skin is a mere husk and I am absent from where I should be inside it. And the thought that always follows: *How did I end up here?*

All those years ago, I blew out into the world like a dandelion seed looking for a place to take root, the horizon ahead immense and unlimited. And then, somehow, cruelly, I landed right back here, being preached to the same way I used to be preached to when I was eight.

"I went in for the meeting at the bank with an Excel sheet on a floppy disk." Dad's words sharpen in my ear. "None of them used a computer regularly and had no clue how to use Excel. I tossed the floppy onto the table and demanded they check out the numbers. It took them half an hour to find a person who could even open the damn document." He chuckles, and drones on about how he persuaded the bankers to give him time until he managed to pocket some money from his own debtors, how he convinced them that great things awaited his company, and how they were swayed, partly because of his imposing personality, and partly because of his, then unparalleled, computer skills.

He puts his cup in the sink. "Have you done your prep work?" he asks.

"Yeah." I run my finger around the rim of my cup, not meeting his eye. Any amount of prep work wouldn't help us now. *Times have changed,* I want to say. *There are policies and structures in place that weren't there in the early years of capitalism.* But I know better than to voice this. Everything was the hardest, toughest, the most difficult when my father had done it.

Which is not without merit, I guess. Dad kept his construction company alive through the war, when no one in their right mind was building anything. He kept it alive through all manner of financial crises that swell like tsunamis here in Croatia, huge waves sent from elsewhere that leave our economy floundering years after all the other countries have recovered. If he hadn't had a stroke, I'm sure he would've found a way to finish the Lovorun project too. Instead, the task of converting my baba's old estate into a hotel fell on me. Then the prices ballooned and the project stalled, and now we owe money, and simultaneously need money to finish the project so we can make money to return what we owe.

Dad walks by me on his way back to the living room where a new bout of television-watching is about to commence. He kisses the top of my head. "You're a smart girl. You'll do fine."

Only I'm not. And I won't.

—

Potential, people used to say to my parents—teachers, friends, strangers on the street. *The girl has so much potential.* I used to believe that great things awaited me. I was reading before I'd turned four. I could calculate before I was five. I recall this vividly because my brother paid me to do his math homework when he was in first grade. I would do the adding and subtracting in his workbook and he would pay me in small coins, gum, and Snoopy stickers. I'll never forget the day my mother found out about our ploy. Before she started yelling and sent me to my room, there was a moment when she looked at me as if she'd never seen me before.

I understood then that knowledge bore power. It made people take notice.

The story became a part of the family lore, something my mother complain-bragged about to the three neighbors she always had coffee with. And I became ravenous, hoarding words and their meanings, facts, and trivia. I wanted more of that power, more of that sense of self. Striving became a hook in my chest, always lurching me upward.

But I've learned the hard way that book smarts mean nothing here. Neither would street smarts, if I had any. It's a special blend that works here, the bureaucratic smarts, paired with a talent for wielding connections and bending rules. Better yet if it comes with a penis.

I can't remember the last time someone said I had potential. But the thing about potential is that it doesn't go away. If you fail to realize it, you don't simply lose it. Instead, it sediments inside you, like tar or asbestos, slowly releasing its poison.

TWO

ZAGREB WAS AT ITS coldest when Vlaho and I met, on a sleety January night, five months after I'd moved there to study biology. The millennium was still so young that its turn felt like a stake in the ground, a moment that would stabilize the world I'd so often seen slip off its axis.

I was only nineteen, yet the country I had been born in had dissolved, the state I was born in had fought its way back to independence through a bloody war. The currency had changed three times before I turned eleven: Yugoslav dinar to Croatian dinar to Croatian kuna. I had been born into socialism and autocracy and was now living under democracy and capitalism, or as close to it as the transitional economy could get.

On top of that had been the broader changes, those of the world in general. Phones having longer and longer cords, until they had no cords at all; computers being contraptions out of sci-fi movies, until they became cubes perched on our desks, getting thinner and sleeker over the years.

And then, of course, the constant changes at home. My parents operating between their three standard settings: togetherness, indifference, and vile fighting. I never knew when I walked through the door after school if I'd find them threatening divorce or laughing over coffee. Me too, morphing over time, from the dutiful daughter always trying to appease them to a rebellious one, until, after the yellow boot incident, I turned into a clammed shell, waiting out the last two years I had to live with them.

Those first months after I moved to Zagreb marked a new start. Everything smelled of freedom and possibility, my lungs stretching out for full inhales, my shoulders relaxing.

I went to classes, met new friends, and partied with the few old ones I had. I ate in student cafeterias redolent of fried chicken, kale, and pasta Bolognese, the smells alone making the space feel overcrowded. In these first months it was easy to believe that I could be a different person, one unaffected by my life back home.

But as the winter tightened its cold grip, the newness of Zagreb started to wear off, and I found myself longing for the stone-built walls of the hometown I'd been so eager to leave, for its blue skies and sea, for its familiar pulse and rhythm. The hole I thought I'd left back in Zadar revealed itself again, and between all the coffee dates and loud student parties and crowded college classes, I couldn't find a way to weld it shut.

That night in January, my best friend Tara talked me into going out. It was her birthday, and she was throwing a party in a bar in Zagreb's center. The bar was small and packed with students, Red Hot Chili Peppers pumping through the speakers as we poured cheap beer down our throats. My boyfriend was there, if that's what I could call him. He was someone I'd been seeing for a month, but I could already tell we weren't going anywhere. I sat next to him with eyes glazed over as he and his friend droned on about some video game.

Suddenly, "One Armed Scissor" cut straight through "Californication."

The room jolted to a halt. Everyone stopped talking and looked toward the stereo behind the counter, where a tall guy with dirty blond hair wearing a gray hoodie was pushing buttons, grinning at his own ingeniousness.

The familiar angry voice yelled the staccato verses through the speakers, reigniting the rebellious spirit of my high school days, and before I could control myself, I was on my feet pushing closer to the stereo. It was instinctual. I wasn't moving with a plan. There was just this need to come closer to the music, to be in the middle of it. Or perhaps to pull it inside me, to fill myself with it.

When I reached the bar, he was still there, the tall guy in the gray hoodie, his back turned to me. I lifted my voice at the refrain. His voice joined mine as he turned to face me.

The moment condensed.

His face was incandescent, as though it were lit from the inside. The room was otherwise dim and filled with cigarette smoke, and of course people don't glow, but that's how he looked to me. There was something in his eyes that offered itself to me. It was so immediate, so intense, it felt almost like voyeurism.

Like I could see more than I was supposed to, looking into his eyes.

Like I was allowing him to see more than he should, as he looked back into mine.

Time snapped back into place, and we were back in the room, at the party, people and music pulsing around us.

"You know At the Drive-In?" he leaned in to say in my ear over the loud riffs.

"Do I know them? I fucking love them," I said, the alcohol making me bolder than I was, the profane word moving something in me, him being so close.

"You may have just become my favorite girl," he said, his words dragging in a singsong accent. I couldn't pinpoint if it was from Herzegovina, or Neretva Valley, or Dubrovnik. All I could tell was that he was from the south, where tangerines and watermelons grow, where beaches are pebbled, and the sea is turquoise blue. "Vlaho." He offered me his hand.

Dubrovnik then, I thought, the name of its patron saint typically given only to boys from that region. We shook hands. Skin against skin, the grip lasting too long but not long enough. "Ivona."

"Do you want to get a beer or something?" he asked, a patch of red igniting his left cheek. I'd never seen someone blush in this particular way.

The song ended. A man, presumably the manager, because he had a pissed-off expression and was mumbling expletives, pushed his way behind Vlaho and turned Red Hot Chili Peppers back on.

"I'd love to," I said, glancing behind my back to the guy I was dating, who was draining his beer in dull light, and I regretted the words before I even spoke them, "But my boyfriend's waiting for me."

Vlaho's lips turned into a lopsided smile, the electricity of the moment frizzing away with my admission. I turned and walked over to my seat, Vlaho's stare trailing me like an echo following a sound.

—

That mistake would haunt me for days. I should've gone straight back to my boyfriend and told him we were over. But I waited until we were alone, later that night, to do it properly. To be considerate, polite. It was still in me, then, that need to appease, to not cause commotion or harm. Not that he cared. He just shrugged at my "I don't think this is working," and said, "Yeah, I agree."

That small courtesy might've cost me my only chance with Vlaho, and that's all I could think about a week later, as I was mustering the courage to send him a text. I deleted the fifteenth version of "hi, this is ivona, the at the drive-in girl from last friday," and before I could challenge myself, I wrote, "send transmission from the one-armed scissor," and hit send.

The same lyrics we'd sung together that night.

I envisioned the text traveling over Zagreb's rooftops, through its grimy smog, and into his dorm room. He lived in Cvjetno, Tara had told me when she'd gotten me his number; he was twenty, and studying economics. That was all the intel she'd had, given that he'd been a friend of her friend, not hers.

The minutes passed. I got up, circled my studio like a frantic cockroach in sudden light. I turned the TV on. The Mexican soap opera that always rolled after the noon news filled the room with heated words that made me feel less alone.

I picked up my Cellular and Molecular Biology textbook, but the words were too fuzzy to read. I checked my phone every twenty seconds even though I'd made sure I'd turned the sound on.

Minutes distended into hours.

I got creative, coming up with excuses for why he hadn't replied. Maybe I had the wrong number. Maybe he didn't have any money on his phone card. Maybe he was in class and he'd left his phone at the dorm. Maybe someone had stolen his phone.

And then the more agonizing reasons. Maybe he didn't remember me. Or maybe he did, and he was choosing not to respond. Maybe he read the text and laughed at my audacity, at the thought of the two of us together.

I went back to that night, dissecting it in detail. That moment, when it had all stilled between us, was it real?

I couldn't tell. I had no idea how that was supposed to feel.

Just a year before, in my senior year in high school, our Croatian teacher had tasked the class with writing an essay on the topic of Shakespeare's quote "To thine own self be true." The quote dug into the pain that had lain dormant throughout my teen years, that duality of life I had embraced—the armor offered up to the world, and the gentle essence it was meant to shield. How I'd learned to hide the soft parts of myself, like a crustacean. Writing that essay, I didn't censor myself. I couldn't bother to; it was our last high school essay, and the teacher only proofread them anyway. It was not like she would dwell on the meaning behind the words. But when she returned the notebooks to us, there was a note inside mine, right under the grade:

Feeling in constant pain is actually quite common, among highly intelligent people.

I laid the notebook on my thighs under the desk, ripped the page with her note off, and folded it in a small square to store in my wallet. I excused myself to go to the bathroom, holding my breath as my legs carried me down the corridor. After locking myself in a stall, I pressed my forehead against the cold tiles and struggled not to cry.

I had been hiding for so long I didn't believe it possible that someone could see me. But someone had. And that felt even worse.

But this had been a coincidental sighting. There was an intentionality to how Vlaho looked at me that night. A curiosity. So much of seeing is in that willingness to look. And, more importantly, it came paired with a feeling that under the careless, messy hair, and tattered Nirvana T-shirt, and love of angry music, he too was someone surprised, maybe even eager, to be seen.

But maybe he'd only been buzzed, and that's what had glinted in his eyes. Only now I couldn't unknow how much I wanted it, to find someone like him.

Three hours after hitting send, the hope grew so oppressive, so overwrought in my chest, that I let it out in low, humming sobs. I didn't cry for Vlaho, not really. I didn't know him yet. I cried because I was only nineteen and I was already so tired of carrying around that jagged grain of loneliness on the inside that always threatened to cut me if I made a wrong turn. I cried because I had all this love inside me, and it had nowhere to go.

The text sounded. "what do you think it even means?"

Then, another one. "i mean, to send a transmission from a one-armed scissor. what is a one-armed scissor anyway? how does it differ from a two-armed scissor?"

I stared at the message through wet eyes. Then I typed, fingers still trembling, "i don't think even at the drive in know what it means. but still, in a weird way, it makes sense, right?"

"i like the part about dissecting a trillion sighs," he wrote.

"and writing to remember," I wrote back.

The phone started ringing then, his name filling the screen. I turned the TV off, cleared my throat. "Hi."

"Hey," he said, and I could see him smiling, pulling fingers through his hair, the way he'd done that night. "I thought this would be easier. Given that each text costs twenty lipa and there are a lot of lines in that song."

"Smart thinking. True economist talking."

He laughed. "You've done your research, I see. I'm at a disadvantage."

"That's a bummer," I said. "That you didn't ask about me."

"Not because I didn't want to know. But I have this policy of not messing with girls who are . . . spoken for."

"Well . . . not anymore."

A beat of electrifying silence. "Want to grab a cup of coffee?" he asked, his words swaying in his southern accent. Relief coursed through me, the first layer of nacre coating that grain of loneliness inside me, smoothing its barbed edges.

THREE

I PARK ACROSS THE street from the bank's main entrance and stare at the large, glass-windowed building as if it's about to swallow me whole. Maybe it is. My thumb rubs the edge of the yellow folder containing all the relevant documents for today's meeting: the original mortgage paperwork, the paperwork on the loan extension, expiring next month. The state of our hefty debt, with zero means to pay it back.

Dad has always been a person of grandiose ambitions, a lover of all things luxurious and extravagant. Soon after Mom died, he tracked Baba's distant cousins, bought them out, and turned Lovorun into a huge building site. It was his way of dealing with Mom's death, I guess, his homage to her. Or maybe it was the fact that her death had reminded him of his own mortality, that his time on Earth was limited too, and if he ever wanted to do something grand, now would be the time. If he restored the ruins and made a heritage hotel out of them, he would've left his mark on the world. His life wouldn't have been for nothing.

I understood where he was coming from.

Lovorun was my grief project too.

In my darkest hour, the olive grove there offered me a way to put one foot in front of the other, even while I was losing Vlaho, even as my whole future was slipping through my fingers bit by bit, like grains of fine sand.

But the documents in my hand are a sure sign we're losing it all.

My phone dings on the passenger seat with Vlaho's message. "ready for the meeting?"

"as ready as i'll ever be," I text back.

"meet you outside the personal banker's office."

I look up at the building, focusing on the place where I know Vlaho's office is, and wonder if he's looking out the window. He works in internal audit and has nothing to do with mortgage handling, but I was relieved when he offered to accompany me to the meeting. I may be out of my depth, but at least he'll be there to help.

At least I'll get to see him today.

I turn the collar of my raincoat up before I step outside the car and into the February cold, and hurry to the bank entrance, where the security guard greets me with a knowing nod. It's the same guard who's been monitoring the entrance since Vlaho got a job here when we moved to Zadar after graduation. I worked as a substitute teacher in the nearby elementary school for a brief period, and Vlaho and I met for lunch in the bank's cafeteria between my morning and afternoon shifts. It was the happiest we ever were in Zadar.

I wonder how much of our story the guard knows. If he's aware that we're divorced now. If Marina had to explain things the first time she came to visit Vlaho at work. Does she ever come? Do they have lunch together like we used to? Neither of them has ever mentioned it, and of course, I've never asked.

As I enter the main building through a revolving door, the dry air gives me the urge to cough. I wave to the receptionist behind the counter, an older lady whose grandkids we always talked about. They'll be finishing elementary school by now. She opens her mouth to say something, probably to kindle some sort of conversation—we haven't seen each other in so long—but I hurry toward the elevator, relieved that it opens as soon as I press the button. Once I'm in, I give her an apologetic shrug. I can't bear asking her about her grandkids anymore, not when the questions on her side have long subsided. *When will you have kids, Mrs. Oberan?* she'd ask. *You and your husband would make such great parents.*

I'm not Mrs. Oberan anymore, but I take comfort in the fact that Vlaho is the world's most wonderful dad. It's the kind of comfort, though, that pricks at the back of my eyes.

—

The personal banker's office is on the second floor. As the elevator doors slide apart, Vlaho appears behind them, standing in the shaft of morning light. The scene looks almost like a painting, a huge weeping fig plant towering above him, the same size as the one he gave me on our one-month anniversary has grown to. I had to move it outside my room a couple of years ago, into the high-ceiling hallway where it'll have room to continue to grow. The irony that it's still growing when our love has long withered is not lost on me.

I push myself against the elevator wall and head out.

"Hey." Vlaho kisses my cheek. He smells of mornings, the wisp of a piney aftershave and mint toothpaste, and underneath, the familiar, powdery scent of his skin. We walk side by side through the corridor toward the offices in the back, our footsteps muffled by the gray carpet that's worn in the middle, marking the people's favorite trajectory on it.

"It'll be fine," Vlaho says, sensing my dismay as he always does. He's just saying that to make me feel better. Or maybe he's referring to the grand scheme of things, where, yes, all will be fine, even if you lose everything except, perhaps, your life and health.

This I believe. The worst already happened when I let him go, and I'm still alive. Still drinking coffee in the morning, brushing my teeth and my hair, cooking lunch, then eating it. Food still gets digested, broken into molecules that get into my bloodstream, then travel where they need to, in order to become building blocks for new cells. This is the way life goes on for me. On a cellular level. "I know," I say.

When we exit the office half an hour later, I'm laden with sweat. We don't talk on our way back to the elevator. The personal banker, a beautiful young woman with brown hair gathered in a high ponytail, the kind of woman who would've made me all kinds of insecure if I were still with Vlaho, didn't tell us anything we didn't already know. The loan cannot be extended, the first payment is due next month, and if we forgo paying, we will have defaulted on the debt, and the bank will have to consider means of forced collection.

My gut twists into knots. How can I go home and give this news to my father, who expected me to perform a miracle, the way he had all those years ago with his floppy disk? A father who's ill and powerless to do anything but watch me ruin it all? It doesn't matter that the circumstances have changed since he turned the leadership of the company over to me when he got sick, or that this downfall was in motion long before I took charge. None of it matters. All that matters is that I've failed again.

"Ivona?" Vlaho touches my hand. "Talk to me."

I stop and turn to him. We're in the middle of the dark corridor and the lack of light softens his face. It makes it easier for me to open up. "I have no idea what to do. There won't be enough money no matter what I do. If the bank isn't willing to give us another extension—"

He leans against the gray panel wall behind him, and I do the same on my side. "I hate to say this but . . . maybe you'll have to sell. That way you'll at least have control over the terms and price." He looks down for an instant then back into my eyes. "I'm sorry, I know how much Lovorun means to you." His voice is supple and low. If I closed my eyes, I could imagine us like we were for years, huddling together in our bed at night, talking.

"Dad would never agree to sell." Sometimes it seems like pulling this project off is the only thing keeping him alive.

"I know, but this isn't about your dad anymore." Vlaho's tone is soft but pointed, the kind he used when he wanted to tell me something without putting it into words. It's these small moments of recognition—a specific inflection of his voice, a particular look on his face, a small gesture no one else might notice—that I live for. Why I swirl in his orbit even at the cost of watching him make a life with someone else.

I reach to squeeze his arm, a touch that will linger on my fingertips for hours. "Thank you for going in with me."

He gives me that look that feels like an intake of breath. An expectation, a wanting. As if his fingers, resting at his sides, are removing a strand of hair off my face. Stroking my cheek.

But a beat longer and the mirage is over. We're back to ourselves, the way we've been for the last nine years. Most of the time, I'm convinced he doesn't even remember the days when we were together. But in moments like this, when silence swallows our words, I wonder.

"It'll be fine." I echo his own words back to him and start walking again. He follows, reluctant.

"Oh yeah," he says, his words dragging slower than his feet. "Before you go. Marina asked if you'll come over for Maro's birthday. It's next Saturday. Nothing fancy, mostly family and some friends. Maro asked if you'd come too."

"Because the little scoundrel knows I buy the best presents," I say to hide how I really feel. Not because it pains me to be in their home, I've grown used to it over time. Not even because Marina's mother will be there, watching me like some sort of tempest, for what could the single ex-wife of her son-in-law be other than an obvious threat to her daughter's marriage?

I dread it because Vlaho's mother will be there. Frana never misses a birthday, christening, or any of her grandchildren's milestones now that she has them. She is the only one who really makes me uncomfortable. The only person who knows the truth behind why I left Vlaho. The only person, besides myself, who I have to blame for it, even though all she had given was a nudge, and the decision was mine, all mine.

"Sure, I'll be there. Just let me know the time," I say, and let the elevator doors squeeze out the image of the man I love.

FOUR

WHILE WE WERE TOGETHER, Vlaho and I joked that we had more anniversaries than Croatia has islands. There was the day we'd met, in that bar on Tara's birthday. There was the day I first texted him, and he asked me out on a date. Then, the date itself, which took place ten days after we first agreed to see each other, because just before we were supposed to go out, Vlaho got the flu.

He basted in a fever for four days, and for the following five, he was too sick and weak to go out. His roommate had gone to stay with friends, so that Vlaho's mother could come take care of him. She had traveled from Cavtat, the small town near Dubrovnik where Vlaho was from. It must have taken her twelve hours to get to Zagreb by bus, because the construction of the A1 highway had only begun.

"She's cooking chicken broth on the hot plate," he messaged me on the third day, in the short intermezzo when the ibuprofen knocked his fever down. "I can barely warm up milk on that thing."

I hadn't been to his dorm room, but I'd been to my friends' plenty of times. Cvjetno was considered one of the better dorms, but it was still dilapidated. Built decades ago, renovated only once since. The furniture dangled off walls, half-ruined by neglect and reckless partying. Each room had two beds with barely half a meter of space between them, two desks, and a small entry hallway with a closet on each side, a tiny sink with a single cupboard, and a counter where you could put a hot plate, providing you had one. Most of the students ate in the cafeteria downstairs anyway.

I couldn't imagine a middle-aged woman sleeping in such a room, in such a bed, and it said something about his mother that she was willing to do that to nurse her son back to health.

Her being there made me jealous. I wanted to be the one on the adjacent bed in his room, running a damp cloth over his forehead, tucking him in, reaching over the void between our beds to hold his hand.

I also wanted to be the one with such a mother.

—

We could never agree, later on, which one of those ten days marked the actual beginning of our relationship. It might've been the day when he said he saw my face every time he closed his eyes. Or the day I told him that not being able to see him was a whole new brand of loneliness. Or the day he said, after a smattering of late-night texts about all the things big and small (your favorite color? the least favorite subject in high school? the one thing you wish you could change in the world?), that I felt as familiar and essential to him as the sea.

Those ten days, the suspense of the wait was so delectable and agonizing, a constant current moving things around in my bloodstream, the whole body a pot of water held over low heat.

I gathered information about him like I'd once hoarded trivia. He was nearly tone-deaf, but he played the electric guitar when no one was around to listen. He loved the sea, unsurprising for a Dalmatian boy. He'd collected mollusks and seashells when he was a child, much like I'd collected pine nuts, acorns, and leaves of all shapes and sizes around Lovorun. He wanted to learn how to sail, but his dad never got around to teaching him. His dad was a first mate on a large tanker ship, sailing the high seas six months a year. When he was home, he couldn't be bothered to do anything sea-related, happy to be land-bound. But one time, his dad skippered a catamaran from Cavtat to Vis and took Vlaho with him. They slept in sleeping bags on the prow instead of in the cabins, and Vlaho said he would never forget the moonlit outline of the island ahead, the expansiveness of that night sky that seemed both unreachable and also like something he could absorb. How he felt insignificantly small, yet important because he was a part of something so much bigger than him, impossible to fathom.

"Yes," I said, remembering the times I spent in my baba's olive grove when I was a child, bura cold on my cheeks, the sea foaming in the distance like a rabid beast, the sharp olive leaves scraping against my face as I reached for the fruits. That sense of being one with nature, of existence itself, in its purest form.

And then I thought of the first time I saw him, his eyes. "I know exactly what you mean."

Sometimes, he'd wait for his mom to fall asleep before texting, because she kept reprimanding him for being on the phone and not resting enough. I wanted him to rest too, but I was too greedy to break off communication, starved for one more message, one more glimpse into who he was and all the ways we might fit together.

Deep into the night, one of us would lose the battle to sleep, and doze off. I would wake up to sunlight filtering through my window, still in my sweatshirt, my neck craned against my bedpost at an unnatural angle. I'd reread his words from the previous night and smile so hard my cheeks twitched, a delicious ache pulsing in my heart.

And so, we were together before we ever saw each other after that first call. Together, before we finally met on Zagreb's main square, under the street clock, his face drawn from the illness but as beautiful as I'd remembered it from that dim bar on the night of Tara's party. Together, before we walked up the narrow stairs along the park that led to the Upper Town, the trees around us bare, the damp smell of decaying leaves earthy and grounding, the hush of the upcoming snow thick in the air. That tender awkwardness of finally occupying the same space, our bodies not yet familiar with each other the way our minds already were.

We stopped under Lotrščak Tower, where we could take in the whole of Zagreb laid out before us, lights flickering as far as the eye could see.

"Do you have trouble orienting yourself in Zagreb?" I asked, looking toward the Lower Town. Apart from the hill we were on, Zagreb was flat, and when you stood somewhere in the street surrounded by buildings, you had no way of knowing which side of the world you were facing. I got lost more than once because I couldn't tell where the north was.

"Sometimes," he said. "It's becoming easier with time."

"This is the only place where I can find my bearings. This hill," I said. "It's so much easier on the coast." We were both from the Dalmatia region, my town marking its northernmost part, his on the far south of it.

"Yeah," he said. "Back home, all things slant towards the sea."

He took my hands and rubbed them between his palms.

"Your hands are cold," he said as if this had surprised him, and then he leaned in to kiss me. And when he did, something inside me reoriented itself, my world softly tipping into his direction, as if he himself were the sea.

FIVE

THE MORNING AFTER THE disastrous bank meeting, I go to the kitchen to dish out Dad's medications into his pill organizer. It has compartments for five parts of each day, seven days a week, and it's still not enough. There are some pills I have to place in the same cube, even though one precedes the other and should be taken in chronological order. A mundane task, this, but it always makes me feel melancholy, the fact that Dad needs so many pills to make it through the day.

The weather has turned to jugo, the warm and wet southern wind that brings rain and joint pains and bad moods. On days like this, Dad's right side hurts more, the pain distracting him from anything outside himself, and for once, I'm thankful for it. It's doing a wonderful job of making him forget about the meeting.

The volume on the TV is too loud. More news about corrupt politicians that no one ever does anything about. This whole society has turned apathetic. Half of our government ends up imprisoned each year, and they just replenish new members from the same unending pool of incompetent, corrupt fools. Unbelievably, there's more of them to pick and choose from, while there's fewer of us living here. I wish the journalists would just stop wasting our time reporting about it.

Dad shuffles into the kitchen. "It's your mom's birthday tomorrow," he says over the voice of the reporter. "We should buy flowers and lamps for her grave."

By we, he means me. They took away his driver's license after his stroke.

"I'll buy flowers, but I won't buy a lamp."

"Why not?"

I stop popping pills from the foil and give him the *we've been here before* look. "Plastic. Why do we keep honoring our dead by polluting the Earth that we're supposed to be saving for our children?"

He pours himself a cup of coffee. "What do you care? You don't have any children."

His words a precise jab.

He's not mean on purpose; he's stating a mere fact. He's always been like this, not entirely aware of the emotional impact his words can have on others, so I take it in stride. It's better than talking about the bank. He wouldn't be able to understand my failure, or to accept it. My dad lifted himself, single-handedly, from unimaginable poverty, and he would not survive tumbling back down into it. And even if the failure of the Lovorun project wouldn't exactly impoverish us, I know this is how he would feel.

Once, when I was twelve, he took me to see the place where his mother had raised him. His father had died when he was a baby, the youngest of four boys. Their home was a small rectangular single-story building made from stone and concrete, with an asbestos roof, thick walls, and a ceiling so low even I had to walk inside with my back and knees bent. On the inside was only one room, and even though it was empty at the time, Dad showed me where the beds had once been, where they'd stoked fire in the hearth, where he'd done his homework under candlelight. Dad was born a few years after World War II, and the electricity hadn't come yet to this village, nor had the running water. His family had so little that once his mother had to borrow a bag of potatoes and turnips, and that's all he and his three brothers ate for a month.

When he was ten, a neighbor gifted him a rabbit for his birthday. Dad kept that rabbit in an improvised cage, and every morning, he got up before school and walked for kilometers to get it fresh grass and clover from the fields surrounding the village. The rabbit was plump, with shiny brown fur and glistening eyes, and my dad treasured it like a pet, a toy, and a friend all at once. But one day, he came home from school to the smell of meat cooking, which startled him because they rarely had meat. Sometimes, his mother would get small dried bits at the butcher's, but when eight hungry hands reached for it, she reminded them that meat was not for eating, it was to give the greens some schmeck. But this time, the scent was overpowering, gamey, doused in the aroma of red wine, and he didn't have to see the empty cage or his rabbit's skin drying on the laundry line to know. He ran away from home, didn't come back until it got too cold to stay out in his paper-thin clothes, the mended hand-me-downs worn almost to shreds by his three older brothers. Afterward, he didn't speak to his mother for days.

This, he told me, is what poverty does. It takes away even what you think is inherent to a human being. Dignity. Pride.

On that day, my father swore he wouldn't be poor when he grew up, and that's a promise he kept. But no matter how much he'd earned, how much he'd accumulated, there was always this need for more. Not because he was greedy; my dad is a very generous man. But because that poverty is still catching up with him, threatening that if he doesn't make more, more, more, it will come and reduce him to what he'd been that long-ago day.

He is over seventy now, but in his core—I can see this clearly as he frowns at the TV news rolling by—he is still a ten-year-old boy getting home to the smell of rabbit stew. And the part that kills me is that he will die, still being that boy.

SIX

MY MOM ALWAYS SAID, "The bigger the love, the bigger the fights." She'd tell me this while making pancakes or an apple pie, or kneading pizza dough, a treat she'd make for Saša and me after a particularly volatile fight she'd had with Dad. Their fights were scary—the aggressive tones and shouting, sharp accusations, the meanness, verging on physical and only miraculously never crossing that line—but I loved these moments of quiet after the storm when Mom would be attentive to me, when she would allow me to get my hands into the flour while she talked contemplatively about life's truths. "It's just the way of things, Ivona," she'd say. "When two people love each other, they care a lot, and so they fight loudly. It wouldn't be good if we didn't care, now, would it?"

She and Dad had met as students in 1971, amid the Croatian Spring and student protests against Yugoslav unitarism, and the times were so combustible that it was impossible to tell their passion for the movement from their passion for each other. It was this passion, Mom claimed, that kept them together still. But what seemed to bind them even more was the never-ending seesaw of upper hands shifting between them, keeping them in tight balance.

I was only a child, so I was inclined to believe everything my mother said. That love was this wild, volatile thing that had the power to both nourish and scar. But at the same time, I didn't want to believe it. In my childish imagination, I envisioned a different kind of love, one that was gentle and kind. Words like *thank you* and *bless you*, and *what is it you need*, its main discourse. A space to rest, reposeful and calm with someone lying right there beside me, equally serene. Someone who sees inside me in a way that makes me translucent; who lets me see inside them too, all the way down to their deepest, most intimate core. Someone who yields to me, surrenders into my hands, while also offering themselves as a cocoon in return. That was the image I conjured as I sat in my room while my parents fought, as I tried to ignore their harsh words, the sound of glass shattering.

—

Hunkering down. This phrase always comes to me when I think of those early days with Vlaho. By the time summer exams came around, he had practically moved in with me. Zagreb's asphalt broiled, a ribbon of wavy heat shimmering above the empty streets. His dorm didn't have air-conditioning, and neither did my studio, but mine at least had windows on opposite walls that could create a draft.

His toothbrush joined mine in the cup, his deodorant took shelter in my bathroom cabinet. His clothes hung off chairs, the backside of the sofa, me. I loved his clothes, the touch of them, the smell, frayed edges, but I loved seeing him shirtless even more. He had the body of an athlete, lean and wiry, though he was a bit underweight, and I kept pressing him to eat more. "You're just like my mother," he'd laugh when I'd shovel another portion of my inexpertly cooked pasta with šalša onto his plate.

We studied in bed together, in our underwear, sticky with sweat, spraying water over ourselves to cool off. He was cramming for microeconomics and I studied microbiology, so we threw words at each other, laughing. "Plasmid," I said, and he retorted with "monopsony." "Quorum sensing," I taunted, and he threw an "isoquant" my way. "Conjugation," I said, and instead of retorting, he kissed me, and we were back to making love. We were always making love back then. His presence in my bed made me feel a little drunk and constantly heavy with want. It was more than just physical desire, this stream of need coming from the pit of my gut. A need that, once it had revealed itself, felt so familiar, like it had always been there, I just hadn't been aware of it. *More of this. More of this!* it demanded.

Early into our relationship—it may have been late March or the beginning of April—Vlaho and I were in Cvjetni trg having coffee. Right at noon, a loud explosion reverberated over our heads, sending the pigeons aflight and both of us cowering under the table. It was only the Grički cannon going off, a cultural testament to events from centuries ago when one such blast saved Zagreb from the Ottoman invaders.

We knew about the cannon, of course we did, and that it went off every day at noon. We had learned about it at school, it was a well-known fact. But still, every time I found myself in Zagreb's center when it detonated, my body ran for cover long before my mind could remind me I was safe.

People sitting near us smiled as we straightened ourselves up. *Dalmatians*, I could almost hear them think. Or perhaps, *Provincials*. Zagreb hadn't been bombed nearly as much as either my or Vlaho's hometown, so people here didn't have the same instinctual response.

Vlaho laughed, brushing off our reaction as if it were dust lying atop his arms, and in that whimsical move I recognized the echo of the same terror that had lurched through me. I thought of my mother's words about love, and my childhood dream about what it could be, and I felt myself on the cusp of something. It would've been so easy, expected even, to laugh the insignificant incident off, and move on. But a fear gnawed at me, that if we did this, if each time we talked we allowed even a dust mote of dishonesty to fall between us, it would eventually gather.

More than losing Vlaho, I was beginning to realize, I was afraid of not being myself with him.

"I hate the cannon," I said. "I hate everything it reminds me of, all the memories it stirs up, and that I can't stop my reaction when it goes off." I said it with such urgency that the air between us trembled. I wasn't talking about the cannon, not really. I was communicating something deeper, presenting him with an offering of almost radical honesty, a chance to be exactly who we are with each other.

He turned serious, then nodded, slowly. "Me too," he said.

Over the course of the following months, I waited for the inevitable. For him to lose interest, to become tired of me. To become overwhelmed with this constant hunger I had for his closeness, for keeping such sharp focus on us. Not letting one thing slip away from me, wanting to get every detail between us just right.

"You will leave me," I would cry to him at night. "You will grow tired of me." There was never a person in my life who hadn't. It was that I thought too much, saw everything myopically. It was that I felt too much. It was that I dissected my surroundings the way no one else did. *Do you have to make such a big deal out of everything?* they said. *Do you have to be so sensitive?* But I couldn't find a way to be something other than what I was. I could only hide it. "You will leave."

Vlaho would hear me out, always a smirk on his face, and say, "But where would I go? You're my person."

Our apartment was a lair, and we lay low in it, allowing the world to rage above us, to come and go as it pleased. Preening, grooming, curling up next to one another, needing each other's body heat like we'd never been warm before.

He never left the apartment unless he had to, and when he did, he left me Post-it notes lying around the house. *You look so beautiful while you sleep*, stuck to his pillow. *You're in the notes of every song I hear*, on the kitchen table, next to a fresh pot of coffee. *I feel you all the time, in my lungs, in between breaths*, on the mirror in our bathroom, next to the reflection of my smiling face.

And from this comfort, this contentment, a new fear was born—of losing the love that I never thought I'd find to begin with.

Some nights, I would climb on top of him as he was reading, holding him so tight he would gasp. Wishing we could meld together, that I could crawl under his skin and stay there. "What is it?" he'd ask, but I couldn't speak, devastated that I would never get close enough to him, that there would always be the skin, the bones, the substance of flesh between us. We would never be one body, there would always be this fear of us breaking into two.

That's when the dreams started.

In those dreams, Vlaho stood with his back to me, and no matter what I did, I couldn't get him to acknowledge me, to look me in the eye. His face, stoic and cold, always angled away, looking out into the distance, anywhere except at me. I would call to him, repeating his name with the sort of desperation that tore my chest apart. Pleading, begging, but no words would come out. My legs were leaden, glued to the ground, unable to move me in front of him, to force him to see me, to hold him to me.

I would wake up from these dreams with a palpitating heart and pain in my stomach so intense it felt like I'd been gutted. Vlaho would sleep beside me, oblivious as I stared at him in the dark, hurt and resentful, even though I knew he had done nothing but sleep. It terrified me that he had such power over me, the power to annihilate me if he so chose. Sometimes, he'd wake up to find me looking at him with dismayed, wild eyes. He'd reach for me, but I'd pull away, curl into myself, caught up in the utter horror of losing him. In those moments, my mother's words would come to me like a whisper in the night. *The bigger the love, the bigger the fights.* Only I wasn't fighting Vlaho. I was battling myself.

SEVEN

VLAHO AND MARINA'S APARTMENT is on the fourth floor of one of the so-called TIZ buildings, built on the former textile factory lot near the town's center. Their building is shaped like a long sail sprawling along the ground. It's only fitting, given that Marina is all about the sea: a scuba diving instructor, a spear fisherman, a sailor, a surfer. It's as if her mother had known this would be the case when she decided on her name, or maybe Marina lived up to the name she'd been given.

I climb the stairs instead of taking the elevator because I need the extra time to gather myself before entering their home, filled with cheer and children. Such a vast difference from where I live with my dad, the land of the scowling and perpetually disgruntled.

On the third-floor landing, I slow my pace further. The apartment Vlaho and I lived in when we moved back to Zadar after graduation was different from where we each live now. It was a tiny one-bedroom ground-floor rental in the suburb. Our room could barely fit a queen-sized bed, two nightstands, and a closet, but we managed to squeeze in his Jackson guitar, an amplifier, and a stack of my books, sans bookshelf. Back then, we used to complain about needing a bigger room, with a larger bed, but really, we were happy to be forced into close proximity. We'd fall asleep in the middle of the mattress, concave from the weight of our embraced bodies. We were so happy there, until we weren't.

I resume my climb and stop at the door that says "Oberan." It's like standing outside my own door. After we'd divorced, I took back my maiden name, figured it would be simpler for Vlaho, for when he decided to start a family with someone else. But going back to my maiden name felt like trying to wriggle myself into my old high school jeans. It didn't fit anymore, and suddenly I was a stranger to all my identities.

I press the buzzer.

Marina opens the door, towering over me with a wide smile. "Hey, lovely." She gives me a hug before she ushers me inside. "Come on in, you're missing all the fun. Let me take your coat."

The thing about Marina is that she makes it nearly impossible for me to be jealous. She's one of those people who have only one face to offer to the world. If people like it, fine. If they don't, fine as well. With her, there are no hidden agendas, no ulterior motives. She shares her opinions unaffectedly and plainly, and while she is respectful of others, she doesn't seem to need other people's appreciation or respect in return. So instead of being envious, I always end up trying to emulate her attitude.

I follow her through the hallway and into the living room filled with blue balloons and kids scurrying around. The adults are crowding around the kitchen island at the center of the open floor plan. The children don't take notice of me, but a few grown-ups sure do. Both Vlaho's and Marina's mothers glare at me from across the room, as if they expect me to throw a temper tantrum or pick a catfight with Marina. Instead of focusing on them, I search the room for Maro and notice him using the couch as a trampoline.

"Hey, birthday boy!" I say.

"Hey, Aunt Ivona," he says, still moving up and down as if his ankles were made of springs. Maro is always jumping, or running, or tumbling. His energy is exhaustless, though he often wears out everyone around him.

I wave my present in front of him. "This is for you."

He leaps off the couch and grabs the gift. A part of me wishes he'd hug me the way he sometimes does when he's sleepy or in the mood for snuggling, to show the audience that I'm not here by accident. I know this kid. I love this kid. But he's candy-fueled, and he just grabs the present out of my hands and rips the paper off. "Pirate ship Legos!" he screams. "Yay!"

Then he's back to his mischief on the couch, and I'm all alone, straightening up before the gun squad on the other side of the room. They look at me with their condemning eyes, no doubt wondering how Marina's instincts have failed to such an epic degree when she's allowing me into her home like this.

I approach Vlaho's mother first. We were family, after all, until we weren't. Her lips are colorless, pinched in a tight smile. "Hi, Aunt Frana," I say, and we kiss each other's cheeks. She gives me a limp hug, releasing me quickly.

"Hi, Ivona. Didn't expect to see you here."

She says this every time. It's not that she doesn't expect me here, it's that she wishes I weren't. We share a secret, Frana and I. She is the only person who knows the real reason why I left Vlaho all those years ago, the truth not even Vlaho knows, and I'm the only one who knows the role she played in it. We're each other's liability, and even though we're both best served not talking about it, we act as if the other one is a loaded gun about to go off.

The front door opens. Vlaho's footsteps fill the hallway. "Here we go, more juice and snacks," he says as he enters the living room, then stops. His gaze travels over the crowd, clearly trying to discern what caused the shift in the atmosphere, until it lands on me. *Ah.* He kicks his lips up in what's meant to be an easy, comfortable smile, but I see the small patch of red igniting high on his cheek. It always fires up when he's feeling insecure.

In moments like this, I ask myself, Why we do this? Why do Marina, Vlaho, and I subject ourselves to this discomfort and judgment? But the answer is always fast and clear—because my being here is the truth of our relationship. Because on ordinary days I'm often the only guest in their home, and we sit at their table or on their carpet talking, and Tena lies in my arms, heavy and half-asleep, rolling a strand of my hair around her finger, her cheek glued to my chest with baby sweat. This is the truth, and none of us is willing to deny it just to make someone else feel more comfortable.

We start the well-trained dance we've perfected over time. Marina, taking every chance to pat my shoulder, or squeeze my arm to show she is okay with me being here. Vlaho, extra engrossed in conversations, keeping things running smoothly. Me, smiling a bit too openly, keeping my voice peppy, averting my eyes whenever they land on him, the love of my life who now belongs to someone else.

But it's tiring, and the first chance I get, I take my beer by the neck and head out to the balcony where the smokers gather. I don't smoke, but the place offers a temporary reprieve, people unwilling to subject themselves to the winter air for longer than it takes to finish a cigarette.

Out there, a couple of mothers complain about their kids' eating habits.

"Which one is yours?" the shorter woman with the pixie haircut asks me, nodding toward the inside of the apartment.

I follow her gaze and realize she means kids. "Oh! None of them." I try to state this as a mere fact, but each time I speak some version of this truth, an essential, pivotal part of me gets chipped away. "I'm Tena's godmother, though." I say this because it's easier to explain than being Vlaho's ex-wife.

"Great," the woman says, then blows soft smoke sideways, and by the way her eyelids drop a millimeter, I know she's lost interest. I can't be included in her mom talks, so why bother with me?

"Want one?" She flicks a pack of cigarettes open and holds it to me.

"No, thanks. I just came out for some air."

"And quiet," the other woman adds. "Just listening to all that rumble . . . " She doesn't finish.

The two of them go on to discuss the best onesies for babies, and which brands use organic cotton, and if buying organic cotton is worth the extra price. After a while, they go in, but I notice it only when they're gone. The night air is whetted, it scrapes against the inside of my nose. The sallow lights delineating the old town peninsula shimmer ahead, dampened by the February mist.

The town is always so vacant in the evenings this time of year, when tourists are gone. When we moved back from Zagreb, Vlaho and I spent countless afternoons strolling the empty streets, fingertips warmed and charcoaled by roasted chestnuts we'd buy from a vendor near the town bridge. The memory makes me languid, sleepy.

"You all right out here?" Vlaho peers in from behind the glass door, then joins me on the balcony. He only has a short-sleeved T-shirt on, and I resist the urge to tell him to grab a jacket. He doesn't mind the cold, I remind myself, his body always so warm, as if the molten core of the Earth itself purls beneath his skin.

"Actually, I have to leave early. Dad is . . . He has—" I stop talking. He knows my leaving has nothing to do with Dad. "I need to pack. I'm leaving in a few days. There's an olive oil fair I'm attending, the Olive Oil Manifestation, in Split." It's the first thing I can think of to give as an excuse, having received an invitation in a newsletter earlier today. Another speck of dishonesty falls between us.

Vlaho nods. "Good. It will be good for you to get away for a couple of days. Take your mind off Lovorun."

The word aches behind my breastbone. "It'll be fine, won't it? Even if I have to sell?" It feels so natural to ask him for reassurance. He was the one I went to for so long. But as we're facing each other on his balcony, the coldness working its frosty fingers up my spine, the audience no doubt on its toes behind the glass, I've never been more aware of the chasm between us. He's staring at me with nothing to say. Nothing at all. Only dead things, skeletons, and I want to weep. "I should go."

—

I've wept over our breakup more times than I'd like to admit. I cried over every first thing that happened after the fact. The first Christmas without him, the first New Year's Eve. The first birthday, mine and his. Then the less consequential things. The time I found a fly-specked moon snail that we were both obsessed with finding in the shallows, but that kept eluding us. The first movie night in the theater alone, sitting with my popcorn in a chair for one, instead of the love seat we used to share. The first Saturday when I had no one to go to the Saturday špica with to drink coffee and roll our eyes at the over-the-top outfits people wear as they run their errands. I cried rivers, then streams, then rivulets, until finally I managed to harden myself. But tonight it got to me, the simple fact that I needed his hug, and I could tell by the look in his eyes that he knew and he wanted to give me one, but for some reason, because of other people's rules, it is now wrong for Vlaho to hug me, so instead, I'm sitting in my car outside my house, unable to go in and face my father, who would never understand, and do the best I can to hug myself.

EIGHT

BACK IN THOSE FIRST months we were together, we often lay in my bed at night, talking. The days were getting longer, spring turning to summer, but they were still too short for everything I wanted to ask him, for everything I needed to say. In the dark, Vlaho's questions became an archaeologist's brush, dusting away denial, oblivion, and restraint, revealing one layer of me after another.

It was in the dark that I told him about the year of exile in high school, the sophomore year when my friends had decided that I wasn't cool enough to hang out with, me with my fancy words like *ubiquitous* or *alacrity*. That I was a drag for refusing to drink and smoke even as their experimenting got out of hand, while I was always too aware and afraid of the consequences. That I had a warped, romanticized idea of what a friendship should be, with my inflated notions of honesty, loyalty, and devotion, as if we were in the nineteenth century, not the late nineties. And how the next time I made a friend, who just so happened to be Tara, I learned to keep my thoughts to myself, and when she suggested that we go get some beers, I was the first one in line in the store, and I bought one more than she did.

I told him about my parents' constant fights, all their near divorces. My mom had always warned me never to air our family's dirty laundry with anyone, but when I was with Vlaho, I didn't feel like I was revealing her secrets anymore, I was disclosing my own. I told him that my dad sometimes got so angry he threw the first thing he got his hands on. A phone receiver, a glass, a wall clock. A yellow boot.

I told him that my mom was the sort of person who reveled in dwelling on problems, and that my father and brother offered enough material for her to always have her hands full. Dad, with his temper, his going out with friends to play cards or bocce, and coming back in zigzags. His unforgiving attitude toward anything or anyone who thought differently, which alienated most of Mom's friends. My brother, who struggled with stuttering, with being the worst at sports because he lacked coordination and was slightly overweight. My brother who, much like Mom, saw a problem to every solution. There was a bit of twisted satisfaction she found, I always thought, in the Sisyphean way she was constantly trying to straighten the bent stems of my father and brother, and never quite managing it.

"What about you?" Vlaho asked. "Were you a problem she needed to solve?"

I shrugged. "Sometimes." Because it would be wrong to say she never helped me or that she didn't care. But there was always a sense that she knew that I could take care of myself, that helping me wasn't as gratifying for her because she didn't think I needed as much attention as Saša, or as much correction as my father.

During those hunkering-down nights, I would ask Vlaho what his parents were like, and he'd say he'd been very blessed, that his parents, especially his mom, were warm and caring. I found it odd. All my friends resented their parents for one thing or another. We were barely out of our teens, our job was to talk badly about them, but Vlaho didn't have anything negative to say. If I'd loved him any less, I probably would have envied him. But Vlaho was my favorite person in the world, and if anyone deserved a unicorn of a mother, it was him.

And yet there was always an inward curl when he talked about his family. And at night, whenever I reached for him to stroke his back or kiss his shoulder, he gave a barely audible whimper. The sound of someone longing to be touched, of someone who hadn't been touched in a long time.

Even while he slept.

A touch—a whimper.

"Why biology?" he asked me one evening in late June, when dusk had settled over Zagreb. He lay sideways on my bed, books, notebooks, and highlighters scattered around him. Outside, the swallows warbled. They'd built a mud nest above my window and their baby birds had just hatched. The air was ripe, fragrant with possibilities.

It was a tough question and had been a difficult choice. Deciding what I wanted to be had needed to be weighed against what was actually feasible in a country like Croatia. Most of the subjects that I could study back home in Zadar felt flimsy. Philosophy, art history, comparative literature . . . all sure ways to end up with a job as a salesperson in the town's mall.

Of course, there were career paths that guaranteed some semblance of job safety: law, architecture, medicine. But I couldn't imagine anything worse than fighting for a living, and couldn't draw a straight line if my life depended on it. And I couldn't fathom cutting into human bodies.

But even then, I understood that those were only rationalizations, and underneath them all was this: for one to know what they want to be, they first need to know who they are. I knew myself only in relation to others: a daughter, a student. I understood myself only in negatives—what I didn't want, who I didn't want to be. Why biology? I had no idea.

Vlaho rested on his elbow, attentive. Waiting for an answer. He always did this, just looked at me and listened. Way past the moment when other people would stop listening. And the silence he laid between us had a way of drawing things out of me that I hadn't planned to say. Things that I might not have even been aware of.

I wound myself around him, contemplating for the first time the real reasons why I'd chosen biology. "When I was six, my parents sent me to spend the winter at Lovorun with Baba while they were renovating our house. Saša had already started school, he had to stay in Zadar, so it was just Baba and me." Closing my eyes, I could still hear the wind howling through the aged windows; smell the sharp, herbal smell of olive leaves when we cut them, the bura wind freezing our reddened hands.

Baba was a woman of few words, not very affectionate, yet I could sense that she liked having me there. She was very much the product of the land she grew up on, rooted in karst's scanty red dirt, made rough by the elements, much like the olives she tended. But like the olives, she still managed, almost unwittingly, to produce something nurturing from that roughness.

There was something soothing about spending the winter in that isolated place, the first one with no chaos or fights, not even the meaningful, loaded silences. Just plain existence, the comfort of chores, teasing out life from dirt and stone. That peace had imprinted itself on me. "It was the only place where I could just be. Where I felt I belonged," I said to Vlaho, turning to face him, "until you."

His body softened into mine.

"The thing about biology," I said, "is that it's predictable. It's like math that way, two and two can't be anything other than four. Only, math is unchangeable, and biology flows. From one season to the next, from birth to death, sickness to health. It's exciting and innovative, and yet, essential and fixed."

Vlaho's face stayed blank, and for a moment I thought I had made no sense. "It's a safe playground," he said, enunciating each word. And a warmth spread through me.

"Exactly."

We relaxed into our pillows, listening to the birds outside. "What about you? Why economics?" I asked, considering it for the first time, and finding it an odd choice. He was imaginative, warm, empathetic, impassioned. Economics sounded rigid and dry, so unlike him.

"I wanted to be a nautical engineer, like my dad," he said. "Travel the world, be on the ocean six months a year."

"Really?" I propped my chin on his chest. "So why aren't you studying nautical engineering? You'd look so handsome in a uniform." I tickled his side, even though an instant shot of adrenaline coursed through me for the near miss of that future. Had he chosen nautical engineering, we never would've met. He would've been studying in one of the cities on the coast, not in Zagreb. And even if by divine providence we did cross paths, we would be spending half our lives apart, him being on the sea for work, and that sounded like too much to take.

"Here's the embarrassing part," he said. "My mom wouldn't let me."

"Wouldn't let you?"

"Well, technically, she asked. Politely. Begged, more like it."

"Why?"

"Because I'm her only child. And seafaring is dangerous. She's been trying to get my dad to stop for years. But it's in his nature. Sailing. The sea. He can't stop."

"So you gave up your dream to please your mom?" I'd done plenty of parent-pleasing myself, but this confession unnerved me. Something lurked beneath it that alarmed me in a way I couldn't yet identify.

"I had a sister," he said. He didn't look at me. He just lay there closing his eyes, as if he couldn't bear for me to see inside him just then.

"Had?"

"She died. Appendicitis gone wrong while Dubrovnik was being shelled."

The footage of bombs tearing at Dubrovnik's gorgeous stone walls and marble streets came to me, the fires burning bright orange against the winter-gray skies. Those images were always displayed on national news on St. Nikola's Day, the anniversary of the most brutal of the attacks, so our nation would never forget this barbaric act. It was a horrible crime, and I never thought about how behind that footage people's lives could've been falling apart for even worse reasons. A surge of grief for Vlaho, for his mother I hadn't yet met, swelled in my chest.

"She was three. I was eight." He said it matter-of-factly, like it was a piece of information outside him, one that couldn't touch him.

"Oh God, Vlaho."

I didn't say anything else and neither did he. Instead, I covered him with myself, held tighter, as if my body could absorb some of his grief by osmosis. Our skins glued with sweat, his breath streaming down my neck, the chirp of the fledglings in the nest above our window now inappropriately cheerful. The pain throbbed inside him, I could sense it, like distant rumbles of a storm on the horizon.

NINE

I DIDN'T REALLY PLAN to attend the Olive Oil Manifestation, but after blurting it out as an excuse for leaving Vlaho's son's birthday party, I find myself scouring the event's website, wanting to go. Not for the companionship of other olive growers, of which there are many, everyone in Dalmatia with a piece of land to their name producing their own oil. But because there's going to be a lecture on olive pomace by a young Italian scientist. Apparently, she invented a way of repurposing the olive residue left after milling into a valuable resource instead of the waste it's considered to be, and this interests me not so much as an olive grower, but as a biologist.

That's what I'd hoped to do for a living before the reality of living in Croatia shot me down. Change the world for the better, one such project at a time.

But leaving home for a couple of days is a challenge. Even though Dad's recovery borders on miraculous, he's far from independent, and for me to go anywhere overnight takes a great deal of planning. This frustrates me, of course, but at the same time, I know I should be counting my blessings.

The stroke had wiped out Dad's entire left-brain hemisphere, and as the doctors were discharging him, they told us he would likely be bedridden and completely dependent on our care for the rest of his life. I panicked. My brother lived a three-hour drive away, and I didn't have the first idea how to provide the kind of care Dad needed. I couldn't lift him on my own, and didn't know how to handle a urine catheter, not to mention that handling tubes in my dad's private parts would embarrass us both to death. I begged the doctors to keep him in the hospital for one more week, until we'd prepared for the reality of this new life. He had been admitted only four days beforehand; the extent of his injuries wasn't yet known even to them. But there was no mercy. "This isn't a physical therapy unit," they said. "Your father is stable, we need beds for other patients." And when I asked if they could get him into one of the physical therapy spa centers, they said they would put him on the wait list, but that it usually takes eight to twelve months to get in. Unless we had a connection, that is.

I remember laughing out loud. Of course, we needed a connection. Never mind that Dad had been paying 15 percent of his considerable income for national health insurance throughout his forty-five years of working.

But despite their drab prognosis, as soon as we brought Dad home, he rose to his feet—his defiant, stubborn nature on display once more. And yet, the extent of his injuries is still considerable and means he is only partially independent, though he would never admit to needing help, not from me or anyone else.

Saša isn't happy when I call him and tell him I need him to come take care of Dad for a few days. "Now isn't a good time, Ivona. The twins had strep throat last week. We just put them back in daycare. Silvija is exhausted. And my schedule is filled to the brim."

It's logical enough. He does have a job, working at a dental practice, and he does have three children, and they are a handful, the twins especially, still in their toddler phase. It's not his words, it's his tone. And what the tone is really saying is: *I have a job, a spouse, children. Would you please?*

But I'm shouldering all of Dad's care as it is, and Saša should help, even if he thinks I have no life to speak of. Dad is his father too. "You could come alone. Let Silvija stay with the kids," I say. "It's only for a couple of days."

"Silvija can't drive. I don't feel comfortable leaving her without transportation, not with the kids still recuperating."

Thoughts like *her parents drive and live three blocks away* and *how 'bout a taxi as an option* come to mind, but I don't mouth them. It would make me sound bitter, and besides, calling Saša out on his excuses usually makes him more combative. "I know it might not be convenient for you, but it's not convenient for me a lot of the time either. And this is one of them. Please, Saša. I don't ask often. This is important to me."

"It's for your *hobby*, Ivona."

As if hobby is a dirty word. "There's an innovator from Italy who's invited to speak. About potential use of olive pomace as a food ingredient." Getting the woman behind this project to give a talk in Croatia is nothing short of a miracle, and I want to be there. I *need* to be there, I feel that in my gut. "Please, Saša." My voice isn't even anymore, it's filled with held-back tears. I can't stand begging him.

Saša sighs with exaggeration. "Okay. We'll be there Thursday night."

And just as I'm about to thank him, he says, "You owe me. Big-time," and I'm back to wanting to slam the phone down like in the old days. Poking a finger onto the screen doesn't feel like much of a statement.

—

Lovorun is where I usually work my way out of these moods, when my chest gets too narrow for breathing, when I get so angry for wanting to say so much but failing to find the right words at the right time, so that is where I'm headed after my argument with Saša. It's been my go-to place ever since the diagnosis, and I don't allow myself to think what I'll do when I lose it, where I'll go when I'll need to clear my head.

Reaching the estate, I park at the wrought-iron gate but don't go into the renovated main house. The humble interior from my childhood memories fades a little every time I see the new layout—the modern reception desk, the small lobby with marble floors, and lighting Dad picked out of one of those Italian interior design catalogs.

Instead, I walk across the courtyard. At the end of it, a small gate leads into the olive grove that stretches beyond on a small peninsula jutting into the sea. As soon as I pass through, I stop to close my eyes, and feel it begin as it always does, the tension draining into the soil beneath my feet, the acid gathered behind my sternum releasing into the purifying air on a long exhale. It's like opening an overcrowded beehive in my chest, this feeling—the bees rushing out to roam free until all there's left is peace.

The branches are thick with light green leaves, the pruning season in full swing.

I take my shears from my backpack. One by one, branches fall down at my feet. Again. Again. Again. The click of the clippers breaking through the branches the only sound. Here, I only think about whether to slide my shears two inches up or down a twig. I don't think about Dad or Saša. I don't think about my sad job at the stationery shop. I don't think about losing this place or even about Vlaho. The fuller my hands are, the emptier my mind is. Here, I'm as feral and primordial as my baba used to be.

TEN

IN JULY, WHEN OUR summer term ended and we were finished taking our exams, Vlaho and I had to go home for the summer. We said goodbye at the fume-filled bus station, and I struggled to let go of him, terrified that stretching our bond in space would make it snap. So when he called to tell me his parents wanted to meet me and were inviting me to spend a few days in Cavtat, I agreed without thinking. Three weeks apart, and I would've agreed to anything just to see him.

We hadn't talked about meeting each other's parents before we'd left Zagreb. Regardless of how we felt about each other, we'd known our relationship was too young for our parents to label it as serious. Of course, his parents had known about me, and I'd told my parents about him. My mother had asked the pertinent questions—who was he ("a student, economics, smart, kind, serious"), his background ("middle-class family, and yes, Mom, they're Croatians"), his parents ("his mom is a teacher and his dad is a first mate on a tanker"), but as soon as she'd gotten the general information, her interest had abated. "Make sure you don't get pregnant," she'd say by way of goodbye in almost every conversation. "You need to finish college first."

Vlaho and I were careful, of course, using more than one kind of protection. I'd always been responsible, and it irritated me that my mother found it necessary to remind me to be what I'd always been. The path of life had long been instilled in me: elementary school, high school, university, job, marriage, kids. In that order, no aberrations. It was the natural order of things, like phases of mitosis. But every time we talked, she'd say: "Opportunities pick strawberries," an old Croatian adage intended to warn me that the more sex I had, the bigger my risk of getting pregnant was, which ultimately had me associating strawberries with sordid sex, until strawberries too started tasting bad.

My mother was chopping onions in the kitchen when I came to tell her I was going to Cavtat to meet Vlaho's parents. She only said, "Oh," and pressed her lips and eyes tight, and I couldn't tell if it was because of the onion tears, because she disapproved of my meeting them, or because they'd beaten her to inviting Vlaho over.

But that afternoon, she came to my room, sat on my bed, and said, "I'm not sure this is such a good idea."

My stomach stirred, though I did my best not to betray it. I turned to my closet, pretending to decide which one of my T-shirts was worth packing. My mother was a defeatist, she saw a cloud to every silver lining, every calm came on the eve of a storm. She saw big emotions, even when they were positive ones, as something dangerous, something inherently about to go wrong. She never missed the chance to tug me down when I was flying too high, warning me—for my own sake—to temper my excitement. Keeping joys moderate made the disappointments that inevitably followed easier to manage.

"You, meeting his parents," she clarified. "It's too soon."

"It's not too soon," I said, sounding like a petulant teenager, a tone that was doing me no favors.

"I know you think you and Vlaho are serious, but you've been together for what . . . four months?"

"Seven," I said, folding a summer dress into my suitcase. "And I don't *think* we're serious. We are."

"You're nineteen," Mom said, resting her hands in her lap. "Things happen. You could change your mind, or he might. You don't want to be meeting the parents of just any boy you date, do you?"

To imply that Vlaho was just any boy grated on my ears, though this was partly my fault. When I'd come home earlier that month, I acted as if nothing of substance had happened in the year I'd been away. My feelings for Vlaho were so powerful and all-consuming, I didn't know how to talk about them in a moderate way. So I didn't talk about them at all. Instead, I'd clutched my happiness close to my chest, the way an octopus folds her tentacles when she's hiding from a trident.

"You were nineteen when you met Dad," I said.

Mom got off my bed, reached for the doorknob, and stood there for several seconds, facing the wall. "Yeah. And look where it got me."

—

The bus ride lasted the entire night. Like the bus, sleep came in fits and stops, and by the time we reached Dubrovnik in the morning, my head was woozy, my skin had absorbed the smell of dusty upholstery, and the doubt seeds that Mom had planted inside me took root. What if the spell Vlaho had been under, the one that had made him fall in love with me, had broken during our month apart? What if we tried to fit together again only to find we couldn't? What if I rubbed his mother the wrong way, and her dislike of me slowly worked its way into him? In Dalmatia, there's nothing more formidable than a mother-in-law, and I'd seen more than one relationship fall apart because of the invisible hold mothers had on their sons.

But as soon as I saw him four platforms away, bathed in the early morning sun, everything else disappeared. The people between us, my doubts, even my mother's voice. It was such a visceral thing, being loved the way he loved me then.

—

We drove in his mother's rickety Opel Corsa over the cliffside road, climbing out of Dubrovnik, southward-bound to his hometown, Cavtat. Only four hundred kilometers south of Zadar, yet the colors were more vibrant, the blues of the sea more sparkly and translucent, the greens of the vegetation more verdant and lush.

"My mom can't wait to meet you," he said. "She's been cooking and baking and cleaning for days. Drove me and my dad crazy."

It astounded me that his mother worried about meeting me, even if it couldn't be a fraction of how much I worried about meeting her. "What did you tell her about me?" I asked.

"Only the truth. That you're smart, kind, beautiful . . . Oh, and that the sex is amazing." He grinned.

"You didn't!"

Vlaho laughed. "Okay, I left that part out."

His smile faded and he focused on the road. The view shot over the small islands, farther, to the gates of the Adriatic Sea, where it married the Mediterranean. After a while, eyes still on the road, he said, "I told her you see me."

We pulled up to their home, a single-story house with a blossoming bougainvillea draped around the facade, tangerine and lemon trees standing guard at the entrance with their glossy, leathery leaves. Vlaho's mother opened the door to greet us, the smell of rožata trailing her. She was almost as tall as her son, same dirty blond hair and prominent nose, only she had pale eyes that seemed sensitive to the light, as if the blue in them could easily be diluted, like watercolor.

She led us into their living room, awash in earthy, woodsy tones, and decorated with family portraits, from those more recent ones to black-and-whites with people I assumed were Vlaho's grandparents or even generations before that. On a credenza stood a photo of a little girl with a plump face. Vlaho's sister. The photo had been taken at a birthday party, Ane's hair made up in French braids, lace adorning the collar of a crisp white shirt below her face. She had been caught at the intake of breath, before she blew out the three striped candles in front of her. She seemed so suspended mid-action that whenever I caught sight of her over the next few days, I held my breath too, waiting for her to exhale.

Next to the photo frame, there were two candles burning, and never once during my stay did I see them go out.

Vlaho's father came in from the garden to greet us. He was the tallest of the three, a boisterous man with a potbelly, thick black mustache, a hearty laugh, and a voice that came not from the throat but some place deeper. He took a liking to me instantly, and kept saying to Vlaho, "Son, if you mess this up, you'll be dealing with me."

As the days rolled by, I felt like I was back in the college lab, a silent observer behind the lens of a microscope, trying to grasp the secret of Vlaho's family. Apart from his father singing arias at random times, their home had a pervasive peacefulness about it. It was the sort of place where you could curl up under a blanket and read, so different from the chaotic vibe of my home, and it soothed me despite the constant strain of being a newcomer, of being the object of observation myself.

With his mother's school out for the summer, and his father home on rotational leave, Vlaho's parents' time was governed by a self-imposed schedule. Every morning his mother would take her coffee into the garden while his dad went into town to have his espresso with friends. Lunch was at one p.m. sharp, a massive display of dishes, savory and rich and plentiful, that made his dad's stomach rounder and left me embarrassed for those poorly cooked excuses for meals I made for us back in Zagreb. Afterward, his father took a nap while his mother puttered around the house and garden. In the afternoon, the smell of coffee would again percolate through the air, and we would lounge around the garden table, watermelon and cantaloupe slices making the air juicy with their honeyed scent.

It was the moments in between these tentpole events that I lived for, when

Vlaho was solely mine. Walking down the hill to the pebbled beach nestled between the pines to play with each other's bodies in the teal surf, and dive to find abalone shells, their inner side a shiny and slick mother-of-pearl. Or driving to a beach farther away, where spectacular sunsets melted over Dubrovnik in the distance. In the evenings, I'd put on a long summer dress, and Vlaho would come out of the shower smelling like lavender crushed between fingers, and we'd walk around the town that had come alive with music and tourists and the smells of seashell buzara and the briney breaths of the sea just before it falls asleep. The yachts and sailboats, moored for the night along the promenade, cast lights under their prows that made the sea glimmering turquoise.

When we walked like this, sometimes he would stop and pull me into him, his face awash in that bluish light, his eyes intent on mine, as if he were checking to see if I was easing myself into this new knowledge of him all right. *More of this*, I wanted to tell him. *More of you.*

"There's an old adage in the Dubrovnik region," my father had told me as he was dropping me off at the bus station on the day of my departure for Cavtat. "Be polite with everyone, and honest with no one." I'd brushed it off—what did my father know about people from Dubrovnik? I knew only Vlaho, but he was nothing like that. And yet, this was exactly what his mother was like. During my stay, she was polite but cautious around me, not showing much of either affinity or dislike, and as much as I tried, I was failing to catch any signals through her impenetrable veneer.

So when she asked if I'd like to help her make pašticada for lunch for what was to be the last day of my stay, I greedily accepted, even though I wasn't great at preparing gnocchi and didn't know the first thing about making the rich, silky gravy pašticada was famous for.

That morning, my phone rang as I was drinking my coffee alone in the garden. Vlaho was still asleep, his father had gone for his espresso, and his mother to the butcher's to get meat for the pašticada. It was Tara calling. When I answered, she was crying so hard I could barely understand her.

"Ivona," she choked on my name. "Ivona, I'm pregnant."

Her words shot down the length of my body. We were not even twenty. "Are you sure?"

"I'm fucking sitting in my bathroom with three fucking positive tests, that's how sure I am," she said. She told me it was with a guy she had met a couple of months ago, before summer term. His name was Stipe, he was from Split, and he studied civil engineering. "We slept together like three times," she said through tears. "Fucking prick. He said he pulled out."

"Tara, pulling out—"

"Don't. Even." She started sobbing again. "I don't even know him. I don't know if I want to date him, let alone have a . . . " She sniffled, checking herself. "I have to talk to my folks. When will you be in Zadar? I'll need a place to stay if they kick me out." She let out a strained laugh. "My mom will hang me by my ovaries when she finds out."

We hung up just as Frana peered from inside the house, announcing she was back and ready to start cooking. I followed her in, doing my best to retain my composure, but my shock must have shown, because as she was rolling the potato dough into a long snake, she asked if I was all right.

"My best friend's pregnant," I inexplicably said, and my face reddened at the glimpse of the simple golden cross swaying off Frana's neck. I didn't want her to think badly of my friend—and me by association.

"Oh," Frana said, her face, as always, unreadable. "Unexpected?"

"Yes," I said, and we worked without saying anything else for a while. She, rolling out and cutting gnocchi, and me shaping them into neat little ovals.

My own hypocrisy left a rancid aftertaste in my mouth. Back in high school during those debates in Ethics class, all of us girls raged against the inequality between men and women when it came to sex, child-rearing, work, pay. We had been so vehement and incensed, it had seemed impossible that any of us would fall prey to the same way of traditional thinking that was keeping women in that subordinate place. But here I was doing just that. By feeling ashamed of Tara's news, I was as good as judging her, and I was sure no one would judge Stipe with half as much scrutiny as they would Tara.

The reality of her situation sank in. Stipe could choose to be involved or not, but Tara couldn't. If she kept the baby, she would have to drop out or at least pause law school. Her body would change and stretch and sag in places where it was supposed to be the tightest and most beautiful now in her early twenties. She had barely learned how to take care of herself, and now she'd have to take care of someone else—a small, fragile being with a tiny pouty mouth rooting at her breast.

At that image, despite reason, a hot flash of jealousy lurched through me. Tara was going to be a *mother*. She would have someone to love unconditionally, someone to be loved by her whole life. I thought back to those days when I sat in my room while my parents fought, taking my babuška apart and assembling it again. How I would cradle the smallest of the nesting dolls in the palm of my hand, a surge of protective love for it overcoming me. How I'd imagined that one day I would have my own daughter, always a daughter, to give this love to. And regardless of the less-than-ideal circumstances, Tara was getting just that.

Frana stole a glance at the credenza where two candles lit her daughter's face. "Children are a blessing, even when they aren't planned," she said. "You . . . do want children one day?" She looked at me, her cheeks flushed, and I couldn't tell if it was because of all the pots boiling around us, or the awkwardness of the question.

"Yes," I said. "More than anything." A vulnerable confession given that I was a young woman who should be wanting more from life than procreating. My own mother would've cringed at this statement and reminded me to build a career first. And even more vulnerable admitting this to a woman whose son I was sleeping with. But it was the truth, I did want children, more than a career, more than anything else, so that is what I said.

Frana squeezed my shoulder, leaving a flour trail on my black T-shirt. "Your friend will be fine." She smiled, and it felt as though what she was really saying was that I was fine. Fine by her.

This is how Vlaho found us when he walked in to grab a glass of water, both of us smiling, the print of her floury hand on my shoulder a stamp of her approval.

—

In the afternoon, Vlaho and I headed into town. It was my last night in Cavtat, the looming separation already sending twinges of nostalgia through me. "There's a place I want you to see," he said, and no matter how much I insisted, his face remained cryptic, and he wouldn't reveal where he was taking me.

The sun was still high in the sky, stringy cirrus clouds floating above us, the air filled with the scent of dried pine needles, the song of cicadas, togetherness. We walked the stone streets of his hometown, which curled up the hill like the lines on a snail's house. Maybe because Cavtat lay on a peninsula like my own hometown, like Lovorun, a sense of familiarity crept up on me and nested under my skin. Every once in a while, we'd stop to say hello to people Vlaho knew. His accent thickened around his own, more melodious than I'd known it to be as he bunched his prepositions with his nouns and made even bigger amplitudes between syllables.

At the top of the hill, we reached a wrought-iron gate that led to a small, white-stoned building amid a cemetery. Beyond it, the view shot over the azure Adriatic Sea, Dubrovnik gleaming in the distance in the golden sunlight. Rows and rows of graves circled what Vlaho said was a mausoleum built by one of Croatia's most famous sculptors, Ivan Meštrović, an octagon-shaped building with two caryatides guarding its entrance. The monumental simplicity of the structure on the outside made me fall silent in awe, its whiteness pristine against the green of the pines and myrtle, and the blue of the sea.

On the inside, a sparse, elegant richness. The ceiling, covered with angel heads carved in stone, the marbled floor showing the stylized symbols of the four evangelists. At the top, a bell.

"I need to show you something," Vlaho said, and this was when I noticed that he wasn't his usual self, that there was a wistfulness about him. Even worse, a reticence. I followed him to a tombstone with many names carved into it, the last name always the same—the same as Vlaho's.

Then, *Ane Oberan, 1988–1991*, carved in silvery letters.

It punched me, the reality of it. Such a short life, such a futile death. I put my arms around Vlaho's waist. "She was so young. I'm so sorry."

His brown eyes darkened into the umber of falling leaves. He unclasped my arms from around him, as if he couldn't stand to be touched, and crouched by the grave. With my hands empty, a surge of loneliness, akin to panic, shot through me.

He played with a blade of yellowed grass, growing against all odds from a crack in the stone pavement between the graves. "The thing is . . . I don't miss her." He said it coarsely, with bitterness, or maybe self-deprecation. "Not really. I know I should, intellectually, in my head, but in my heart, I just . . . don't." He looked up, a challenge in his eyes. *So, what does that tell you about me?*

I held my own waist. "You were eight, she was three. I barely remember anything from when I was that age."

He shook his head, like I'd misunderstood. I ached with the need to slide down to him and hold him, for a physical bond to bridge whatever it was he was putting between us. "The truth is . . ." He pulled his hands over his face. "I resent her."

"Resent her? How? For what?"

He rose to standing, his gaze glued to his sister's name. Her eyes, young but soulful, forever caught still before blowing out those birthday candles, pierced me, as if her name itself were watching me.

"Things changed after she died," he said. "My mom changed. Ane died, and my mom was as good as gone because of it."

With those words, everything I'd witnessed over the last few days rearranged itself before me. I saw it then, the veil that hung above Vlaho's family. That atmosphere I'd thought was calm was actually subdued. The laughter, stifled when it reached a certain number of decibels, both Frana's and Vlaho's. At meals, the clock on the wall striking evenly through quiet conversations, its beat a metronome of grief. I realized then, for all the love Frana had for him,

Vlaho was second best, just as I was. Whatever he did, no matter how good he was, he could never quite make his mother as happy as she had once been.

Striving was a hook in his chest too.

Vlaho locked eyes with me and I could see him more wholly, more truthfully than ever before. *I need to show you something*, he'd said when we came up here. And what he was showing me was the last piece of himself he hadn't already surrendered.

In his eyes, a question, the same one I'd seen in the mirror so many times. Waiting to hear if he was still good enough, lovable enough.

I took his hand and pressed it into my chest, where there had once been a hole inside me, now welding itself shut. I pressed my other palm against his heart, closing the circuit between us. I could sense his yielding, the way his heart nestled into my hand. With this final confession we had worked our way through our pasts, it seemed. Now we were both free, like fennel seeds shaking from the stem. Now we could look for a place to take root, and as long as we did it together, we would be fine. We turned to the horizon. Below us, beyond the graveyard, the Adriatic Sea scintillated, as vast and as clear as our future promised to be.

ELEVEN

THE NIGHT BEFORE I leave for the Olive Oil Manifestation, I take a long bath and wax my legs. As I put on a sheet mask, I stroke the few gray hairs silvering in my chestnut-brown hair and touch the few lines that don't fully go away when I stop smiling. I don't mind these small tokens of growing older. They give a sense that there's some life behind me. Enough smiles to etch themselves onto my face. Enough worries to streak my hair.

But as I'm grooming, I see it. A single gray hair, down there. I stare at it, hot-and-cold sweat climbing up my spine while my brain ping-pongs, confused, because what does it matter that I have a gray hair down there, when I have them up here where anyone can see?

And I cannot explain it, cannot rationalize it, my body is acting of its own accord. I'm suddenly freezing in a bathroom filled with hot mist, and everything feels blurry, like it isn't real, like this is another person's life, not mine.

I realize, with a start, that life has scurried past me.

In all my musings about getting older, I never thought about pubic hair. It never occurred to me that it too would go gray. That it too would grow old. That this most private part of me that no one ever sees but me—because there is no one, there was never anyone before or after Vlaho—will be the place I mourn my youth the most.

As I'm standing there bending over myself, I feel, very distinctly, something inside me snap. I can literally hear the sound of it, something essential inside that I don't have the words for, snapping.

I fight the feeling off, splash my burning face with cold water. I open the bathroom door to let the steam out, to let that feeling out, but it doesn't go. Instead, as I climb into bed, it climbs in after me and sits on my lungs when I turn the lights off.

TWELVE

I DID BRIEFLY GO to therapy. Twice.

The first time, I was sixteen. My father came home early from work one day and told me to peel the potatoes for lunch. I was watching TV in the living room and saw only his shadow in the hallway behind the glass door where he was taking his shoes off. It irritated me that he had barely entered the house and was already barking orders. I don't quite remember what I said to him, but there must have been some sass in my voice, because the next thing I knew, he'd kicked my boot, full force, through that glass door.

I will never forget the shock of it, my yellow Lumberjack lying in front of me in a pile of broken glass. My voice caught deep in the back of my throat, unable to form a gasp. The waiting. For him to walk in. To see what he would do to me. He had never hit me, but I didn't know if he would do it this time, if my rudeness had crossed some sort of imaginary line. So I just stood there, eyes on the yellow boot.

He told me to piss off to my room, and I did so without making eye contact. The rest of the day, I waited, suspended in horror, for my mother to come home from work and find the glass scattered there, because my father hadn't bothered to vacuum it.

When she came home, I waited for her to come for me, my voice still caught deep in my throat, now forming a lump, glued with panic. She took her time, each second its own punishment. Standing behind the door of my room, I could hear the swooshes of glass being swept into a dustpan, the conversation between them that wasn't elevated the way it would be if they were fighting, and that is what made me sink completely.

Later that evening, Mom sat me down, and before she even got a chance to say anything, I launched into an apology. I was rude, I said, and that was only because I was having a hard time at school; it was hard for me with the other kids shunning me, and sometimes, it was hard for me to control my emotions, so I was rude, and I was so sorry that I disrespected Dad, I should have peeled the potatoes when he asked, I should have put my boots away after coming home from school to begin with, and I knew the two of them worked very hard, and that life wasn't easy on them, I had made a big mistake, and I would never do it again.

Worry streaked Mom's forehead. "What are you really saying, Ivona? Are you depressed?"

I nodded.

My mother was a natural worrier, and some issues scared her more than others, depression and mental illness topping the list. Admitting to being depressed would make her compassionate, and maybe more attentive, and hopefully a lot less angry that I'd made Dad smash the door down.

But she put her hands on her face, like she couldn't deal with one more thing that day. And then she said, "I'll get you to see someone." And suddenly, I wished she had yelled at me or punished me, anything but this. How easy it came to her to wash her hands of me.

—

A week later, I sat in the psychiatrist's office. I had sneaked into the building like a burglar, dread crawling up my spine for fear of someone recognizing me, someone who might tell my former friends at school that I was crazy on top of everything else they already disliked about me.

Most of all, I was afraid that I really *was* crazy. That the psychiatrist would see whatever it was that was wrong with me as soon as I opened my mouth, and she'd have me locked up. I was sixteen, and this was what I thought happened to crazy people once a psychiatrist determined them certifiable. This was what everyone in Croatia thought back then, that's why no one went to psychiatrists no matter what they were dealing with.

The psychiatrist was a nice woman in her mid-forties. She asked me question after question, and I answered with panicked honesty. She had a flicker of a smile as I told her about my friends shunning me, as I spoke in detail about what happened that day when Dad had launched my boot through the living room door. As the session came to an end, I couldn't stand the anticipation anymore. "So, am I crazy?" I asked.

She lifted her head from her scribbles and said no.

"Am I depressed?"

She said no again.

"So what is wrong with me?" And by this I meant, Why was it so hard for people to love me? Why had I been born with all these feelings inside me when they had nowhere to go, when there was no one else who wanted them?

She said, "Nothing is wrong with you."

"But those girls in my class hate me," I said. I wanted to add, *my family hates me too*, but I knew that technically wasn't true, so in my panicked honesty, I refrained.

And she leaned in and said, "Well, maybe there's something wrong with them."

I took those words and deposited them inside me. They got me through many a storm later on, a proof that my internal compass wasn't completely defective, that I wasn't inherently faulty for being the way I was. They gave me hope that one day I might find someone who'd shuck me like an oyster and find all the pearls I was hiding within, and this hope became my bread, my water, and my air.

It wasn't until years later that I saw her words for what they really meant. If people want to love you, they do, no matter how flawed you are. But if they aren't inclined to love you, nothing you say or do, no amount of your own goodness, can make them change their mind.

THIRTEEN

THE OLIVE OIL MANIFESTATION is held in one of Split's biggest hotels, nestled on the beachfront, with a dizzying labyrinth of floors, amenities, and conference rooms. People roam about, most of them men in their fifties or sixties, typical olive oil producers I've become accustomed to meeting during the milling, eyes drunk with Dalmatian melancholy and self-significance, voices booming when they talk to one another all knowledgeable and important, and just so dismissive toward females that you can't quite call them out on misogyny because it's all jest and banter.

I don't care, I'm not here to mingle. What interests me is the lecture by the Italian scientist, whose exciting research innovates ways of turning the olive pomace into a valuable cosmetic and food resource, rich in antioxidants, vitamins, and minerals as it is.

Although I expect it to be full, the small conference room where the lecture is to be held is half-empty. I take a seat in the middle, not too close, but near enough to be able to hear everything.

When the scientist enters the room, my breath hitches. She is so young. I can't imagine she's a day over thirty. Her tiny stature and short, boyish hairdo only add to the impression of childlikeness. But when she starts talking, in decent but heavily accented English, she commands attention. Her every sentence is a light-bulb moment. I'm swept inside the world of Florence-based labs, research, and making the world a better, cleaner place. I feel, for the first time in a very long while, the energy of life pulsing through me.

This, I think with a pang, *could have been me*. Had the beans scattered in a different way, had I been born somewhere else, or just a decade later, I could have been the one giving this lecture, enticing people's minds with these valuable concepts.

It's only when I glance around that I notice that other people aren't as impressed. Their heads are bowed as they scroll through their phones. Given their age, their English is likely too rudimentary for such a sophisticated topic. Or they couldn't care less about the pomace or where it ends up. Whatever the reason, they're not paying attention, and that's probably why the scientist is making eye contact with me as she speaks.

—

After the lecture, the attendees are ushered into the hotel bar to mingle. The bar has been converted into a refreshment zone for the duration of the Manifestation, with a buffet table showcasing finger-food versions of the best Croatian sweet and savory dishes featuring olive oil from various olive varieties. I haven't gone inside yet, didn't feel comfortable entering alone, standing aloof in the middle of the room, but that's exactly what I do now.

When the crowd around the scientist dissipates, I walk over to her and thank her for the inspiring lecture. She gives me a pointed look, a dash of recognition in her eyes, then offers me the seat next to her. "You were one of the rare ones who listened," she says. "Tough crowd."

And I tell her, "Right. Welcome to Croatia."

—

We talk for what feels like hours. She tells me about the project, where the idea first came from, how she was lucky to be backed by an institute she worked for, how she got EU funding and has spent years doing this research. I'm enthralled by her youth—she's in her late twenties—and by her knowledge. I wonder, though of course I don't ask, about her private life. If she's married, if she wants to have children. A part of me can't help feeling that women can never have it both ways and are always forced to choose one at the expense of the other, when men, doing the exact same thing, don't.

When she asks me where my passion for the topic of pomace comes from, I tell her about my grandma's olive grove that I now tend myself and also mention my education as a biological engineer. I relay that sadly, by the time I'd finished college my hometown no longer had job openings in my field. She dwells on this as she swishes the wine in her mouth, and then asks, "Why didn't you go someplace else?"

I take a swig of beer to steal some time. Sure, it looks easy now to simply pack up and leave. But back then, Croatia was a clenched fist, you couldn't leave just because you wanted to. No point in explaining that, though, so I shrug, but at the same time I'm afraid that acting casual paints me in the worst of ways, like someone who didn't care, who lacked the ambition, or even competence, to aspire to greater things.

We talk more about the pomace, polyphenol oxidase, and hydroxytyrosol, and I don't think anything about it at first. But at the end of the evening, when we hop off our stools to go our separate ways, she tells me she's applied for more funding, and if it goes through, they'll be able to scale the project. "We'll be hiring if that happens," she says. "I don't know how you feel about moving to Italy, but we could use someone as passionate about the project, and as qualified, as you." She takes the receipt and writes down her email and phone number on the back, then gives it to me. "Let's keep in touch."

Back in my hotel room, I tuck myself into bed. Behind the floor-to-ceiling window, the sea in the Split Channel roils. The rain splatters against the glass in loud thuds, muffling every other sound but my thoughts. *Why didn't you go someplace else?*

What a simple notion, to go. How stupid it seems now, to have stayed.

I could've told her that it was difficult to leave, almost impossible, because Croatia wasn't in the European Union, and getting a work visa for any place was a bureaucratic nightmare. That even if you wanted to leave, information as to how was hard to come by. Google was rudimentary, there were no Instagrammers or bloggers to follow like there are now, showing the way out.

But the truth is, I did have the opportunity to leave. I just turned it down.

Back in my fourth year of college, while I was doing lab work in parasitology, Professor Tomašek came to inform me I had gotten a perfect score on my midterm exam. He was taking a team of students to a competition in New York, and if I was interested, I had a place on the team. "It's a great opportunity," he said. "Many top-notch research labs monitor this competition and recruit students to intern for them after graduation. One of my students from last year's competition is working in Basel now, and a couple more from previous years are in Germany and the UK. It could be a good starting point for your career."

Even back then, I knew career opportunities like these didn't present themselves often, not in Croatia. This was my chance.

But as I walked back to our apartment, my thrill tapered off with each step. Fears crawled out of their hiding places, growing steadily and inevitably, like mold. I had never been separated from Vlaho, except when we went home for the summer, and even then, we were never apart for more than ten days at a time. What would it mean, if I took off to New York—New York!—for two whole weeks? If I got on that plane, and visited another country, another continent without him?

Reticence gave way to something heavier. The place I didn't like to visit, but that still lurked within, even though he had loved me so well, so fully for more than three years. He'd never given me a reason to doubt him, but it was still there, that disbelief that he continued to choose me day after day after day. And the fear that something could snap him out of whatever kept him tethered to me. If I went to New York, would it make him itch to travel too? Without me? Would he start looking for opportunities to go somewhere as well? How long, then, would it take for our bond to snap? *Far from sight, far from heart,* my mom always said.

I unlocked our apartment door. The February drizzle clung to my coat as I hung it over the rack. I unzipped my boots and went into our living room. Vlaho beamed at me, the way he always did when I entered a room.

I lingered there, taking him in. They say that being in love fades after you've been together for three years. I'd often wondered if we too would become as mundane to one another as a pair of scissors—the way couples do when the initial spark dims. But standing there, I couldn't help thinking that people just forget how to be present with one another. They forget to really look at the other person, see them the way they used to, in the beginning. And what I saw that day from the doorway, beyond the šalša-stained, wrinkled T-shirt, and socks that revealed we should clean our floors—was everything. Everything.

I wasn't aware of it then, but that was when my decision was made. I wanted a career, I did. But I wanted him, what we had, more. I wanted to make a family together, add more people, our own tiny people, to this bubble of ours.

I put all my money on that, and lost.

And if I had taken time with this decision, if I'd known that it would turn out to be a pivotal one in my life, I would've really dug deep into what each of those things meant, and if I could, somehow, have both. I would have questioned the very premise of *out of sight, out of heart,* and why the hell I feared it so much. I would have imagined who I could have been if I had gone. Someone stronger perhaps, more self-assured, someone who had the courage to keep Vlaho in her life.

Now in the darkened hotel room, I rub the receipt with the scientist's email and phone number between my fingers. She put the offer of leaving Croatia on the table again, like Professor Tomašek had years ago. I laugh into the darkness, marveling at the fact that the only job interview that has ever gone well for me was the one I wasn't even aware was happening.

I imagine myself in one of the labs she talked about, the centrifuges, spectrophotometers, fermenters, flow cyclometers as far as the eye can see. I feel the hardy fabric of the lab coat pressing against my chest, the pressure of the protective eyewear behind my ears.

But then a letdown, a sense of free-falling.

Of course I can't go. Who would take care of Dad?

FOURTEEN

FOR A TIME BEFORE we graduated, Vlaho and I discussed where we should live. If we should stay in Zagreb, or go to his town or mine. The thought of staying in Zagreb wasn't palatable to either of us, even though we both had better chances of finding jobs and building meaningful careers in the capital than either of our towns. But we longed for home—for the oxygenated skies, the centering that is the sea. It is deeply ingrained in us, Dalmatians, this yearning to return home. Like we are born with a homing beacon, this need is always present, a rope tightening, pulling us back.

Vlaho and I were also practical, or so we thought back then. We wanted to have children sometime down the line, and we knew that, with the way childcare worked in Croatia, it would be wise to be close to at least one of our families. My hometown was bigger than his, and it was also one of the rare cities, apart from Zagreb, that housed the headquarters of a bank where Vlaho could find the kind of job he'd hoped for.

He had gone in for exactly one interview at the bank, while we still lived in Zagreb, and that was that. He got the job, and the matter of our relocation was settled. We were moving to Zadar.

But over the few years I'd been away studying, Zadar had changed. It used to house several chemical plants, factories, and labs, and opportunities for employment abounded. This had been something I'd taken into consideration when I'd decided to become a biological engineer.

What I hadn't known, because I'd only been eighteen when I left, was that the process of decay had already been underway. Transition from a planned to a market economy had started before the war, along with the privatization of state-owned companies. But, as often happens in Croatia, noble ideas gave way to sordid execution. Many of the companies had been bought for mere kunas by corrupt individuals who'd then sold the assets for personal gain and declared the businesses bankrupt. Hundreds of people were left unemployed.

By the time I finished college, the once-prosperous industry already lay in ruins. The whole economy of our town and region took a sharp, unsatisfying turn toward tourism, the beauty of these parts the only thing we still had to offer to the world.

Another hard truth about potential is that it needs favorable conditions to materialize as the best version of itself, just the way the bacteria cultures in a petri dish grow better if the conditions are just right. And here was the truth about my petri dish when I returned home:

Zadar's multiple labs and chemical plants closed in the transition.

Interview after interview at the few state-run places that still hired biological engineers, with committee members nodding, seeming impressed with you as a person and your knowledge, and, oh God—*potential!*—and then finding out the person who got the job was the mayor's semi-illiterate nephew, who had probably purchased his way to a diploma as well.

An occasional gig in a school teaching biology, but permanent placement out of reach because the ruling party had made sure only "suitable" people got the coveted permanent positions.

Vlaho's wage barely enough to subsist on, covering rent and utilities, and not much more than food. Standing in front of a storefront, eyeing a nice jacket you can't afford, feeling ashamed to ask either your husband or your parents for money to buy it.

Having only one handbag with straps so frayed that, during the next interview, you fold them in your hand to try to hide them.

The shame of asking for a bit of money from Mom to buy new panties because the old ones have holes in them (and the shame of undressing before your husband in panties with holes in them in the first place), only to hear her venting to her neighbor friends a few days later about how she is still supporting you because this country is beyond repair—but the emphasis always on her still supporting you.

Finally, you're the problem your mother is solving, but your brother managed to get it all right at last—a job, a functioning relationship—and now your mother is turning into a person who loves solutions more than she loves solving problems.

People telling you to ask your parents for money, because your parents aren't exactly poor, but all you can think about is your mom's venting to neighbors about supporting you. Not asking for a dime as a matter of principle, because you do still have your pride, until you ask for a few carrots because you can't make lunch without them that day, and she buys you zucchini and peppers, and potatoes, and parsley too, and you're grateful in the way that makes you loathe yourself.

Your husband coming home from work with a satisfied look on his face—he learned something, proved himself to his superiors in some new and exciting way, but gradually, he stops sharing stories of his workday, and you don't know if it's because the novelty of the job wore off, or because he feels sorry for you.

Him, getting a raise, and then a promotion, and you're happy, but your happiness tastes bitter, until you can't stand the duplicitous nature of this new reality between the two of you. How you want only the best for him because you love him so much, and how you simultaneously resent him for his success, and then hate yourself for resenting him.

People telling you to have children—if you can't get a job, why not at least get that out of the way?—and you fuming because how easy it comes to them to propose that when they haven't considered that you need to accrue at least twelve months of work within an eighteen-month period to qualify for maternity benefits. And how could you afford having a baby otherwise, except by asking for your parents' help, but then there would be more venting to the neighbors.

Dad's story often came to me in those days, the one about rabbit fur and poverty. I had always thought of it in black-and-white terms, like an old movie, a story from times long gone. But here I was, living the twenty-first-century version of it, the dignity and pride I thought inherent to me obliterated.

—

Six years, and I was done.

By then, Mom had already died, and I was in the process of divorcing Vlaho, and everything felt even more irrelevant. I found myself at the counter of a stationery shop near my old elementary school, copying documents to apply for yet another pointless job interview, and I saw a small note on the counter. *Workers needed.* Something inside me spiked, sharpened like the tip of a pencil. What was the point of playing the game if the rules were rigged against me? The joke had been on me, sending the same résumé, the same required documents again and again, hoping against hope for a different outcome.

So, when the saleswoman approached me, I pushed the last copy she'd made of my CV back into her hand and asked her to give it to her boss.

Dad thought getting a job at the stationery shop meant I was settling, but I wasn't.

It was an act of defiance.

I was done catering to the logic of this twisted system.

I was flipping it the middle finger.

—

When Mom died and Dad resolved to turn Lovorun into a heritage hotel, he was convinced it would be a silver bullet for us both. He would have left a mark in the world, and I would *finally have a real job*.

"You'll see, Ivona, it's going to be the best thing that ever happened to you," he said.

But the hotel was never my dream; I never wanted to work in it, the introvert that I am.

So much energy went into our confrontations over this: "Can't we just renovate and leave it be?" I'd ask, and he'd tell me we can't invest so much money only to use the estate for our own enjoyment; investments don't work that way, where is my instinct for business?

"You'll finally be able to quit your job at Indigo," he'd say.

But I didn't want to quit my job at Indigo, not to become a hotel manager, at least.

Dad couldn't understand this. Why wouldn't I want to make use of this opportunity he was creating for me when I didn't have anything better going than selling pens and staplers? He thought working at a stationery shop was beneath me, and he wasn't wrong. I was capable of so much more, had worked with rigorous diligence throughout my school years toward so much more.

But if there was one way of becoming less myself than by selling stationery, it would have been by *pretending* to have a semblance of a life, a semblance of success, just because someone else had installed me in a better-paid position.

FIFTEEN

THE DAY AFTER THE conversation with the Italian scientist turns out to be one of those glorious Dalmatian days that fill you with gratitude for life so deep it's almost painful. The air clean and fragrant after the storm, the sun high in the sky, the colors as lively as if it were late spring already.

I've been looking forward to having coffee with Tara while I'm in Split. I don't see her as often as I used to, not since she married Stipe and moved here after she'd learned she was pregnant. It always seems so recent, until she mentions that Marko, that fated baby, is now in college himself, like we had been when he was conceived.

We meet on Split's riva, the sea promenade adorned with a string of coffee shops that look over the seaport. The view shoots toward the faraway islands, ships big and small cutting through the tranquil sea in between.

Tara rocks their youngest on her knee, a three-year-old daughter who too came as a surprise in the moment when they were so close to finishing their job raising their sons. Tara always rolls her eyes when she tells the story, but it's obvious how enthralled she is by her daughter. "There is something about girls," she says, "that engages a more tender part of you."

I don't tell her that I wanted a girl, and always thought I would have one. I also never told her about the morning before her wedding, when Vlaho and I went to Kaufland to buy a greeting card, and, as we passed the baby aisle, I slipped in, drawn by the doll-sized garments in pale blues and pinks. "Maybe I could get her something," I said to Vlaho. I had already bought Tara a baby swing, I didn't need to buy anything else. But I wanted to feel the clothes—Tara's pregnancy had left me with a sense of unexpected longing. I picked up a pink onesie with a mushroom print. The fabric was soft to the touch; I could almost smell the baby's powdery scent as I brought it to my nose. When we came home, I put it in a box under my bed, the intention of giving it to Tara only an afterthought. To this day it's there, though I take it out only when I am in the mood of completely undoing myself.

I don't share this with Tara, because she is different than I am, less emotion-driven, more reasonable than I could ever be.

"Why do you still cling to him?" she asked once a few years back, her tone a little annoyed, when I mentioned Vlaho in a context I can't even remember now. "You've been divorced for years." A rotten feeling surged up my throat, a sense of being deeply flawed for catering to these emotions, for being a part of his life and allowing him to be a part of mine. How could I explain what Vlaho meant to me? How could I illustrate what it was like for someone like me—someone who'd kept herself so shut for so long—to be unpacked so fully by someone, and be loved for what he found inside? How can I explain even now, years after our relationship ended, that being loved by him, being loved like that, is the most life-affirming experience I've ever had?

I'd made light of Tara's question at the time because I knew she'd never understand, and made a pact with myself never to mention Vlaho to her again.

Because, ultimately, she was right.

Vlaho and I broke up, while Tara is going on twenty years with the guy who didn't think to pull out.

Now when Tara asks me, "What's up?" I smile and rattle the little stuffed owl her daughter insists we pass back and forth. I talk about my dad, the looming foreclosure of the hotel, and how I might need to find a way to sell it if I can get him on board with that.

"You know," Tara says, breaking a cracker for her daughter, "Stipe is supervising a reconstruction of an old building here in town that's being turned into a hotel. He's meeting the investor as we speak. As I have it, they've been looking to buy more property in Croatia. If you want, I can call Stipe, see if the investor might be interested to meet with you."

She dials her husband, and within three minutes, it's done, a meeting arranged between the investor and me, without us ever exchanging a word. A strange combination of fear and excitement pools inside me. What if I mess it up? What if I get it right? What if getting it right is messing it up?

SIXTEEN

THE SECOND TIME I went to therapy was when my world was collapsing in full force, a year before Vlaho and I got divorced. The panic attacks had gotten bad, and I felt unhinged, like a train in the midst of derailing, suspended in the air in those few moments before it hits the ravine.

Sometimes, I'd curl up next to Vlaho at night and beg him to help me. "Please," I pleaded. "Please. I don't know what to do." What I was really asking for was a solution. To show me a way out. To undo the diagnosis that had slipped between us, split us in two like a merciless chisel. Vlaho held me close and stroked my hair, and kissed my temples, but he couldn't do anything for me, not really, and that hurt even worse.

My therapist, Astrid, was an older woman with a bony face, sharp nose, and even sharper observations. She seemed judgmental but kept her judgments to herself, which disconcerted me, because all my life I'd depended on my ability to read people, and she was giving me nothing to decipher. She was a cognitive-behavioral therapist, so she was trying to teach me about the connection between thoughts and emotions and actions, and how I could use rationalizations to stop the vicious cycle of panic. But it wasn't helping, the part of me that was negative always had more arguments to offer than my positive side.

And time after time, I asked her—pleaded with her—to tell me why. Why was this happening to me? Why was I so fragile? I knew many people who'd gone through worse things, but who were still functioning. I was nowhere near functioning.

Astrid didn't like this question. She'd deflect it by saying that we can't know what's going on in other people's lives, that many of them might think I was doing okay if they saw me out and about, and that it doesn't matter how other people deal with problems, what matters is how I deal with problems. But one time, I might've pushed the question too far, because Astrid folded her notebook, looked at me, and said, "Do you know what a color wheel is?"

I said yes.

"Not everyone has the ability to see all the nuances," she said. "Some people, those with Daltonism, see only shades of gray. Some people, the majority, see the basic colors. But a few have this incredible gift," she leaned in, and for the first time I felt warmth emanating from this woman, "and see all the glorious hues and gradations of gold, teal, turquoise, peach. You, Ivona, are one of those lucky few who see the whole spectrum."

She said it as if it were a perk, but I couldn't see any benefits if it caused me this much pain. "Is there any way I can change that?"

She sat back, shaking her head. "It's like the color of your eyes. You're just born this way." Then she smirked. "Tell me, though. If you could change it, would you really want to?"

I sunk into the couch, considering this. What came to me weren't exactly images of Vlaho, but a palette of emotions tied to otherwise invisible moments we'd shared. The way something opened in my chest when he'd sink his fingers into a tangerine, offering a part of it to me. The suede feeling of hearing him whisper in the dark. The slight tug I always felt when I was around him, a sense of centering, of my world getting aligned.

These moments rushed through me like paint exploding on canvas.

I looked at Astrid, and God help me, I said no.

SEVENTEEN

AFTER MY COFFEE DATE with Tara, I walk to a hip bistro in Split's town center, where I'm supposed to meet the investor interested in discussing the purchase of Lovorun for lunch. When I step inside from the cobbled street, I have to stand in the doorway for a moment to let my eyes adjust to the dim light. Inside, everything is velvety. The purple upholstery on the chairs, matching heavy drapes embroidered with gold framing the floor-to-ceiling windows, hardwood floors brushed into softness.

I try to calm the tremors in my fingers. I'm not equipped for this. For all my supposed intelligence, I'm no match for the cunning and guile of a professional negotiator, someone who facilitates the buying and selling of hotels for a living. Whatever tactical advantage I have, I'll ruin it as soon as I open my mouth.

He's easy to pick out among the few scattered patrons. He occupies the corner table, one hand swirling a teaspoon in his coffee cup, the other on his laptop. His face is mirthless, with clean-cut edges, exactly what I'd expect a businessman of his caliber to look like. He can't be more than a few years older than me, but he oozes the sort of authority that reminds me of Astrid and the fearful respect I had for her, how my stomach always clenched before our sessions, then almost imperceptibly unclenched after them, because I could never tell what she really thought of me. When he looks my way, his crinkle-less eyes scrutinize me until I feel unstable on my feet despite wearing flats. I expand my lungs to make room for the anxious feeling rising inside.

He gets up from his seat and I offer my hand for a shake. He takes it in an exacting grip. "Asier Henry," he introduces himself.

I mutter my name, and he splays his hand toward the chair I'm supposed to take. "Please."

The waiter hands us menus. The bistro is one of those places that have started popping up recently, a combination of hominess and haute cuisine. Dalmatian comfort food, reimagined as high-end. The menu is short, only a handful of offers for each course. It takes thirty seconds to scan over it, but I take my time, grateful for the chance to gather my composure.

The investor orders brancin carpaccio with blackberry cream and capers, and I opt for mussel buzara deconstruction. When the orders are placed and there's wine on our table, the investor leans back in his chair, playing with the stem of his glass. He has that scrutinizing look again. "I'm assuming Stipe told you that we—the fund I work for—are in the process of scouting a couple of hotels here in Dalmatia to add to our portfolio. In fact, I just came from Vis island. Have you been there?"

"I haven't," I say.

"A stunning place. We were looking into a property there. But there was a legal issue, a dispute over the ownership of the land. So our attorneys flagged it as a no." There's an accent to his English that I can't place. Not quite American, but not British either.

"Courts here are very slow." My own English comes out a bit rough around the r's and the w's, which is frustrating because it flows so seamlessly inside my head.

"So I've been told."

"May I ask one thing, though?"

He nods.

"Why heritage hotels?" As poor as my understanding of the hotelier business is, I know it's a numbers game. Mass consumption makes for the biggest profit. Four-star hotels with hundreds of rooms are the real cash-makers. Everything is more expensive to run on a smaller scale.

Asier gives a half smile. The skin on his cheeks is pockmarked, pitted with long-ago acne scars, and it makes him look even more severe. "Well, the fund's founder started this business with a heritage hotel in the south of Spain. He built his whole empire on that premise. And frankly, the pandemic has been favorable for our niche." He leans in, twirling the stem of his glass between his palms. "The market is changing. New generations—Millennials, Gen Zers—don't want to lie idly on a beach somewhere, like their parents did. No matter how beautiful the beach is. They want a full, immersive experience."

I bite the insides of my cheeks to prevent myself from smiling. Dad doesn't know the first thing about Millennials, but he hit the nail on the head with his heritage hotel idea. "I see."

The plates arrive. His food is assembled like a piece of art on a porcelain canvas. A Miró painting, with clean edges, and vibrant colors rimmed by blackberry sauce. My food is served in a bowl, with what looks like tomato soup in the center, lined with smoked mussels on one side, and some sort of tuile on the other.

"Bon appétit," Asier says, seeming unimpressed. Eating food like this, in places even more lavish and opulent, must be his norm. He scoops some of the brancin on his fork, and I do the same with my shellfish. When it hits my palate, the taste ricochets in my mouth. The smoked mussel is tender, the tomato sauce creamy, infused with garlic, parsley, and wine. I close my eyes, and for an instant, I'm transported to my mom's kitchen, aged six, or eight, or ten, eating her scampi buzara on a Saturday, because that was the day she frequented the fish market. "Mmmm."

I open my eyes, warmth creeping up my ears for letting out an audible moan.

Asier smiles, the first sign of humanity. "That good?"

"It's like tasting my childhood," I say.

"That," he points a finger at my plate, "is what we're going for with our hotel experience. Not eating to quell hunger, but for the sake of the experience itself."

"Tell me about Lovorun," he says.

I scrape the last bit of sauce from my bowl. The balance between what I should reveal and what I should withhold is porous, but comes with a barbed edge. I need to tread the line with caution. "It's a remote little hamlet that my family renovated recently in order to turn it into a hotel," I tell him, sticking to the facts. "It lies on a seafront, the main building has ten rooms. Other cottages, still in need of some final touches, make for separate apartments, each suitable for a family of four or five. The estate is surrounded by a vibrant, verdant olive grove." My throat expands delivering those last words. I'm going to miss those olives.

He nods, satisfied. The bistro has filled with more patrons, the clamor making the atmosphere less austere. "What about you, are you in the hotel business?" he asks, finishing his wine.

Ah. Masked in this inquiry is the mother of all questions. *What do you do for a living?* The only question I hate more than *When are you planning to have children?* Though, with being divorced and approaching forty, that one is becoming so infrequent I almost miss it. Much as I hated being asked, at least it signaled that people still thought it could happen for me.

Asier's eyes probe me. They are gray, the color of the abaxial side of an olive leaf. He has a calmness about him, which I'm sure brought him many a victory in contentious negotiations. And a poker face that could coax you into revealing your cards before it's good for you.

Neither my job at the stationery shop nor my running Dad's company sounds like an adequate response. They're what I do to make ends meet, or because there's no one else to do it. The only thing I do for *living* is pruning those olives with care, teasing life from their branches. Using my otherwise useless knowledge of biology to make the best oil possible. A negligible contribution to the world compared to what the Italian scientist does, but one I am proud of nonetheless.

I reach for a small bottle of olive oil among the condiments and twist off its cap. I swirl it under my nose, the way a wine connoisseur would her wine, and take a whiff, then swirl it again. I offer it to him. "What does it smell like?"

He thinks a moment, then says. "I don't know—olive oil?"

"This oil was pressed from olives that had been stored in the seawater before milling. The bioactive phenolics are only partially preserved. It still has some health value, but not nearly as much as oil from freshly pressed fruits."

Asier sniffs the oil again. "How can you tell?"

"Extra-virgin olive oil smells like cut grass, or olive leaves; or fruit. Sometimes like green almonds. It's pungent and spicy. This one is mild, doesn't sting the inside of your nose when you breathe it in."

He looks around the bistro, as if wanting to file a complaint with the staff.

I twist the cap back on. "It's a common practice here. Back when there weren't as many mills, people had to preserve the olives in seawater so that they wouldn't go bad before it was their turn in the mill. Now there are mills everywhere, but people still put their olives in seawater. They're accustomed to the milder taste."

"But are they aware it's of worse quality?"

"Some are. And some are convinced that the traditional way must be the best." A lot could be said about the inability of people from these parts to latch onto progress, I want to add, but refrain.

"I see," he says.

I sit back. "That's what I make. Oil. The kind that's the equivalent of your hotels," I say. "Not a product, but an experience."

There's something liberating about saying this aloud to a man like him. Someone who must have trodden the streets of every major city in the world, who's reached a level of professional success I can only dream of. It may be simple and lowly, and unrefined. But so is sales. And isn't that what he's in? Sales? A bit more sophisticated than the kind that happens in a stationery shop, but commerce nonetheless.

Asier's eyes widen ever-so-slightly, like he's going *huh* on the inside, and for the first time since we met, the terrain between us evens out a notch.

—

After our meal, he invites me to the construction site where Stipe's company is working on the renovation of the fund's latest acquisition. "To show you what we're going for," he justifies, but I sense there's more behind it, a current of curiosity passing between us in both directions.

After I'd mentioned olive oil, he seemed to stop rushing through the conversation. Instead, he ordered another coffee and asked me a set of questions. How come I own a hotel if I'm not in the hotel business? How did I come to run the construction company? Am I a civil engineer? Normally, questions like these would've made me nervous. But my thoughts kept going back to the gray hair I discovered in the bathroom. And the need that emerged after that, to move, to live, to grow.

I'll admit I'm curious about him too, how he got into this line of work, his accent, the origin of his unusual name.

When I ask him about the latter, he tells me that it's Basque. His mother was Basque, but she fled to the UK when she was twenty, supporting herself as an au pair. "A bomb," he says, "exploded near her, miraculously leaving her unharmed. Her decision to leave was sealed as soon as she counted all her fingers and toes." He says it in a practiced way, like reciting a stanza by memory. It must've been repeated the exact same way in his family for ages.

People tend to do that with painful memories, I think, remembering the night Vlaho told me, in pretty much the same way, about his sister dying. They reduce those painful events to a set sequence of words, so that it's easier to get them out. I wonder if this helped Asier's mother at all, or if she too would duck under the table if she found herself in Zagreb's center at noon, when the cannon goes off.

"Sorry, you said your mother *was* Basque?" I ask.

He tells me she died when he was seventeen. His father is American; he worked for the Foreign Service when Asier was growing up. His parents met in London, had him, and then spent their life moving around. "My mother died in French Polynesia, of all places." His voice doesn't inflect or deepen when he says this, and it makes me think of Astrid's color wheel and how she said some people saw only basic colors. I wonder if Asier is one of those people or if it is true that time heals all, because whenever I mention my own mom dying, I have to rush through words. They always threaten to reel me someplace deeper.

"It must've been awful to have to move all the time," I say as we walk up Marjan, the hill on the side of the old town. But what I really mean is, to have to leave her in a place that far away, if that's what they did. I struggle visiting my mother's grave, and reduce my visits to a sequence of tasks, much like Asier reduced his mother's trauma to a sequence of words. But it puts my mind at ease that I can go to her whenever I like. That I will be able to go there and talk to her one day, when I'm ready.

Asier looks at me with an air of surprise. "Not at all. It was a great way to grow up."

We arrive at the construction site, and he shows me around. The historic structure is barely visible behind the scaffolding and tarp, but the building, I can already tell, will have an ancient, ethereal feel, with its elongated windows, blue shutters, and elaborate stucco decorations under the roof.

"We are restoring it back to the way it used to be," he says. "Our architect did a substantial amount of research in the National Archives to reconstruct its original appearance, inside and out." He turns to me. "I wanted you to see that we treat our investments with respect."

His eyes are olive-green.

His voice has a deep, masculine timbre to it.

I haven't had sex in nine years.

The thought is so sudden, so raw, I almost choke on it.

"It looks beautiful," I say, turning away to rebound. "We have villas like these in my hometown, along the seaside near the center. We call them Italian villas, though I'm not sure why. Maybe because they were influenced by Italian architecture, or perhaps they were built during the Italian occupation."

I often walk by those villas on my way to the town center, daydreaming of waking in one of the rooms with high ceilings, gossamer white curtains swaying in a gust of sea air, framing a view not unlike this one. Not because I dream of being rich, but because there's something about waking up to such a view that makes you take life in big gulps. "You've done it justice," I say.

Asier smiles, then looks toward the sea, and nudges me to do the same.

In front of us the navy-blue mass rolls slowly. It's chilly, the air cleansed and sharpened by last night's storm, the islands ahead seeming thrice closer than yesterday. I tighten the lapels of my coat across my chest. "Gorgeous," I say.

I'm not looking at him, but I can feel his eyes targeting me as he says, "Gorgeous, indeed."

EIGHTEEN

THERE WERE BRIEF PERIODS of contentment in those first few years after Vlaho and I moved back home from college, when I would get a substitute teacher gig at one of the schools and we'd live the semblance of a normal life for a while.

Early in the morning, we'd dance around one another in our miniature apartment, getting ready for work, and when my morning shift ended, I'd go to the bank and we'd have lunch together in the cafeteria, talking quietly under the clamor of his coworkers. At night, a satisfying exhaustion would come over me, my throat achy from talking too much and too loud in the classroom and breathing in the dry, seborrheic school air, but it was the exalting type of tiredness, one with a purpose, and I would curl up on the couch next to my husband, and he would massage my feet, sore from standing in front of the blackboard all day. He too, satisfied in the way he wouldn't be in the periods when only he worked, not because he resented the fact I wasn't bringing in any money, but because he wanted me to have what he had too.

But those moments of satisfaction were rare, and more often than not, our lives cleaved apart. He had somewhere to be every day. He had colleagues, fulfilling work, and I spent endless days cooped up in our ridiculously small apartment, the feeling of life slipping through my fingers both numbing and dizzying.

One foggy November day, four years into this ordeal and after another one of my job applications had been rejected, Vlaho and I sat in our kitchen eating breaded fried chicken and Swiss chard. He asked me if I wanted to talk about it, and I found I couldn't speak. I looked at him over the scanty lunch I'd made for us, feeling sure he would have rather eaten in the cafeteria with his cheerful colleagues than at home with his silent, depressing wife. It struck me that this was only one of the many concessions he was making for me. I hung off his neck like a boulder, making his life miserable when it didn't have to be. I realized all this mid-bite, and I couldn't say anything, and he must have seen something—terror, pain, whatever it was I was displaying—in my eyes, because he put the fork down and got up. "Get your jacket," he said in a determined tone he rarely used. And I was so unmoored, so lost, that I stood and did as he instructed.

Vlaho drove us to Billiard Bar, and we drank beers, and there was rock music playing and laughter and raucousness all around us, and it reminded me of the night we'd met. He hadn't changed a lot over the eight years we'd spent together, his face only a touch more defined now that he was twenty-eight. That same incandescence illuminated him from within, and it touched the same nameless place inside me as it had back then.

We talked about inconsequential things for a while, his mother's new car, my brother's upcoming wedding, the new album that one of our favorite bands had released, and it seemed to me that this was his point. This was why he'd brought me there, to prove that we were still here.

The alcohol slowed my blood. We started touching again, the way we used to, the way we hadn't for a while. My fingertip on the soft skin between his thumb and forefinger as he held his glass. His hand cupping my knee under the table. A brush of his knuckles against my cheek as I talked.

"We don't have to choose this life," he said, his accent heavy after the third beer.

"What do you mean?" I asked.

"This whole concept. The way our parents' generation did it. Eight-to-four jobs. Saving up to buy an apartment with a loan that will kill us for decades. Working for a wage that's not enough, just to earn a pension that's not livable."

"Oh yeah? And what would we do instead?"

He shrugged. "Go to Tarifa or something."

"Tarifa?"

"Spain," he said. "Near the Gibraltar Strait."

I scoffed. How weirdly specific and unusual a destination, a place I'd never heard of. It made the conversation even more bizarre. "What's in Tarifa?"

"Sailing," he said, then he straightened up and added in a more deliberate tone, "Freedom."

We launched into a conversation, as if we were truly considering it, even though it was ridiculous. Croatia hadn't joined the European Union yet, and we couldn't just pick up and go wherever we wanted. There were visas and work permits to be considered. There were all kinds of obstacles, most likely insurmountable, because people would be leaving this country en masse if it were that easy.

But I let Vlaho paint an image for me, of beaches stretching as far as the eye could see, wind sweeping through the sand, cold cervezas at nightfall, crowded tapas bars, and us, making love late at night, relaxed, untethered. He would learn sailing, he said, and become an instructor. Maybe over time we would buy a used sailboat and live on it. I could do whatever I wanted, maybe own a seashell gallery?

I chuckled, imagining what my parents would say if I told them I sold seashells for a living.

But Vlaho didn't smile back, and I felt odd suddenly, like there was more being communicated than my brain was wired to grasp. It zigzagged around us, this unsaid thing, like a gnat I couldn't catch.

"I mean, is this what we wanted?" he said. "Me, working all day to bring home barely more than an average cashier? You, not even able to get a job? Relying on our parents to help us with bills just so we can pretend we're independent. Is this really *it*?"

He didn't have to explain what "it" meant. I knew. It ached in my bones, burned in my blood. It was the place where all my striving went. Where all of it went unanswered.

"All I'm saying is, we could blow off the script," he said, and I leaned on my clasped hands, and truly imagined him this time: tanned, breeze tousling his hair, bleached white at the ends by the relentless sun, hanging off the side of a boat as the sails catch the wind. I could see him, so unlike him, but so much more like him at the same time, undomesticated, and the image filled me with longing for this version of Vlaho I had never met.

We drained our glasses and got up to leave. We exited the bar, the smell of cigarette smoke that clung to our skin and clothes even more striking against the crisp winter air. Vlaho turned me toward him and said, "All I want is for you to be happy." He rubbed my upper arms and corrected himself. "All I want is what we already have."

We went home that night and undressed each other with care, and lay down together, and when he was about to enter me, we didn't stop like we usually did, and he didn't reach for protection. Instead, his eyes bored into mine, and we were agreeing to blow off the script, perhaps in a different way than we had talked about earlier that night. "I am happy," I said to him as we were moving together. "Right here, with you. I don't care if I never get a stupid job. This is all I need."

But it wasn't entirely true, though I didn't know it back then. Having him was not enough. And I often wondered in the years that followed, if it would have made a difference had we gone to Tarifa. Or if we'd still have cleaved apart, like we did because we stayed.

—

Six months later, I lay on an ob-gyn's chair, legs in stirrups, a probe stuck in my vagina, the faint smell of alcohol and latex saturating the air. The gynecologist, a woman in her fifties with a flushed face, moved the probe around, her eyes glued to the screen.

My uterus, a dance of light and shadows on the monitor, came and went from view. As much as I tried, I couldn't make out its contours, so I focused on the vase of pink tulips on the doctor's desk across the room. Their long stems, delicate petals, the subtle way they made the room less clinical. And inside their flower heads, even though I couldn't see them, their own reproductive organs, the gynoecium; a pistil consisting of an ovary, a style, and a stigma.

The conversation about Tarifa had sealed the decision without us ever discussing it. Maybe it wouldn't be the perfect order of things (get a steady job, access to maternal benefits, then get pregnant), but we didn't care about the order of things anymore. That night he hadn't used a condom, and the next day, I'd taken myself off the pill.

All those years of using double, even triple protection, and I couldn't believe I hadn't gotten pregnant when we so much as touched. But six months, and here I was. I had read on the internet that it was normal for it to take up to a year to conceive, but after getting off the pill, my periods were turning out to be anything but regular. This didn't worry me, I'd had irregular, light periods before getting on the pill, and when I'd asked my family doctor about it, he saw no cause for concern. "You're thin and athletic," he'd said. "It's normal."

But now that we were trying, the impatience had gotten the best of me. In six months, I'd only had two cycles. If it could take up to a year for women who were regular, it might take me five, and I wasn't willing to wait. I'd done enough waiting by then.

The doctor finally looked at me, pulling the rod out. "Alrighty then. We're done here. Why don't you get dressed and we'll talk." Her tone was breezy enough, but her eyes carried a note of something that made my navel pull inward.

I closed myself in the small dressing cabin in the corner of the room, attuned to the sounds on the other side of the door. Out there, the doctor whispered a few instructions to the nurse, who then closed the door behind her as she left the room.

I pulled my panties up with shaking hands, and came out to sit on the chair across from her. She didn't acknowledge me until she finished typing, using only her two forefingers. Then she faced me. "All right. Was this your first time getting a transvaginal ultrasound?"

I nodded.

"Ivona, there's no easy way to say this. You have a condition called uterine hypoplasia." She paused, and I thought, *Okay, that doesn't sound that bad. Not like* cancer.

"That means your uterus is underdeveloped," the doctor clarified, and I could see I was in trouble by the intense way she was observing me.

She proceeded to explain what the condition meant. That there were different levels of severity, but I happened to have an extremely rare type that's also among the most severe. That this was the reason my periods were light and infrequent in the first place, and that being on the pill had masked the symptoms until now. That my uterus was too stunted to carry a pregnancy. That I would not be able to have biological children of my own.

Her words bounced off me as if I were a tree trunk. The doctor put her hand on mine. Her fingertips were so hot she almost burned a hole through me. I focused on the tulips, as mute and stumped as me.

"But there is treatment, right? A surgery, something we can do?"

The doctor's eyes softened. The same note in them as when she'd told me to dress. Only now I could interpret what it meant. Pity. "Surgery is an option in some hypoplasia cases. Unfortunately," she sighed, "your particular case isn't compatible with surgical repair." She turned to the computer screen and began typing again. "I'll send you to do some more tests. MRI. HSG. That should give us a clearer picture."

"So there might still be a chance that—"

The doctor shook her head, resolute. "I don't want you to get your hopes up, Ivona. I truly am very sorry."

Outside on the street, a perfect Dalmatian spring day. Warm sun in the deep-blue sky, a gentle breeze, blackbirds and swallows singing in the branches of freshly leafed trees. But my mind twisted and corrupted the image until it turned ugly. The broken asphalt, the overflowing garbage cans. Cars double-parked on the pavement, blocking the way for a mother with a stroller.

A mother. A child.

I reached for my phone, then stared at its dark screen.

I wanted to call Mom. Funny how this impulse always stayed with me no matter what, this conviction that she could make things better if only I asked. As if I were a four-year-old with a scraped knee, crying *Mommy, Mommy, make this better*, and her kissing it would fix me right up. But she couldn't make this better, no one could. She'd likely make it worse, her catastrophizing as instant and consuming as a sandstorm. I could see myself offering this burden up for inspection, and her taking it, making it her own. I wasn't ready to hear any of it, I couldn't bear to comfort her over my loss.

And I couldn't call Vlaho either. How could I break it to him over the phone that we would never conceive a child of our own? How could I tell him that he'd married a woman who not only couldn't find a job, but who didn't even have a functioning womb?

A thought impaled me, so acute it almost brought me to my knees: *What will become of us?*

I stood there, in front of my ob-gyn's building, on that incongruently beautiful May day, and I knew in my gut, in the marrow of my bones, that I was once again alone.

NINETEEN

WHEN I RETURN HOME from the Olive Oil Manifestation, I find that I can't fit myself into the same old routine anymore. Something changed, though I can't quite put my finger on it. The juices of life are on the move inside me, rising, accumulating, taking up space. Infinitesimal, microscopic growth, but it's all I can think about as I'm calling the doctor to send my dad's prescription to the pharmacy or making kale stew for lunch. It's all I feel while I'm fielding Dad's protests that everything I cook needs more seasoning. He always needs more seasoning these days. His taste center burned out in the stroke, making everything chronically bland. I tell him that he needs to eat less salt, doctor's orders. He grumbles and salts his dish anyway, but I don't even get upset about that.

I email Asier the documents he asked for: the deed, the blueprints, architectural projects, and the general information about our company, and then I text him some of the photographs of Lovorun from my phone. He's in Portugal, he says, has some business to attend to, and when the team goes over the paperwork, and if the board finds Lovorun interesting, he'll be in touch to organize a viewing.

And just when I think this is all I'll hear from him in weeks, he texts me back one of the photos I sent him, with the olive trees visible to the side of the main building, circled in yellow highlighter.

"Are those the olives you told me about?" the text says. "The ones you make oil from?"

I answer, "yes."

And he texts, "They look well taken care of, they're beautiful," and I text back, "i know."

"If the transaction goes through, I'll kind of feel bad for taking them from such capable hands," he texts.

And my gut squeezes and expands at the same time.

—

It's innocuous, except it's not. The next day, he texts me a photo of a Portuguese bacalhau dish, saying that Croatian brancin tasted better, followed by a wink emoji. Later, I text him a photo of mussels caught onto the underside of the town bridge, asking, "think these would taste good smoked?" with a laughing emoji, and he asks, "why the laughing emoji?" I tell him that one should never eat mussels from ports, doesn't he know that? And he says that I'm the seagirl, he'll abide by my instructions.

—

His texts start coming more often during the vigorous spring days, warm and lengthy with sunshine, animated with birds' chirps. With the winter veil lifted, the colors around me explode in their vibrancy. Lime-green of the newborn leaves on the Mediterranean hackberry. The borage-blue sea in the Zadar Channel, the sky deep and powdery against the dandelion sun. I refuse to think about what the texts mean, to overthink this time, whether I'm reading them right, what is it he wants, what is it I want, what sort of future we could have anyway. I don't want to look at any of that. I embrace the spark it gives me, and let it rest inside me as a mere fact.

TWENTY

MY MOTHER'S DEATH WAS sudden. It came on the heels of the diagnosis, not a full year after the doctor had handed me the cruel truth. It was a stupid death. Mom fell off a ladder and hurt her head while she was cleaning a high window on our home. It left us shell-shocked, Dad and me. As we arranged for the funeral, for Mom's death announcement to be put up on the town's notice boards to inform our acquaintances of her death; as we received the condolences and prepared the house for the wake, we were detached, suspended in the aftershock. I did not cry. Not even when Vlaho held my shoulder so tight it hurt as they lowered her coffin into the grave. Not even when they slid it on the ugly concrete shelf where she would forever rest.

I was not there.

I wasn't anywhere.

—

It had been that way since the diagnosis. For days afterward, I lay in bed, unable to get up. Vlaho took sick leave and laid himself beside me. We kept the curtains drawn, shutting out the spring and the susurrus of birds building nests and feeding their progeny on the outside, the illustration of the very type of family we would never have. The darkness and silence were inky. If I closed my eyes and inhaled the familiar scent our bodies had left on the bedsheets, for a moment I could pretend that none of this had happened, that we were still in Zagreb, at the beginning. Going somewhere, together. But the heart pain was too sharp, it always drew me back.

We burned through the options quickly. "We can adopt," he said on one of the first days.

"Yeah," I said. "If we put a rush on it, we might get a ten-year-old by the time we're fifty-five." Adoption was often the hot topic in the news because it was one of the most preposterous, most obvious examples of bureaucracy ruining people's lives. The courts favored biological parents and rarely revoked parental rights even when children were openly neglected or abused. The procedures took forever. For every child available, there were dozens of couples waiting. Kids often spent their entire childhood in the system, while prospective adoptive parents' arms went empty.

"We're young," he said. "We can wait. It's bound to happen eventually. Even if the kid is ten when we get it."

I wanted to punch him for the nonchalance in his tone. "Maybe I don't want that, Vlaho." Meaning, waiting for a child for what could be decades, without a guarantee of ever getting one. Relying on our toxic country's bureaucracy to give me what I desired most in this world, when it had let me down in so many ways already.

"What about international adoptions?"

I huffed. "Oh, so you're suggesting we fight the bureaucracy of not just one but two countries, one of which we've never even been to or know anything about?" I turned my back to him. I could feel him lift his hand, feel it hovering over my shoulder. And the exact moment he drew it back.

"We'll use a surrogate, then. Your ovaries work, don't they?" His voice was thin. He was begging me to grab hold of this absurdity, but I was so porous I couldn't possibly latch on.

"There are no surrogates in Croatia." Even if by some miracle we found a woman who would agree to carry our child for us, legally the baby would be hers, not ours. "*Mother is the woman who gives birth to a child*," I quoted the Family Code to him with a cold voice.

No, there were no options.

I turned to Vlaho, his brown eyes floating with impotence. "I want my own child," I said to him. A child I would carry in my own womb. A child that would be conceived between the two of us, born of our love, carrying within itself pieces of generations that came before us, the smallest babuška in the long line of babuškas. "I want to be someone's mama," I said, and when I voiced that truth, I couldn't stop saying it. "I want to be a mama, I want to be a mama, I want to be a mama," I repeated through snot and tears. This is what I had wanted all my life. My truest, deepest desire.

But there would be no children.

Inside me, I could feel my useless, stunted uterus.

Vlaho returned to work. I used to wake up before him, make coffee, sip it as I watched him go through his morning rituals. Kiss him to taste the coffee and mint toothpaste on his lips, to brush my nose against his clean-shaven cheek, to press my body against his until I'd convinced him to undress even though he'd be late for work.

But in this new life, I pretended to sleep. I would hear the wardrobe shriek as he slid it open, the sound of his shirt as he flapped it over his back, the squeak of his shoes against the tiles as he left. Most days, he'd sneak out so as not to wake me. But sometimes he would stop in the doorway, as if the weight of our problem had rendered him immobile, and I would feel him watching me. It would last for a moment or two, and I would wonder if he knew I was only pretending to be asleep. I'd steady my breathing, make sure my eyes didn't move under my eyelids. In those moments, there was nothing I longed for more than his touch. There was nothing I dreaded more, either.

He'd never come over, though. Instead, he'd turn and go about his day, his relief almost palpable when he'd close the door behind him.

And with him, all the warmth spooled out from our apartment too. The space between the walls stood, heavy and devoid of life. I lay there, with nowhere to be, nothing to do, hours of emptiness ahead.

He was giving me time, I knew. He wasn't the type to ever demand that I feel anything other than what I *was* feeling. To convince me that I should be grateful or happy for the small things in my life when the life I had dreamed of had so wholly disintegrated. He had spent his childhood with someone whose feelings he couldn't negotiate but only coexist with, and he'd learned then that there was no point in trying to force grief out of people, not until it was ready to come out on its own.

A part of me was grateful. And yet! And yet, a part of me was screaming inwardly, wishing he would grab me by my shoulders, kiss my wet eyes, and say, *Enough!* I would've resisted him if he'd done that, of course. I would've pushed him away and retreated to my wallowing. I had fallen too deep, too abysmal was my loss. But I still wanted him to try.

When he'd come back from work, we'd both make the appearance of an effort. I'd make myself presentable. Brush my teeth, comb my hair, sometimes even shower. I'd throw something in the pot, though it was obvious my heart wasn't in it. I used to love cooking for him. But in this new existence, my food was flat and so was his face.

We'd talk. There was always an anecdote up his sleeve to relieve the silence. His tone would border on bright, so I knew he was faking it. I'd poise a smile he knew I struggled maintaining. He'd ask about my day. I never had anything to report, save for poring over the Employment Office ads, and sending occasional CVs for jobs I didn't have a chance of getting. I didn't tell him about the hours spent staring out the window, overlooking the overgrown fields outside our building. Scouring the internet for faraway places, not because I wanted to travel, but because somewhere else, maybe I could reinvent myself, be more than a Woman with a Faulty Uterus.

At night, I'd let him go to bed first, no matter how late it got. He'd ask me to come with, but I'd tell him I wasn't tired. And I wasn't. All I did was lie around. My body was weary of resting, my mind sluggish with under stimulation. I'd watch vapid shows until he fell fast asleep, and only then would I sneak in next to him. Most nights, I'd turn my back to him, but sometimes I'd torture myself by watching him. He deserved more. This wasn't what he'd signed up for. I despised myself for it.

And then I'd think about time. How it isn't only relative to happiness, racing when you're happy, dragging its feet when you're miserable. It's also gender-biased. If things were reversed and Vlaho were the infertile one, all he would have to do is wait a decade or so, until my eggs dried up and we were barren together. But a man's fertility doesn't have an expiry date, he can conceive a child until the day he dies.

Vlaho could promise to stay true to me. But the truth of the matter was, twenty, thirty years later, he could change his mind. If we hit a rough patch; if he fell for someone younger than me, he would still have a chance to father a child. He would always have that chance.

That truth loomed over me like a guillotine.

He'd lie there, the face I loved so much mellowed with innocent sleep. The only person who ever made me feel safe now held a blade over my neck. All I could do was wait for the rope to snap and the sharp edge to fall.

—

In early November, six months after the diagnosis, I got a teaching gig at a village school twenty kilometers outside Zadar. It was only temporary, covering for a teacher getting a hip replacement, but it was the only thing that had gotten me out of the house since May.

As I drove inland, the bura wind howled around my car. It poured down Velebit mountain, picking up speed, lifting the particles of salt off the sea in Velebit Channel. The bura has a way of getting through however many layers of clothes you're wearing. There's something clinical about it, disinfecting, and I raised my chin toward it when I exited my car.

The school was a shabby old two-story building, yellow paint peeling off in stripes. But around it, there were olives, pregnant with fruits, their color a mix of green and purple. I stopped short when I saw them, as if someone had opened a door to let air inside the vacuum in my brain.

That weekend, I went to Lovorun for the first time since Baba had died. The bura had subsided, leaving the air behind chilly and the sky clean-cut blue. The olive grove was covered with weeds and brambles, some as high as my waist. The tops of the trees bulged thick as a lion's mane, with hardly any space left between the branches. I circled around them, inspecting the fruits. Most had fallen off and lay rotting on the ground. It had been so different when Baba was alive, the orchard groomed, grass cut short, branches hanging low enough to reach without using a ladder, each one trimmed as carefully as an old gentleman's beard. Driving back home, I made a promise. I'd restore this place to its rightful glory.

Come pruning season in February, I filled my thermos with boiling-hot tea, and my backpack with sandwiches. Vlaho leaned against the kitchen doorway. He had his gray hoodie on, the same one he wore the day we'd met, and the image filled me with tender longing I didn't want to acknowledge.

"I can come with you," he said. "It's Saturday. I don't have anything better to do."

"No, thanks, I'm fine," I said, stuffing the thermos in my backpack.

"I guess . . . What I'm saying is . . . I'd like to go with you."

I zipped up my backpack. So hard to form the words, and harder still to admit the truth, even to myself. And the truth was, the diagnosis had tanked me into a nameless, despicable place I was unable to claw myself out from. And even though the source of my pain was within me, it had his face. When I thought of infertility, when I thought of the children I would never have, it was Vlaho's face I saw.

The olive grove served as the beacon of a faraway lighthouse, drawing me ashore. I needed the light for myself. I couldn't bear to have him there. "I want to do this alone. I need some space to think."

He walked over to me. In the sallow light of the kitchen hood, his skin looked pale, the circles under his eyes purple-blue like bruises, and it was the first time I noticed what a toll this situation was taking on him. But instead of making me compassionate, it filled me with frustration. He wasn't doing anything to stop the pain. The last nine months, all he'd done was hover there like an apparition, telling me, without the zeal of conviction, that everything would be okay. Assuring me he would never leave me over this. I wasn't buying the first, and the latter I knew was true, but only because he didn't have the guts to make that call.

Which I knew was unfair, because what *could* he do? What could either of us do? But his inertia made me feel like I was the one supposed to find a way out of this mess somehow. That his giving me time was in fact him *waiting* for me to snap out of it and fix us somehow. I didn't know how to fix us. The deadweight of his expectations pressed down on me like a slab of stone.

"It's . . . I don't know. I can't remember the last time we talked," he said. "Like, really talked."

I grabbed the pot of tea off the stove and it burned me. "Fuck!" I turned to the sink and ran cold water over my hand. "You really want to do this now?"

"And when would you like us to do this?" His voice had an edge. "It's been months."

I turned to him, steadied myself by grabbing the back of a chair. "There's nothing to talk about."

"Ivona—"

"Vlaho."

"Please."

"Can't it wait?"

He leveled his stare at me.

"I've been lying around this apartment for nine months. And when I actually want to go somewhere, that's when you want us to bare our souls?"

"It's not like I planned to bring it up now. And for the record, I wanted to talk to you all this time. I just didn't want you to think I was pressuring you. Or blaming you."

"Blaming me?" Bile rose up my throat, hot, hot, hot. "If you're saying you're not blaming me, then that's exactly what you're doing."

Vlaho rubbed his face. "That's exactly what I didn't want you to think."

"Well, kudos!" I hated myself for all the venom I was spewing, but I couldn't stop. "Of course you blame me. It's my fucking uterus that's not working. It's me who can't have children, not you."

"It takes two to have kids, last time I checked. It's not just your problem."

"Yeah?" I faced him off, challenging him. "For how long?"

Inside me, the hole reopened, throbbed. The pain was so bad that for a moment I wanted him to admit it, to eviscerate me completely. To end this agony once and for all.

"What does that mean?"

"It means that you can fuck someone else, and *your* problem is gone." I lowered my voice, and added, "I wonder how long it will take you."

He slammed the chair under the table. "That's a fucked-up thing to say, Ivona. I'm not the enemy here."

"You know what?" I took the backpack, flung it over my shoulder. "I really don't want to talk about this right now." I stormed out of there, riled up like a kettle about to boil. *I'm not the enemy.*

Oh, but you are.

When I got back home, he was waiting for me with a bowl of maneštron, a hearty vegetable soup his mother had instructed him how to make over the phone. I apologized. We held each other in bed that night, lying in the dent we'd formed in the middle of the mattress. He whispered he loved me and that we would get through this. I echoed it back to him, wishing for it to be true. But how could it be true? How could we go on when the backbone of our world had broken in half?

The days got longer. The sun got warmer. The colors turned brighter.

The darkness inside me spread.

This was where my mother's death had found us. This was where we were when he was holding my shoulder tight as they were lowering her coffin into the grave.

—

After the funeral, countless people came to our home to share stories about my mom over wine and charcuterie. I wondered if that was the point of this whole custom, to keep the grieving family busy with entertaining so that they wouldn't have the time to process the loss. I couldn't stand being around people. Couldn't stand their pitying glances, their saccharine words of consolation. I kept to the kitchen, arranging one plate of food after another.

Ten days beforehand, Mom had cooked a Sunday lunch in that very place. She had outdone herself as she always did: roasted a rooster with potatoes and homemade mlinci, a type of baked dough she briefly cooked and then swirled in the gravy. Salad, of course, and steamed broccoli. And rooster soup with semolina gnocchi, the kind that lifted you from the dead.

Vlaho's mother came into the kitchen. She had traveled from Cavtat the previous day. She stroked my back, and the tenderness of her touch reminded me of Mom and all the things I'd wanted from her. Of all that I hadn't told her, all the things I hadn't asked. All the things I'd resented that I'd never be able to talk out with her. I turned to Frana, buried my head into her chest, and, for the first time since Mom had died, I cried.

And Frana kept me close and rocked me, the aquatic color of her eyes diluting behind the ripple of her own tears. "I'm so sorry, dear. I'm so sorry," she said. "Losing a parent is hard. Almost like losing a child."

She'd never mentioned losing Ane before, not to me. It put me on edge, made my tears retract. She inhaled, then let the breath go. "I wanted to die so many times," she said. "But I also had Vlaho. He was what kept me afloat. The fact that I'd see him finish high school one day. Graduate. Get married. Have kids of his own."

Those words, a precise cut.

The air around us shifted. "Being a parent," she said. "It makes you protective, you know?"

I didn't know.

I would never know.

But I understood what she was saying. She could be a grandmother if it weren't for me.

A simple truth we both understood lay between us. Vlaho would never leave me over my infertility. He was too good, too kind to do something heartless like that.

I knew this because I knew him.

She knew this because she had raised him.

"Please, Ivona," she said, her voice strangled. "Please, set my son free."

"How can you ask me that?" I rasped.

"I'm so sorry," she said. "I'm sorry for what happened to you. But Vlaho . . . He deserves to be happy. He's the type, Ivona, always has been. He was never like those other boys, running around, partying, chasing adventures. Always the happiest to be at home." Her face closed up, and I could feel her detaching herself from me, from whatever feelings she might have had for me, her daughter-in-law of ten years. As she recast me, from family to nemesis. "This half life," she said. "It won't be enough for him. He will never be reconciled to it, no matter what he says."

Our eyes held in a horrible lock I couldn't withstand or pull away from. I was agony, burning from within. I wanted to hate her, but her face reflected all kinds of pain, all kinds of loss as she was begging me to revoke one of them. It was unbearable, the weight of the burden she'd unloaded on me.

On this of all days.

But that must be the thing you learn when you lose a child. You don't wait for second chances. You don't wait for the right moment. You act when action is necessary. It's animalistic and natural, even when it's completely inhumane.

"There you are, you two," Vlaho said, entering the kitchen. Frana's eyes and mine were still wrestling. I could feel myself faltering.

There was a slight dip in Vlaho's tone when he said, "Everything all right here?"

Frana nodded. "Yeah, sure. Just refilling the plates." She lifted one up and walked out.

I turned to the charcuterie, not breathing. Vlaho kissed my shoulder, rested his forehead on the top of my head. "What was that all about?"

"Nothing."

"You sure you're okay?"

"I'm fine," I said.

A dust mote, upon dust mote, upon dust mote of dishonesty. Until it gathered.

PART TWO

MARINA

TWENTY-ONE

I NEVER EXPECTED TO meet anyone after Vlaho, never attempted to date after we'd divorced. Not just because my heart still belonged to him, but because I couldn't see the point of starting out with someone new only to come to the same miserable end once the man realized I couldn't give him a family. And this is the thing about Asier. He'd tiptoed into my life so softly that he was already in it before I could ask myself, *What's the point?* If he'd been any louder or pushier, I might have jolted and fled, but he entered gently, his influence visible only as it accrued.

And by the time the question emerges, I don't let myself dawdle on the answer, because it's so hard to resist this newfound aliveness.

Not that Asier and I are *together*. Neither he nor I have said anything that could be unequivocally interpreted as more than friendship. But there *is* more. In the focus we've put on each other, in the fact that we talk and text every day, even if it is about things of little importance. It's in the words with delectably hidden meanings, and the fact that my day feels unremarkable until my phone lights up. Until I light up with it.

When he texts me at night, he asks, "How was your day, Gorgeous?" A simple question, but it makes me spend my days scouring for things worth sharing, the appreciation of life that had long eluded me once again making everything around me more meaningful.

One glorious morning that I'm off work, I put on a lighter jacket and head to town on foot, with no plan, nothing to do except absorb the beauty and promise of the season. The road snakes along the seafront, where wooden ships sleep in small coves. The sea is calm, smells of seaweed; iodine and salt. Cormorants stand on small piers, their black wings stretched wide as they dry, their heads turned up to the sun, as if saying, *I am here, I embrace you.*

I walk by the Italian villas that I mentioned to Asier when we were in Split and take a photo of each one as I pass. "i would drink coffee each morning on this terrace if i lived here," I write, sending him the one with the balcony resting on high columns, from which I'm sure one can see the entire Zadar Channel. "or sleep in the room on the second floor of this one," I send with another, "with this big french window open to the sea."

Asier doesn't answer, he must be busy or asleep. I don't know, and what surprises me is that I don't fear not knowing, like I used to, with Vlaho. I walk over the bridge and settle in one of the coffee shops on the town's main square. The sun is warm on my face, painting everything behind my eyelids in gleaming red. I'm like those cormorants. Here, embracing.

A pair of hands closes over my eyes from behind. "Look what we've got here. A lizard!" Marina says in her boisterous tone. She removes her hands and bends down to kiss my cheek before she eases herself into a chair next to me. "Waiting for someone?"

"No," I tell her. "The seat's yours."

She takes out her phone. "Let me just tell Vlaho we're here, he's doing some grocery shopping at the market."

It's Monday. "Shouldn't he be at work?"

"He took the day off. I needed some help with the sailboat. Prepping it for the season."

The waiter comes and Marina orders a latte for herself, and I ask if we should get Vlaho his macchiato. She nods, and I order it for him, tell the waiter to hold the foam, because Vlaho hates when he has to dig through it for his coffee.

"So, how was Split? Was it nice to wag your tail elsewhere for a bit?" Marina asks.

"It was all right," I say. I think of Asier, and it takes some effort to suppress the grin that escapes me. I tell Marina about the scientist and her project instead, and how she said I might get a job in Florence someday, if the money from the EU funds goes through.

"Ma dai," Marina says, with a fling of bunched fingers, so even though the words sound exactly the same in Croatian, I know she's speaking Italian. "Ma che successo epico," she adds with her over-the-top accent. I laugh. We met while learning Italian, and hers is as awful as ever.

She pushes my shoulder. "I told you a long time ago that you should get out more."

"I know," I say, and that's when our coffees, and Vlaho, arrive.

He bends down to kiss my cheek, and the warm smell of his skin, the realness of it, flips my stomach. It's a small failure each time, this reminder that I'm not over him, but today it hits differently. For the first time, someone else is on my mind, and it softens the blow.

Vlaho settles into the chair opposite me, easing plastic bags with sardines and Swiss chard to the floor.

"Guess what. Our girl here got invited to work in Florence with some Italian hotshot scientist," Marina says.

I give her a look. "You're telling it like it's a done deal. And even if it were, it's not like I can go anywhere, not with Dad in my care." I wince at my own words, because I don't want them to think I'm resentful of my role as my father's caregiver. "But I might have a potential buyer for Lovorun," I say, turning to Vlaho. "Tara's husband connected me with this guy, this investor." I become self-conscious, telling him about Asier, for acknowledging that I met someone else, even though I'm not exactly owning up to it.

It's almost imperceptible how he tenses up.

"Anyway," I continue, in a quieter voice. "He—his fund, the fund he works for, I mean, runs a chain of heritage hotels and they're acquiring new property in Croatia, and it sounds like Lovorun might be a good fit. They were looking at an estate on Vis, but it didn't check out, legally." I'm rambling now, so I turn to Marina, hoping she'll pepper the conversation with one of her wisecracks, but she too is eyeing me with suspicion. I'm hyperaware of my body, it moves with exaggeration. "Anyway, chances are they'll buy."

Marina glances at Vlaho as she takes a sip of her coffee. "And this investor. Is he . . . our age?"

"He's about . . . " I start, but then stop myself. "What does it matter, his age?"

Marina shrugs. "Just asking, I guess." But I can tell she isn't just asking, she is *asking*, and Vlaho is too, with his tumultuous eyes.

Their reaction to something I haven't acknowledged even to myself, let alone said, gets under my skin. All these years I've watched the two of them together. I saw their kids get born, celebrated their birthdays and christenings. I've seen them exchange hugs and warm looks, inside jokes, and language loaded with the shared familiarity that had once been reserved for him and me, and I endured it all.

So what is it they're calling me out on, exactly? For flirting with a man I should be professional with? For believing that I still have a chance to meet someone new? Or for failing Vlaho? For not being true to him—or at least to my feelings for him? Him, looking at me with those turbulent eyes.

I straighten in my chair. The thing about feeling too much is that sometimes you have to force yourself to feel less. That in order to preserve your heart, you have to close it off, deliberately deny it its main function, and reduce it to a mere pump. The first time I did this was after the boot incident, when Mom sent me to the psychiatrist. Her dismissal had drilled a hole so deep, so angry, that I couldn't stand it. Shutting myself off was the only way I could manage to share the same space with her. And I had to do it countless times since, with Saša, Vlaho's mom, even Tara. I'm an expert, really, by now.

So I look at Vlaho, straight into his eyes, and steel myself against the wounded look he has no right to.

Then I turn to Marina. If anyone should be happy that I'm moving on, it's her. But what startles me is that her face looks even more dismayed than Vlaho's.

TWENTY-TWO

FOR A TIME AFTER my mother died, Vlaho did his best to put me back together. He lay next to me stroking my back while I stared at the wall, mourning the mother I no longer had, the mother I had never had, the mother I would never be.

He cooked for me on the days he wasn't working and tried to lighten my mood by bearing small gifts. A book on olive oil production, a special blend of coffee, a packet of roasted chestnuts from the vendor near the town bridge. At night, he would press himself next to me, and whisper in my ear, "Don't worry, baby, we'll get through this. It's going to get better." Platitudes that made me close up even tighter.

Sometimes, he would try to paint the future for us, a bright one, but I could hear him struggling between words, each turn a road we couldn't take. "We will travel," he would say, because he couldn't say we would have children, but we didn't have money for traveling, and he knew me well enough that he could hear me calling him out on this even if I wasn't saying anything. "We'll build a small house on one of Zadar's islands and spend our weekends and vacations there," he'd say. Which only reminded me that he had weekends and vacations, because the rest of the time he was working, while for me the time was always the same, a block of indistinguishable minutes, hours, days.

Slowly, it must have dawned on him that it wasn't wise to paint such a rosy vision of our future, and maybe it even dawned on him, as it had on me, that we didn't have much of a future at all.

On some nights, he would reach for me the way he used to, the need growing inside him, obvious in his heavy breath and lingering touch, but this reaching felt useless now that I knew it would lead to nothing, a mere carnal chore, and most times, I would just stiffen against his touch, and he would pull back, and turn toward the ceiling, and I would feel the weight of his disappointment sitting heavy on top of him.

In those moments, I hated myself for not being able to give him what he wanted, but there was also a spiteful part of me that almost rejoiced in his pain. He should suffer too, I thought. But no amount of his suffering ever felt enough, he would never suffer as much as I did.

His mother called often, and sometimes, after catching up, he would grow serious, monosyllabic in his answers, and he would slant his body away from me so that I couldn't hear what she was saying, and then he would try to look casual as he got up and went to our room, as if to look for something. But I could hear him whisper-consoling her, telling her that he liked his life the way it was, that he did have a family, that he knew she was alone, with him living so far away, his father being away for work, with Ane gone, and he was sorry that was the case, but that couldn't be helped; there was nothing he could do about it. And he would end the call, but wouldn't come out of the room for minutes more, and I could feel him suspended between the rock and the hard place, and I hated the fact that I was the hard place.

His mother's words came to me often those days, that request that had shocked me into stupor on the day of my mother's funeral. I wished I could yell at her, strip her of humanity the way she had stripped me, and tell her how utterly unfair and selfish her request had been. That day had felt like its own kind of death, her words a rogue wave that slammed me into the sharp rocks below the surface, cutting open, letting blood, mauling me. I had been so angry for so long because of this, but the truth is, after that first tumble, the wave started receding, and what was left was this: a glint of relief. Slowly revealing itself, over time, in the rare moments I was ready to look.

A way out of this agony. For both him and me.

Even though it had been building gradually, the last of the fog lifted in an instant, and in this one moment I knew, beyond any doubt, that I had to divorce him. It was a Saturday morning, four months after Mom's death, and as always, the town filled with people for Saturday špica, the aimless ritual of cruising around, showing off cute outfits and made-up hair, pretending not to be posing for the photographers who were snapping shots they would later upload to online galleries titled *Walk Around Town*. These galleries that everyone pretended not to care about, but secretly hoped to be caught in.

The frivolity of this ritual annoyed me, but I liked going to the town's center on Saturday mornings for reasons all my own. When I was a child, my mom frequented the farmers market there on Saturdays. She worked Mondays through Fridays and the farmers market closed on Sundays, so this was the only time she could do her shopping. She'd take me with her to help carry the plastic bags filled with vegetables and fish and meat, a full week's worth of provisions. The bags would strain the muscles in my arms until I worried they'd snap off, and the handles would dig so deep into my palms that it would take hours for the grooves to recede.

After we'd lifted the heavy load into the trunk of our car parked on the city wall, we would descend back into town, where Mom would treat me to a slice of cake while she had her coffee and a cigarette. I don't remember us talking much, apart from her always asking if the cake was good, but there was a shared closeness in those minutes.

After she died, I felt a need to reenact this ritual from my childhood. I thought it was more fitting to honor her this way than by bowing over her grave. And Vlaho liked that this was something we could do together, that I was agreeing to leave the house and be with him.

It was August. Vlaho and I had coffee on the old Roman Forum and were weaving our way through throngs of tourists on Kalelarga, the main and widest street in the old town, when we ran into one of his colleagues, an office-mate from the days when Vlaho first started working at the bank. The man was pushing a stroller, a toddler sleeping inside, and his wife held both her palms against her visibly pregnant belly.

Vlaho shook hands with him, and introduced me, and the man introduced us to his wife. Her smile was wide and her skin seemed to be shimmering in the noon sun. The expression "pregnant women glow" sounded true to me for the first time.

"Congratulations," Vlaho said. "I knew you had a baby, but didn't know there was another on the way."

"Yeah," his colleague said, "we're not getting any sleep anyway, and let's just say we're on a mission to get out of the diaper phase as soon as possible."

I traded a fake smile with his wife. It annoyed me, this bragging by way of soliciting sympathy. *Poor you,* I almost said, *I can't imagine how hard that must be.*

But what Vlaho did next imprinted itself on me forever, marking the beginning of our end. He kneeled down to look into the stroller, and put his hand over the sleeping child's ankle, tenderly, the way a flower falls into a grave. It lasted only a second, but there was such warmth to the gesture that it split me in half. I had never seen Vlaho show interest in other people's children, and after the diagnosis, he'd been adamant that he was fine with us not having any. But in that moment, I saw that he carried inside himself the immense potential, if not desire, to become the world's best dad.

For the first time, I could see his mother's point clearly. And the worst part was, I agreed with it.

The realization might have been lightning quick, but acting on it took time. I couldn't just tell Vlaho I was leaving him. He would never have accepted my reasoning. So I bided my time, slowly receding, the way the tide retreats from the shore. My inability to find a job had already built a barrier between us; I only had to deepen it.

And I did. I "forgot" about his next birthday, and I "wasn't in the mood" to celebrate any of our many anniversaries. I went to Lovorun more often, even when there was nothing to do, and never asked him to come with me. I pretended to have a headache on Saturday mornings so as to avoid going for coffee together. I refused to go with him to Cavtat for the All Saints' holiday, saying I needed to visit Mom's grave, which of course I didn't end up doing. And he took it all in stride, because he understood that the diagnosis, and my mom's death on top of that, had devastated me, and he was giving me time. I had known he would, I'd counted on it. I had seen him give all the time in the world to his mother, hovering, *waiting* for something to change.

I had known the essence of him, is what I'm saying.

And I used it against him.

The day I told Vlaho I wanted a divorce was a bleak November day. We were eating lunch in silence—there had already been so much silence for so long between us. I looked at him over the mist rising from the hot chicken soup, that face I loved so much, and I forced myself to utter the words: "I don't want to be married anymore."

He must've not taken it seriously, because he raised the spoon to his mouth, emptied it, swallowed. "What are you talking about?" He put the spoon down.

I told him I didn't love him anymore. It took my all to keep a blank face through the lie, to him who knew what every twitch on it meant. But the shock must've blinded him to the nuances of my expression. "You can't be serious."

"It's been happening a long time now. Coming on gradually, for years. You must have noticed. I—I'm sorry." And to illustrate my point, I could easily summon all the distances growing between us ever since we moved from Zagreb, his career and the lack of mine, his reproductive health, and the lack of mine, but between these tentpoles of our unhappiness, hundreds of hours of missed connections, intimacies turned down, conversations not being had.

He stared at the wall, his eyes turning hazel behind the veil of tears. My heart squeezed and I almost balked. But the small voice kept saying, *You're doing it, you finally said it! If you hang on for just a minute, you will have set both of you free.*

Thus began the long months of back-and-forth. Our relationship undulating like a wave.

Him, trying to reach me. *It can't be true. You're the love of my life, and I know I'm yours. I know it even if you're saying it's not true. A love like ours can't just disappear. Please, Ivona, look at me. Look me in the eye and say you don't love me.*

His anger when he couldn't get through to me. *Why are you doing this? Why are you pushing me away? Won't you at least try? Is what we have not worth putting in a tiny bit of effort?*

The bargaining. *What if I take an unpaid leave and we go somewhere, reinvent ourselves? What if we move back to Zagreb, where our love was strongest? What if we go to Tarifa, or someplace else—you choose!—and start anew?*

The devastation. Him curling up in a ball, his shoulders heaving. These were the moments that were the hardest for me, that tested my resolve the most. Seeing him like that, I couldn't help wrapping my body around his, eager for it to convey what I'd banned myself from saying through words.

We would make love in those moments, the kind of love we had never made before, the desperate, beseeching kind that left our souls bare and flesh tender and achy. And as we lay in the exhaustion of it, the wave would start again. *I know you love me. I know your soul, and you couldn't make love to me like this if you didn't.* And I would reach deep into the cruelest part of myself, one that resented *him* for all my losses, and tell him that I did care for him, but didn't love him the way he deserved to be loved. Not anymore.

Having your heart broken is a clean, even righteous kind of pain. But intentionally breaking the heart of someone you love—there's no filthier, uglier task. It felt as though I had taken my own essence—the deep feelings, the empathy, the compassion—and mangled it into something morbid and disgusting. The kind of person I hated, the soul I didn't want to call my own.

It was on anger that this ordeal finally ended. We were having breakfast, and he declared that he'd gotten us plane tickets, a surprise trip to Madeira, where there was a botanical garden I'd always wanted to see. It would be our first plane ride, and mark the new beginning of our life and he didn't care that he'd spent our last savings on it. I didn't even look at him when I said no. And for a moment, he didn't say anything back, but I could feel his frustration swelling, so overpowering that it made me look at him. His face was at once distraught and livid, and he reached for a pen lying on the table, and stabbed his thigh with it.

He froze, as if he too couldn't believe what he'd done, but then a new influx of resolve came from somewhere deep within him, and he stabbed himself again. Again and again.

I yelled for him to stop, and ran to him, dropped to my knees to pry the pen from his hand. Once I did, he just sank into the chair, stunned. And I was stunned too, because I'd never seen him like this, never thought him capable of inflicting self-harm. I went to take the alcohol from the cabinet, horrified at what he'd done, at what I'd made him do. The pen had left small blue punctures in his skin. I ran a cotton ball over them, disinfecting them, and he didn't even wince. He felt unreachable, out of it, and this is when I realized my presence there wasn't making the transition easier for him, it was making it harder.

That evening, I packed up and left.

TWENTY-THREE

THE NOTICE COMES FROM the bank. We have officially defaulted on our mortgage. I set the letter on the dining room table, fear roiling in my gut. Over the last few weeks, I allowed myself a reprieve of blissful denial, deepening the communication with Asier, holding on to the joy it gives me, while ignoring the fact that he is someone I met because I've made steps toward selling Lovorun, a course of action my father would vehemently oppose.

Even though it's afternoon, I make some coffee. A poor attempt at appeasing Dad so that he takes the news better. He shouldn't be getting worked up. The doctors have warned us it's imperative his blood pressure stay under control. What they didn't tell us, though, is how to shield him from life, or how to stop him from being himself once that life inevitably happens.

But as I'm placing his cup on a saucer—he takes his coffee in those unnervingly tiny espresso demitasses—I realize my fear is not so much for him as it is for me. He's been a different man for many years now, his rages tamed by time and age and illness, but my stomach hasn't caught on to that change. Memories loom alive, of him exploding over things that were impossible to predict. How quickly you got—or failed to get—out of the car, how long you talked on the phone, how loud you listened to music. His rage would come so fast it engulfed you before you'd even realized it, and by then, it was too late, you were already inside his furious tornado.

By then, your yellow boot had already been sent crashing through the glass door.

Dad sits down and raises the demitasse to his lips with both hands. I slide the letter to him. He takes it even though he can't read it. It's one of the oddities of how he chooses to endure his illness. He's lost the ability to read, but he still buys newspapers on occasion, or opens a book.

I guess pretending you haven't lost something is easier than facing the loss head on.

It shouldn't surprise me, that's where I excel too.

Through a dry mouth and words barely audible, I explain what the letter says. We have defaulted on our debt, and if we forgo two more monthly payments, the bank will have to charge it off and move into foreclosure. The only way to avoid that is to sell the estate and settle the debt ourselves.

As I'm talking, Dad's eyes neither emit nor receive anything, but when I say I might have a potential buyer, he snaps and hits his open palm against the table. "We're not selling," he thunders, much louder than a man in his condition should be able to.

"I don't think it's a matter of choice anymore," I say, my head sinking between my shoulders the way a turtle slips into her shell. A humiliating thought comes unbidden—what would Asier think of me if he saw me cowering like this? "We don't have the money to open. We're neck-deep in debt. I can't get the hotel up and running without a fresh influx of cash, and we don't have any."

"I said, we're not losing the hotel and we're not selling it." Dad gets up and hobbles to the living room to rummage through a console where he keeps some of his documents. I wait, like the chastised child that I am.

He comes back with an envelope. "There," he says, shoving it my way. "This should be enough to cover the initial costs and get everything going."

I extract a contract between him and the bank about running a savings account. It's his "safe stash," for when he's too old and too sick for me to take care of him by myself. "It's enough to get started." His voice is gruff as he eyes the envelope. This time, not because he is disappointed in me, which he still undoubtedly is. His tone has a different undertone now, one of loss.

One of a rabbit fur hanging off the laundry line.

My throat clenches. I place the papers back inside, my fingertips leaving sweat marks on the documents. "Dad, we're not spending your last savings."

He looks at me with tired eyes. "Call Saša."

—

His request saddles me with an unnamable type of sadness. That he would congregate with Saša against me is a special kind of defeat. Their relationship has been askew since I can remember, as if the two of them spoke different languages and failed, time after time, to understand one another. Saša was a whiny, needy boy, and whenever he'd done something wrong, or failed to do something right, it was always someone else's fault, someone else's wrongdoing. Dad believed in doing things for yourself, in being responsible for your own actions, failures and achievements alike, so he despised this trait of Saša's, deeming it a brand of weakness unbecoming of anyone, let alone his son.

And even though I never liked seeing Saša twitch in pain for failing to live up to Dad's standards, I savored these small victories when Dad would tell me I was his pride.

Because, Saša had Mom.

It was Mom I wanted too, not Dad with his droning and temper. Not Dad with his impossible standards and negativity. But Dad is whom I got, and while it wasn't perfect, this was one truth of life I could depend on. And now he tells me to call Saša and it feels like someone has kicked the knee on my one good leg.

—

I get up from the table and move into the hallway to make the call. When Saša picks up, I do my best to relay the conundrum in the few minutes he has mentally assigned to me.

"Look, Ivona," he says once I'm finished. "I talked to Dad a few days ago. He may be old and sick, but he still has his business acumen. If we sell the hotel, the best we'll be able to do is retrieve the original investment. All the work that went into Lovorun will be lost. And we would lose the property on top of that."

The way he speaks about it gets under my skin. He hasn't been to Lovorun in years. Even before Baba died, he didn't like going there. The place means nothing to him. He understands its value only because every Croat knows that land is the only resource worth owning.

"But if we invest Dad's savings," Saša continues, "and start doing business, we won't only keep the land. Eventually, we'll make money. With any luck, a lot of it. And then we can put *that* toward Dad's care."

"Everything Dad has in savings isn't enough to cover what we currently owe. And there's a myriad of additional costs we would need to cover to get the hotel up and running."

"So, I'll invest. I'll lend you what you need, and you can pay me back when the business starts making a profit. With minimum interest."

I wipe my hand down my face. My brother, the benefactor. I look toward the dining room, Dad's bald head only a shadow behind the glass door. He isn't the one to eavesdrop but I measure my tone anyway. "I don't think that starting a business with that much debt, owed to family or not, is such a good id—"

"You're only saying that because you don't want to do it."

Saša says this with disdain, and immediately, I'm on the defensive, wanting to refute what he's implying. It's not about what I want, it's about how imprudent it is to not have any money set aside with Dad being as ill as he is. That his condition could deteriorate overnight, and he might become dependent on other people's help, the type of help I'm not trained or able to provide. Or does Saša intend to swoop in to help when that happens? Because I'm not seeing him putting in his fair share even now.

But then I stop. I stop, because, Saša is right. I don't want to do it.

A plain and simple truth I've been too afraid to voice for too long.

I start back toward the dining room. It's an impulse more than a decision, coming from the gut, not the head. There is a pressure building up in the back of my head that scares me, but I won't—can't—stop myself. I'm an avalanche tumbling downhill, one that's been a long time coming. I sit across from my dad and switch the phone to speaker.

"Listen to me, both of you. I don't think investing all our money and leaving Dad high and dry is a reasonable thing to do, given his condition. You can both well disagree, but I won't be the one taking any of your money to the bank or any other place. I won't be the one running the hotel or hiring a hotel manager to run it for me. Saša—" I pick up the phone and hold it in front of my mouth so that he can hear me loud and clear. "I have no problem with you taking over as the director. In fact, I'm happy to make all the necessary arrangements with the public notary and sign the company off to you." I pause, already feeling the deflation swooping in, the inevitable fall from the adrenaline high. "But if you choose to keep me on as director, I'll do what *I* think is right. Sell the property, settle our debts, and liquidate the company."

Without waiting for either of them to respond, without even taking my phone, I get up and leave.

TWENTY-FOUR

I EXIT THE HOUSE before I have the chance to self-sabotage and concede. If I stay, it won't be long before they snatch this small victory from me. It is the way of my family. I resist, and then I question myself into submission.

Doubting myself comes so easy. How could it not when so many times in my life I've seen my perspective differ from others'? Sometimes it feels like my inner compass is set to a different north than everyone else's. Vlaho was the only person who never questioned my sense of reality or the truth. The only one who never thought that my rivers ran too deep or that my skies stretched too wide. But look how that ended.

Maybe there's something wrong with them, the psychiatrist told me long ago when I asked what was wrong with me, and I folded her words inside me to validate my instincts when I doubted myself. But now I see them for what they are. Everything is relative. They're not right, and neither am I.

My feet move in time with my frantic thoughts as I walk the same street with the Italian villas I'd texted photos of to Asier a couple of weeks ago. I'd been brimming with excitement then, the kind only the prospect of a new relationship can bring. If Saša and Dad knew about him, they'd think he's the reason I want to sell. They'd assume I'm desperate for this man's affection, lecherous after years of being untouched and neglected in this particular way. The thought makes me feel dirty.

All those flirty little texts we exchanged, the need for Asier to like me, to be attracted to me, to find me funny or smart or beautiful; all the late-night daydreams, imagining how it would feel to put my arms around his neck, or fold my curves against the lines of his body—they open a cavernous shame now, as if my dad and brother can see inside my most intimate thoughts. I can hear them mocking me with the type of contempt reserved for lonely old maids who can't help but be swayed the first time someone throws a crumb their way.

The worst part is, now that I see it through their eyes, I cannot unsee it, cannot unsee myself as this pathetic creature selling her family's most cherished heirloom to the corporate devil for the sake of what? A few compliments?

I think of Asier's murmured *gorgeous*, standing before that hotel in Split, and feel ugly in every conceivable way.

I reach Branimir's Coast, but instead of walking across the bridge and into the old town, I move onward, farther along the promenade, and then across the park with the big bronze statue of a sailor gripping the helm. The sailor has a determined look on his face, and it strikes me that even like this, somewhere on the imagined brassy high seas, he seems to have better bearings than I do.

I walk around him and toward the white building that sprawls along the road like a sail. The light is on in Vlaho and Marina's apartment. I stand in front of the lobby door. As I put my finger on the buzzer, I imagine myself going up, entering their home, sitting on their couch. Vlaho would make me mint tea, because he knows it always calms me down, and Marina would sit cross-legged beside me on the couch, her hand squeezing my knee as she she'd hear me out. And then, in her signature way she'd say something funny like *Way to deal a blow to the patriarchy*, and I'd feel a momentary irritation that she was turning my distress into a joke, but before that moment even elapsed, I'd be laughing, grateful for the new perspective.

All this plays out in my head, as real as I am, standing here, but I let my hand drop to my side.

There was a weird energy passing between us the other day, when they sensed something might be happening between Asier and me. If I go up, I will have to circle around the truth—the fact that I did think of Asier that way. It feels pivotal, this thought, like the end of an era. My miniature world is losing its breadth, becoming even smaller.

I skulk away, blending with the evening shadows. I find refuge on a bench in the crook of my town's neck, at the bottom of Jazine cove, from where the old-town peninsula resembles a woman's bowed head resting against the bosom of the sea. The dark-blue hues of dusk fall over buildings of different styles—some ancient, some medieval, some socialist—rising above the city walls. Her buildings are her scars. She has been destroyed almost completely several times in her history that spans three millennia. Last time, in World War II, when she was carpet-bombed to the ground, and less than a tenth of her old, gorgeous buildings survived intact. But she rose again, and here she is, pulsing with life.

TWENTY-FIVE

WHAT I'VE COME TO think of as the era of Marina started at the Italian-language course I took one September, a smidge under two years after Vlaho and I had divorced. Marina was the only other woman my age in the class, so we naturally gravitated toward one another. She was a sailing and scuba-diving instructor, and much of her clientele was Italian. She wanted to become fluent because few Italian tourists spoke English, and even fewer spoke Croatian. I wanted to learn because I was immersed in olive oil production research, and Italian was its official language. I didn't really need to learn it, but it gave me something to do in that lonely time after the divorce.

Our teacher, Šime, was a dry little man with a wiry mustache who raised his hands like a conductor when he talked, a sight that was difficult to watch with a straight face.

"Ancoraaaa," he'd draw out at the end of each class. "Che ore sono?"

"Mezzogiorno," the class would say in unison.

"Tempo di salutarsi!" he'd say.

"E ora di bere un caffè," Marina would whisper with an eye roll. It had become a ritual of ours. We'd stroll around the town after class, then have coffee in one of the sun-bathed piazzas.

What I liked about Marina was that she was the only woman our age not obsessing over men. Living in a town that's oriented toward raising children will do that to women. Whenever I met a single woman in her thirties, she was spiraling in a panicked need to pair off. To avoid becoming a spinster, an old maid—the kind of woman society took pleasure in deriding the most.

Marina never talked about men or wanting a relationship. I never even saw her check a guy out. For a while, I thought she might be gay, but she showed no interest in women either, so there was that. What she did talk about, and profusely, was sailing and the sea. The sun-streaked depths and the fish, and this suited me just fine. I countered her blue with my olive-green.

I had told her that I was divorced. It was the only time we mentioned relationships and marriage. When she asked me why, I said it just didn't work out, and didn't offer more. She said, "That's why I'll never get married." Her parents had divorced when Marina was thirteen, but her sister, Irena, was nine and she ended up developing both an eating disorder and depression in her early teens, which Marina attributed to the divorce. Irena lived with a much older lover somewhere in Sweden now, accepting a very small and contained life, as though she could take the world only in miniature dosages. Which meant their mother was pressuring Marina to have children, as Marina was the only one of the two siblings who seemed capable of it. "I will never get married," Marina said to me that day. "But if I did, I would never divorce. It's the worst thing you can do to your kids."

"Luckily, we didn't have children," I said, marveling at the levity I managed while saying it. And that was the only time we ever touched on that topic.

After one class in December, we exited the building, the tower bells all across the town greeting us with their brassy noon song. "Let's have some coffee and fritule." Marina linked her arm through mine.

December in Zadar meant one thing: Advent. Small wooden cottages sprung up along the Five Wells Square as they did every year at Christmastime, offering mulled wine spiced with clove and cinnamon, sausages with mustard on bread, and fritule—a deep-fried yeasty dough covered in powdered sugar. It was hard to score a table this time of day. We circled the square three times until one cleared.

"My shift starts at two, I can't stay long," I said.

"Well, if you can kill half an hour of my time, I'll be much obliged," she said. "Winter is destroying me. I hate waiting for the season to start."

"You're missing the point," I taunted her. "Everyone who works in tourism milks the season for three months and then takes the rest of the year off. Minimum input, maximum output, baby." I snapped my fingers three times, the way our Italian teacher sometimes did.

Marina huffed. "I guess I missed the memo."

"Ivona, hej." The familiar voice came from behind me. Even in the few syllables of his hello, his southern accent tinged his words, and the bright color of it streamed into my veins.

We hadn't been seeing much of each other since the divorce. For all the hurt and pain leading up to it, the divorce itself had been a fairly dispassionate, bureaucratic process. By then, Vlaho had moved out of our apartment as well, and found a new place closer to the bank. When we met at the courthouse, he appeared less gaunt, less hollowed out. He was somber, but calm, reconciled to the situation, and this broke my heart in a whole new way. We'd had coffee from time to time since. Not often, because there was always that balance to strike, wanting nothing more than to be around him, and knowing I needed to let go.

"Oh, hey," I said, a little too eager, as I turned to him.

His face was more angular, starker, than when I'd seen him last, seven months ago. He'd grown a two-day shadow that pricked my face as he kissed me on both cheeks. But he still smelled the same. That scent, always the scent snapping me back to who we'd once been.

He looked over the cheery throng of people around us enjoying mulled wine. "You're the last person I'd expect to see here."

"Likewise," I said. Neither of us liked crowds. That's why we'd spent our college years holed up in my apartment instead of going to rowdy student parties.

"I'm just passing through. I parked my car under the city wall." He pointed his thumb behind him, toward Vladimir Nazor park.

"Shouldn't you be at work?"

"I'm on vacation as of today. Going to Cavtat for the holidays. So I thought I'd buy some presents before I go."

He looked between me and Marina, and I realized I hadn't introduced them. "Oh yeah, sorry, this is Marina. We take Italian together. Marina, this is my . . . um . . . Vlaho."

"Buongiorno," Marina said with a mock flourish.

They shook hands with polite disinterest. He turned to me again, took a moment to inspect my face. A thousand questions vacillated between us. *Where have you been? What have you been up to? Are you okay? Are you, really?* Questions we couldn't ask, but that burned inside us nonetheless.

Being locked outside his life was the worst kind of punishment, yet so fitting for the crime I had committed against him. I ached, as I always did when I saw him, to put this whole charade behind us. To get up from that chair and sink into his embrace, holding tight until he surrendered to me. To tell him the last two years had been a mistake. But of course I couldn't do that. He was bound to move on sometime, and when he did, he'd be happier than I ever could have made him.

If he hasn't moved on already. The thought struck through me.

"Well then—" he said. "Wish me luck. I have no idea what to buy. I can get away with a nice bottle of wine for my dad, but my mom . . . " He shrugged.

"Frana loves that peony perfume from L'Occitane," I reminded him. "The one in the round red bottle." It stung to be so familiar with his family yet removed from it at the same time.

"Oh, yeah. Right. That's a good idea." He loitered for another second, his hands deep in his pockets, looking like he wanted to say more but hadn't found anything worth saying, and I felt the same way. "Well then . . . "

I wasn't ready for him to go. I needed a few more minutes. Why the beard?

What was going on at work? Did his father get that gout under control? Was there someone else already?

"Care to join us?" I asked.

"Thanks. I haven't had coffee today." His acceptance as quick and eager as my invitation. He glanced at Marina, as if asking for her permission. She slipped her phone inside her backpack. "By all means."

"Thanks," he said.

"How do you guys know each other?" she asked.

"We used to be together," I hurried to say before he managed to beat me to it. I waved my hand in a nonconsequential way, and Vlaho gave me a *Is that what it was?* look. "We're just friends now," I added, and Vlaho's lips curled into a smile soaked with quiet hurt.

"I see." Marina seemed mildly amused by the display of awkwardness between us, but she didn't press us for more. It wasn't her thing, prying.

"Marina owns a sailboat," I said.

"Oh, really? That's amazing," he said.

"You sail?" Marina asked.

"No, but I've always wanted to learn."

What happened next happened in a flurry. Marina offered to show him the basics, and at first, he declined. He didn't want to be an imposition. But Marina said she had to take the boat out before the season anyway, and that it wouldn't be a problem if he tagged along. She'd do that for a friend of mine. I relaxed in my chair, kind of proud that my friend would be instrumental in fulfilling Vlaho's lifelong dream. This way, I thought, I was still a part of his life. I still mattered. It never occurred to me that Marina would turn out to be the woman I had feared since the day I learned my uterus was useless, and in some way, since the very day I'd met him.

Next September, Vlaho called to tell me she was pregnant. That they were getting married. I knew they had been hanging out since she'd given him sailing lessons the previous spring, but the idea of them being together, sleeping together, shattered me to pieces. For weeks afterward, I couldn't straighten my back. I walked bent around my center as if I'd taken a literal blow.

If there had been any attraction between them the day I'd introduced them, I'd completely missed the clues. In my naïveté, I thought of love only as a tsunami that pulls you under with brute force—like it had been with Vlaho and me. But sometimes, love can work more like osmosis, it can imbue you slowly. Vlaho and Marina must have connected like that, two fluids of different densities: steadily, drop by drop.

It would be a church wedding, he said, not because either of them was religious, but her mother was traditional in that sense, and Marina had given in. Marina hadn't struck me as much of a people pleaser, but I'd obviously missed some clues there too.

Ours had only been a civil wedding. I wasn't religious either, but it felt like God's blessing would make their marriage more real than ours had been, more substantial. The one that mattered. The one kids were born into. That was the blow that was hardest to stomach.

It would be a small ceremony, he said. He sounded congested, like he had been crying. "I'm sorry," he said. "I'm so sorry."

I clenched my stomach to prevent the dismay rolling upward. "You have nothing to be sorry about," I said, but really, I was thinking, *You bastard, you bastard, you son of a bitch. How could you, how could you, how the fuck could you?* The pain was so searing I couldn't speak. When I managed them, my words sounded venomous. "I left you, remember?"

"Yeah," he said. "Yeah, you did." That hollowness of voice. That defeat.

We hung up.

It was done. The worst thing imaginable, the one thing I'd dreaded since we parted ways, had happened. Vlaho had someone else. Someone else was entitled to kiss him, love him. Make her life with him, share his bed. Decode the endless number of his facial expressions, his tender smiles. Listen to the sound of his deep melodic voice when he pillow-talked, a voice that carried the scent of tangerines and watermelons and all things beautiful and painful.

Someone who could curl his silky hair around her finger when he lay in her lap. Someone who could look for his nose and downward-sloping eyes—that look that always read a bit melancholy—on a child that had her cheekbones and lips.

I curled up on the floor in my room, and cursed the day I'd enrolled in Italian, the day I'd met Marina, the day I'd introduced them to each other, the day they'd made love and gotten her pregnant. Images of him pushing into her tore into me, snapshots of them lying naked on the stern of her boat, becoming one under the light of countless stars. I wanted to claw my eyes out, but the images were mental, burned into my brain.

The wails within me flared, and I had to let them out or they would rip right through my chest. I started howling. The ugly, loud way, the way animals growl when they're injured. I held myself on the floor, on my knees, rocking back and forth.

"What the hell is going on here?" Dad, who never came into my room, stormed through the door.

I saw myself through his eyes, a grown woman kneeling, sobbing, and felt ridiculous. I straightened up and wiped my tears and nose with the back of my hand. "Nothing, Dad, sorry. Everything's fine. I just got a little upset about something, that's all."

"Thought someone had ripped your head off," Dad mumbled and shut the door as he left the room.

I sat on my bed, all those beastly howls still roiling inside me, with nowhere to go. Once when we were children, my mom said that Saša's tears always broke her heart. "When Saša cries, he never lets out a sound," she'd said. "There are only these enormous tears rolling down his cheeks." What she hadn't said, but implied, was that because I cried with sound, my sorrow wasn't as real, wasn't as heartbreaking as his.

I lay on my bed, the roars frozen inside my chest, and thought of my mom up there in heaven. Big fat tears came and went, rolled and rolled, but there was no one to be heartbroken for me. I was that tree, felled inside the forest, that no one had heard fall. That tree that didn't make a sound.

TWENTY-SIX

WHEN I FINALLY RETURN home that evening after giving Dad and Saša my ultimatum, my phone is still resting where I left it on the dining room table. There are two new messages. The first one is from Saša. It says simply, "You win."

Meaning, go ahead and sell the property since you can't be reasoned with. Meaning, he disagrees, but apparently not to the extent of shouldering the burden of Lovorun Heritage Hotel himself.

You win, it says.

At what, I have no idea.

For days, Dad speaks to me only when he can't avoid it. When he needs me to get him something from the store, or to take him to the doctor. Our lunches together are long, silent marathons, punctuated only by cutlery hitting the plates and overly polite requests to pass him the salt. The rest of the day, he takes to his bed, as if my decision is making him physically sick.

A constant need to apologize sits amid my chest, but if I do, I'll have to backtrack on the words I finally found the courage to say. And I'm not willing to do that, even while I'm still questioning them myself.

My mom often comes to mind, those moments of quiet after her fights with Dad, when the two of us would be kneading pizza dough. "Sometimes, we have to make sacrifices for the greater good," she'd say. She never elaborated on what she meant, but it was implied she was referring to her staying married to Dad so that Saša and I would have a normal family. A sacrifice I was grateful for because I couldn't imagine being a child from a broken home, not in a time and society that still stigmatized divorce. But now I see the truth neither of us could see back then. Our home wasn't any less broken just because we lived in one household.

It begs the question, then, where is that fine line between sacrifices that make sense and those that don't? And how do we tell them apart?

At night, I lie awake in my bed, wrestling with myself. It's always so much easier to question oneself in the dark. I'm split in two—the person wanting to apologize, and the person observing the person wanting to apologize. *It could be a good life*, the Apologizer says. *You could be your own boss, finally earn a decent salary. You could even keep the olive grove. It's a sensible thing to do.* But even as I'm saying these things, my very essence screeches and bolts as if it were a car careening into a wall.

I spent years watching the upstream swimming my father had to do just to keep his business afloat. I saw his frustration over the shifting regulations, the quagmire of indecipherable codes and bylaws, needing connections that he never seemed to have or that were never as strong as other people's connections. How all of it had made him first miserable, then angry, then bitter, until it took the worst kind of toll on his health.

Many people start businesses in Croatia, the Apologizer protests.

Yeah, the Observer retorts, *but maybe their skin is thicker than mine.*

But when all the other arguments fall silent, there is this: an amorphous feeling of doom for tethering myself even more tightly to a life I don't want. A life where I have no say.

A position in which I am the executor of someone else's dreams.

The ultimate concession.

There's so little of me left. If I stretch myself any thinner, I will disappear.

The other message I received that night was from Asier. "The board is interested," the text said. "Let's set up a viewing." And then, "I'm really looking forward to seeing you again."

For a couple of days, I didn't answer.

"Everything all right?" he asked then, but I haven't answered that either. I'm being childish and unprofessional, but if I answer him, I'll have committed to a particular course of action, and I'm not ready to do that yet.

TWENTY-SEVEN

MARINA ASKS ME TO give her a hand cleaning her sailboat. She has a tour coming up, and her young cousins, whose help she usually enlists, are getting ready for their prom. I don't think much of her request; I've helped her now and again over the years, and she and Vlaho have helped me with the olive harvest in return. Besides, it's better than spending time in the caustic atmosphere reigning between me and Dad, between me and Asier's unanswered texts.

It's a beautiful mid-April afternoon, the sky so low and thick-weaved I could comb my fingers through it. Marina is waiting for me on her boat, moored in the marina near the town center, two buckets of soapy water laid out before her, and a couple of bottles of our favorite craft beer sweating on the aft deck. The boat looks suspiciously clean, but we take our long-sleeved shirts off and get to work, running sponges up and down the lengthy teak-wood beams.

"You look different somehow," Marina says after a long stint of working in silence. We haven't seen each other since that day in the town when the three of us had coffee and I told them about the hotel sale. I can't help feeling she's still fishing for answers.

"Different, how?"

"I don't know, just . . . different vibe I guess." She is scrubbing away, not making eye contact. "Does it have anything to do with that man, what did you say his name was?"

She looks at me now. I sit back on the freshly washed gunwale, ignoring the moisture soaking into my pants. I want to ask her, *What's it to you? Why do you in particular—you, Marina Oberan, the current wife of my ex-husband, ask me that question with such obvious discomfort?* But of course, I can't ask her that.

I squeeze the sponge dry, gathering thoughts that scatter like beads of soapy water over the ship's beams. I don't know if over the years she sensed my yearning for her husband, the gaze I'd let linger on him sometimes, when a conversation stalled. That sense of possessiveness that still haunts me, this flawed belief that he's mine despite being married to her. I tried not to let it show, but who knows what my body reveals when I let my guard down. If she noticed, she never said anything. Why would she? At the end of the day, I went home to my father, and Vlaho was making his home with her.

"I fought with my dad and Saša about Lovorun," I say, unwilling to answer the question she's really asking. Telling her that I like Asier the way she suspects would be as good as telling her I've moved on, and I'm not ready to absolve her, whether she needs absolution or not. I'm painfully aware that it was my decision to leave Vlaho, and I got over myself in so many ways to be able to be near them, but a small part of me is still resentful—will always be resentful—that the two of them paired off. "They don't want to sell, and I don't want to run the hotel. But I don't know if I'm just being selfish."

Marina fetches us two beers then rests her back against the stainless-steel railing. The setting sun creates a halo around her blond hair, and a thought occurs to me, that she looks kind of beautiful.

"Weren't you eager to sell?" she says.

I exhale all the turmoil that's been pressing hard against my chest these past few days. "I was. But does it make sense to sell? Is it the right thing to do?"

She shrugs. "Does it feel right to you?"

"I think so. But that's subjective. The real question here is, does it make sense, objectively? Saša has a full-time job and lives a three-hour drive away, and Dad's sick. So my decision seals the deal for us all. If I accept what they're proposing, everyone wins. Dad gets to see his dream come true and, in time, all three of us get recurring revenue. We keep the land. I keep my olives. Instead, if we sell, we get money that will melt away over time. Dad loses this one last chance to do something big before he dies, my brother loses a second income, and I lose the grove." I let out a long breath, tallying all these losses. Seems like I've answered my own question.

Marina gets up and throws a shirt over her back. It's become chilly now that the sun is setting. "Sometimes, when it's really important, we have to do what's right by ourselves. It sucks, I know. I've hurt some people I care about deeply that way." She holds my gaze for a beat too long. "But it's the God's honest truth."

The skin along my spine pricks, but before I can say anything, she pushes herself against the railing and goes into the cabin to put away the cleaning supplies. Just as well. We never talked about the fact that she took Vlaho from me, and this oblique apology, if that's what it was, is likely the most I can bear to talk about it without giving away too much myself.

I breathe in, looking around the marina. A cool breeze sweeps in from the park across the street, raising the hairs on my arms. The evening is so beautiful it hurts. It feels abundant, like raw potential, like everything is possible, but nobody knows better than I do how misguiding potential can be.

I take a swig of beer and watch the diamonds glint on the sea surface. There one moment, lost the next, hard to fixate on, forever elusive. I mull over what Marina said, and the decisions I made. Refusing to go to New York for that competition all those years ago for fear of putting a wedge between Vlaho and myself. Moving in with my dad, and taking over his company, because there was no one else to do it. Leaving Vlaho so that he wouldn't be punished for my infertility, so that his mother could have grandchildren. Decisions I felt forced, even coerced into for the greater good.

For the first time, they reveal themselves to me for what they were. Choices. My choices.

Because even conceding to someone else's wishes, giving in to meet someone else's needs—even sacrificing yourself—is a choice.

These decisions then became threads, that became strings, that became ropes, wound tight around me, and Dad, and Vlaho, and all the other people I love, braiding into this particular reality we are living now. And who says this reality is any better than any other reality could've been, had I braided my ropes differently?

When I get back into my car, I reach for my backpack and take out my phone. With my pruned fingers, waterlogged from all the washing, I open the text thread to Asier that has been sitting silent the whole past week. "I'm ready for the viewing whenever you are."

TWENTY-EIGHT

IT SURPRISED NO ONE as much as it had me, that I could be friends with Vlaho's wife. That I would be able to witness him forming a family with someone else without completely disintegrating. But life serves bitter dishes sometimes that, after you've chewed on them for a while, start to taste good, and become good for you. Kind of like taking a sip of olive oil, its piquancy biting down your throat, but then working healing wonders in your stomach, intestines, veins.

The dish was bitter for a long time. After Vlaho called to tell me Marina was pregnant, I didn't want to see either of them. For some time, Vlaho continued inviting me to meet for coffee, but I couldn't stomach it. That guillotine still hung above me. Seeing him would've snapped the rope.

A part of me hoped they would pack up and move to Cavtat so I could roam the town without fretting I'd run into them. In a town as small as Zadar, with its one cinema, one theater, one mall, one vendor near the town bridge selling roasted chestnuts in winter or corn on the cob in summer, it was bound to happen sooner rather than later.

I ran into Marina on the town bridge of all places, when Maro was three months old. I noticed her a moment before she saw me, but there was nowhere to go to avoid her unless I wanted to throw myself into the murky water below. Her face opened in a smile as she stopped, blocking my way with the rosemary-colored stroller.

She was puffier than the last time I'd seen her, she'd obviously retained much of her baby weight. But despite that, her face was drawn, dark circles under her eyes showing she wasn't getting much sleep. A new-mother face.

A face I would never have.

The town bridge undulated under the footsteps of people treading past us, a movement you could feel only if you stood still. It destabilized me, made me unsteady on my feet. The pram was luckily facing away from me. I couldn't imagine what would happen if I saw his son, the son he'd had with someone other than me.

"Hey," Marina said. She reached for me and kissed both my cheeks. "I'm so happy to see you."

I could tell she meant it, but I couldn't pretend I returned the sentiment. Nights and nights of agony, imagining them across the town, sharing a bed. Nights and nights of cold-sweat terrors, sharp images of them loving each other. Worst of all, nights upon nights of feeling his lips on mine, the pressure of his head nestled between my shoulder blades, his center against my center, only to wake up empty-handed. Phantom pain, they call it, when a limb you've lost still feels like it's there, hurting.

"Where are you off to?" she asked.

"Just buying new flip-flops for the summer."

"Oh," she said. "Do you have time for coffee?"

The baby cooed. She put her hand inside the pram and rocked their son back to sleep, her eyes never leaving mine.

"Congratulations on your baby," I said, my mouth desiccated. "I don't really have time for coffee."

Marina looked at her watch, her lips breaking into that same conspiratorial smile she'd flash when we mocked Šime, our Italian teacher. "It's eleven. If you're out and about, it either means that you have a day off or you're working the afternoon shift, which doesn't start until two." She pushed the stroller a step forward, then reached for my arm. "Come on."

I was too stunned to say no, so my legs followed her. We walked in silence for a while. "How've you been?" she asked me as if I were the one who'd produced another human being since we'd last talked.

My impulse was to lie. To hide how this whole business of them marrying and having a baby stretched the very fabric of me to the point where I wasn't sure anything was left but the holes. That a veil had come over me, even darker than it had been when I first learned I was infertile. But another part of me, a wicked part, wanted to dump all this on her. Make her rot with guilt and remorse. Caught in between those two options, I said nothing.

A gauze hung over the pram, shielding Vlaho's son from the June sun, and protecting me from seeing him. Still, my eyes glued to it, drawn by its irresistible magnetic force.

"Still learning Italian?" she asked.

"Yeah, right. We barely made it to our first-level exams, the class was so bad."

"True," she cackled, a clean, untethered sound. It reminded me of why I'd liked her when I first met her, how at ease with herself she was. "Signor Šime made us laugh so hard we almost started speaking Italian through our asses."

We were on Kalelarga now. There was bustle around us, people rushing about, shopping, just like when we'd strolled the town in search of a non-occupato table for our coffee after class. I could almost hear the echoes of our giggles as we spoke Croatian words with an Italian accent. She'd been the only friend I'd made in Zadar since high school.

It hit me, this truth I hadn't been aware of.

I didn't only resent Marina for taking Vlaho from me.

I resented Vlaho for taking Marina from me too.

Our sandals synchronized their tapping against the cobblestoned street. Despite wanting to break the pattern, I couldn't make myself fall out of rhythm with her.

"I've missed you," she said. "We both have."

I snorted. It was so sudden and piglike that Marina started laughing and so did I. A strange sense of release streamed between us. We fell into an easier silence from then on.

He had missed me.

We found a table on the Forum and ordered our macchiatos.

"I'm sorry," she said, stirring a packet of sugar into her cup. "We never planned for any of this."

A tremor started deep in my bones. Last thing I wanted to hear about was how they were consumed by a sudden flame of irresistible passion. How was that any better than slowly giving in to it? "Look, you were both single, and you hit it off. I get it. Neither one of you owes me any explanations."

"It wasn't like that. It's . . . " She sighed, looking toward Ugljan island across the Zadar Channel, as if that's where she'd find the words. "We were both—"

A buzz hissed in my ears, my whole body blaring at the impending doom. If she said one more word, I would get annihilated right then and there. "Please." I put my hands over my ears, staring down at the pram's wheel. "I really don't want to know."

In my peripheral vision, Marina nodded her agreement. Funny how we could carry on an entire soul-crushing conversation without ever looking at each other.

The tower bell above us sounded half past, and the baby stirred and started bellowing its throaty, nasal cries. Before I could react, Marina lifted him up and pressed him against her chest. He was unbelievably tiny in his onesie, his thin froggy legs splayed apart, his bum covered in a diaper that was much too big for it. His feet were pink and chubby and crinkled, each of his toes the size of a single lentil. Marina was saying something I couldn't hear.

"Would that be okay?" Her voice sharpened at my ear.

"What?"

"Would you mind holding Maro while I run to the bathroom? I swear my bladder shrunk to half its size since this fellow elbowed his way out."

There was no way I was taking him. "I, um—"

But Marina was already handing him over, adjusting his miniature head against my breastbone, to the side so that he could breathe. She was gone before I could say no. And just like that, Vlaho's baby was resting against my heart.

He was weightless, yet I'd never held anything more substantial. His gossamer hair tickled my chin. He made the funniest little expressions, as if he were going through a roller coaster of emotions but was unbothered enough to open his eyes. He looked goofy and wise at the same time, a pink Smurfy sage. He had his father's nose. I put my lips on his soft head. He smelled like baby powder and innocence. To my horror, my chest expanded to usher him inside. "Hey there, little one."

Marina stood at the cafe's entrance with a sneaky smile. She took her time walking over. "You want to give him back, Aunt Ivona?"

I shook my head, breathing the baby in again. "You witch. I bet you didn't even have to pee."

PART THREE

ASIER

TWENTY-NINE

I WATCH THE AIRPLANE land from the parking lot behind the airport building. It's the last day of April, but the weather has turned, as if to prove that it can manage one more bite before it gives in to the spring warmth. The wind rustles through the tops of nearby cypresses, the stormy clouds low and threatening on the horizon.

Something akin to stage fright—excitement mixed with fear—pulls in my gut as I'm waiting for Asier. I don't know where we stand, where I've left us. After that fight with my family, I was short with him. Not just because I didn't know if I wanted to go through with the sale, but because that shame for wanting him tainted whatever it was growing between us, and I couldn't cleanse it.

So when he sent me a photo of the sun setting over Hyde Park, glistening in millenary hues of green, I didn't answer. A few days later, he sent a photo of his neighbor's mutt, an adorable dog he said he talked to when he sat on his balcony, to which I replied, "a good-looking friend you have there." A couple of days later, he sent me a poem about an olive tree he had "accidentally come across" online, as if one can stumble upon poetry without intending to, and I sent back only "lovely," even though the poem chiseled its way into my heart, its verses about resilience and sturdiness both sparse and humbling.

He stopped texting me after that.

It felt safer that way, getting us back to the realm of business acquaintances negotiating a deal. There was so much in the ether already, all kinds of grief, anticipation, and anxiety because of the upcoming sale, incredible muscle work needed to keep my head straight. Piling more onto it felt unwieldy.

What were we, after all, but two worlds briefly touching? We were leading such different lives, often in different parts of the globe, and I couldn't imagine anything meaningful emerging from this.

So I replaced the new habit of texting with him at night with my old habit of stalking Vlaho's socials, but poring over his photos wasn't landing the same way. Something had been lost, the painful thrill of it subtly shifted to the side, and I found myself scrolling through the abyss of my feed instead. One night, I came across a post with a photo of two lemurs hugging, saying that a person needs eight hugs a day for regular maintenance alone—to reduce stress, lower blood pressure, and tone the vagus nerve. Eight hugs, in other words, just to keep functioning.

In the near darkness of my room, I turned on my back and tried to recall the last time I was hugged. Not a passing sideways embrace at hello, or the pat on the back Dad gives me when he's in a good mood. A real hug. I thought back and back, and there was nothing as far as the eye could see.

So when Asier said he was coming for the viewing, I offered to pick him up. He said I didn't have to, he could take a cab—by then the distance I'd put between us had festered—but I insisted.

I have no idea if this hug deprivation is a hoax or a scientific fact. All kinds of half-truths float on Instagram, there's no way of telling if it's true.

But it is true.

So, here I am.

I tighten the edges of my jacket against the wind, make one more swipe to try to comb my hair behind my ear, but it refuses to stay put. People start exiting the double glass door and spilling onto the parking lot. It's hard to breathe despite the wind blowing gusts of air into my face.

The crowd dissipates and still no sign of him. But then the door slides open again, and there he is, absorbed in his phone as he's rolling his suitcase behind him. He looks up, and even though I don't move or wave, he spots me instantly. His smile is measured and fleeting.

We walk toward each other, then stop with a meter between us. I feel every molecule of the space we didn't cross.

"Hey," he says.

"Welcome to Zadar," I say, sounding like a taxi driver picking up a tourist.

My whole body is sensitive as he reaches and gives me a not-too-near one-sided hug. It feels anticlimactic. As he recedes from me, I catch a whiff of a citrusy, manly tang under the stale smell of airplane. A small thing, this scent, but something inside me gathers.

"I hope you had a good flight?" I ask.

"It was fine," he says, unsmiling.

—

As I drive us into the city, lightning cracks on the horizon, and the first fat raindrops hit the windshield. The town is gray and lifeless as we descend into it, as if it's not ready to show itself either. "I'll take you directly to the hotel," I say. "You must be tired, and, well, the weather is—"

"Yeah," he says.

"I can take you to see Lovorun tomorrow. The storm should clear by then."

"Sounds like a plan." He's looking out the window. I take note of the first impression my town must be making. Junkyards, car dealerships, warehouses, and bathroom supply stores with glass windows that glint like golden teeth in a mouthful of cavities. Houses interspersed in between, made of concrete and not even painted, their gardens filled with rusty old car wrecks and rototillers, and patches of overgrown cabbages and spring onions. I have the urge to tell him there's more to my town than this, its center is old and beautiful, and it will take his breath away, but he's more absorbed with the sights—the neighborhoods thankfully getting neater the more westward we go—than maintaining a conversation with me.

His reserve drills holes in my excitement, until it sinks completely.

Until I sink with understanding. I've really screwed this up.

We enter the hotel complex and drive down a narrow road surrounded by a pine tree forest. I round a fountain and stop the car, but don't shut down the engine. The rain is pouring now. It's like a curtain, isolating us in the car, hiding us from the outside world. It makes the moment intimate, acute. I'm aware of every part of my body and his, of even the softest sounds of our breaths.

"When would you like me to pick you up?" Only now do I dare look at him, and he does the same.

"I'm an early riser. Just text me when you're here." He reaches for the handle to let himself out. I want to stop him, but don't know how. "Thanks for the ride," he says.

A split-second movement. I lean in, aiming for his cheek, but kiss the corner of his mouth instead. I pull back, mortified, pinpricking all over, drawing back the smell of him—mist and citrus, with me.

He looks ahead of himself for a moment, barely containing a smile. He's not a beautiful man, but his angular features have a way of arranging themselves into something pleasing when he smiles, as if the sharp contours are only inflicted on him, and there's something warmer underneath that aches to get out.

"See you tomorrow," he says, and exits into the pouring rain, goes behind the car to get his suitcase, doesn't even hurry to retrieve it. He closes the trunk, then taps twice against the window, and I press my foot against the clutch, but don't go yet. Instead, I watch him walk to the hotel entrance, his blue shirt soaking through, and when I finally shift into first, I realize I'm barely containing a smile too.

THIRTY

THE NEXT MORNING IS deceptive in its calmness, a quiet anticipation building beneath the surface of our polite exchanges as I drive us to Lovorun. Asier is pensive, and I can't tell if it's because he's focused on the scouting job he's here to do, or because of that near kiss that still hovers between us like a specter. I fight the urge to bring it up, to apologize for my clumsy move. Maybe it's best to pretend it didn't happen. Maybe he doesn't think much of it at all.

When we arrive, I tour him through Lovorun, show him every nook and cranny, lead him behind the reception desk made of smooth olive wood, its grain wavy and curved and irregular. It is rare, I tell him, because olives are rarely harvested for wood in the Mediterranean. They're much too valuable. He slides his palm across the lacquered surface but doesn't say anything. I take him through the dining room with its ten tables; the kitchen in the back, small but equipped with shiny, state-of-the-art stainless-steel appliances. He says nothing, his face reveals nothing. Then upstairs through the rooms, one by one, beds bare, mattresses covered in plastic, curtains shielded with wraps so as not to catch dust.

"Want me to tear one open?" I ask, and he shakes his head.

He takes note of everything, though: the beige carpets, the double vanities in the bathrooms and claw-foot tubs. The crystal chandeliers, the art decorating the walls. He stops by each painting, and I'm dying to ask him what he thinks of the choices I made, my small contribution because everything else reflects Dad's taste. I commissioned the art from a local painter who uses colors and shapes so simple they tease the eye, to depict the typical Dalmatian motifs: fig leaves, piers, church towers.

We make our way out of the main house and into the small cottages surrounding it, their terraces ensconced behind crawling jasmine and rosemary hedges. "These have finished exterior, but still need some work on the inside," I say.

From there, we proceed to the main yard, where we stand side by side, all without him saying a single word.

Asier crosses his arms at his chest, lost in thought. I want him to love it, to be in awe of it, and I also want him to say he won't take it, and then it scares me he'll say he won't buy it, that it's not on par with the gorgeous hotels they already have in more sought-after places like Porto, and Pisa, and Crete, and Corsica, which will mean I'll have to find some other way out of our financial conundrum.

When I can't take the uncertainty anymore, I draw nearer and ask, "So, what do you think?"

He takes a while to turn to me, as if I'd summoned him from the depths of spreadsheets and calculations. "Hmm?"

"Do you like it?"

He inhales slowly. I can tell he knows he's keeping me on edge taking his time with the answer. "I don't know . . . ," he says, and just as my legs turn to liquid, he breaks into a grin. "Are you kidding me? It's exactly what we're looking for."

"Show me the olive grove," he says after I'd recited all the legal details about the hotel.

Showing him the house wasn't hard. Over the years of renovations, it has morphed into something I don't feel as connected with, something alien. But showing him the olive grove—as a selling point at that—feels no better than offering your child up to a potential kidnapper. It's been a faithful companion throughout my life. A place where I lay in the grass as a child, watching the cottony clouds amass on the horizon. A place where I followed Baba around, hearing her grumble as she picked dandelion leaves for salad between the trees with her gnarly hands. A place where I let all my sorrows leak out of me once I'd found out I was barren. A place that taught me that even though I was infertile, I still had the ability to make something grow and thrive.

I extend my hand over the small iron gate. "You can see it from here," I say.

He gives me a pointed look. "No. I want you to show it to me."

He's serious, and when he's serious, his face can look almost cruel.

"Not much to see," I concede, walking through the gate, not wanting to make a thing out of it. Gnarled old olives lie beyond, forming three neat rows, sleepy in the sunlight. "The terrain that belongs to the hotel stretches all the way to the end of the peninsula over there," I point southwest, "and upward to that dry wall."

I walk with my back to him. It's only a grove, but the care I've put into it shows. Every leaf and blade of grass in its place, the ease with which the trimmed branches sway in the wind. It is beautiful in an unspoken, quiet way. There's a hush in this place that has a way of seeping into your soul if you make yourself still enough.

Midway through the grove, I falter to a stop, as if saying, *There, that's it, you've seen it all.* Asier saunters past me before returning to stand right in front of me, close, past the line where a business partner or a friend would stop. He's not as tall as Vlaho, so our eyes are almost level, but despite that, he has a way of taking up space and occupying attention. "What's the one thing you like most about this place?" he asks.

He reaches for my arms, crossed at my chest, and starts playing with the loose thread on the hem of my sleeve, as if it's perfectly normal for him to be doing that. But I can sense his alertness, his whole body's sharp vigilance that mirrors my own. I stop breathing when his fingers trace over the fabric and onto my skin.

It is so soft, his touch. Human.

It's also a door.

I can't make myself look at him, because if I do, something will happen. A recognition, an acceptance. Here, in this place, of all places.

Pressure builds behind my nose and eyes, burning hot. I uncross my arms and move past him. "Why do you want to know?" I look out into the distance. My face is aflame.

"I don't know," he says. "I just do."

He's prying into a part of me that's too personal to share, and from the tone of his voice, he knows it. "What's the point? It's not like I'm keeping it."

"Indulge me." Side by side, we face the sea, the place where it opens between the mainland and islands, onward to infinity.

I take a deep breath, and when I let it out, I tell him, "Okay, close your eyes."

"Me?" He asks, puzzled.

"Yes, you."

"All right . . . " He spreads his legs for balance and shuts his eyes.

"Now, what do you hear?"

The sound around us is as clean as the vitreous air, uncluttered, unpolluted by civilization. Atop silence, only birds gossip, flying in and out of branches as they build their nests. The sea laps the nearby shore in murmuring hums. Receding, it disappears between rocks, blooping and whimpering.

"What do you smell?" I ask, before he's even answered. I focus on the scents now, the smell of juicy grass, the scent of earth after yesterday's rainstorm, now evaporating in the warm sun, sweet like baby breath.

"What can you feel on your skin?" An enveloping of air cleansed by rain. The sun, hot as it kisses the skin. The brine of the sea.

Asier's eyes are still closed. "Spring," I tell him. "In summer, everything changes. There's a relentless hum of cicadas, smell of wild oregano and fennel. Soil parched, too hot to stand on barefoot. In fall, the dry smell of immortelle and rosemary, dampened by dewy, foggy mornings. Windless calms binding the sea in place. And in winter, sharp chilly winds, piercing through however many layers of clothes you have on, the skin on your hands chapped and red until you can't straighten your fingers. Salt lifted off the sea, filling your nostrils, purifying you."

He opens his eyes, a drowsy look lingering in them as he orients himself.

"Seasons," I say. "That it's forever changing, but always stays the same. That it makes you feel alive like nothing else can. That's what I love the most about this place."

It happens so fast afterward. When we get into the car, we're kissing. It's urgent and hot, and necessary. The gearshift and handbrake form a barrier between us, not allowing us to get closer. It's all futile grabbing, inability to hold on to anything, always at odd angles, never in a complete way. The drive back to Zadar is both agony and a heartbeat. His hand on my hand, my hand on his knee. His kiss in my hair, his murmur in my ear.

THIRTY-ONE

AS WE APPROACH ZADAR, the traffic thickens and so do my nerves. For all the kissing before we left Lovorun, neither of us has mentioned our destination. Perhaps he expects me to drive him back to the hotel, but he hasn't asked, and I'm afraid if I take him there, I'll give the wrong impression. That spending the night together is a given, when I'm not ready to do that. But I don't want to leave the flame between us unattended either. I haven't been held or kissed in years, the mere warmth of his skin against mine is a salve. So, when we reach the outskirts of the town, the ugly part where all the car dealerships and warehouses are, I ask him if he's hungry, if he wants to go sightseeing.

"Sure," he says, and I flip on the turn signal to steer us toward the center.

We park in the lot at the neck of the old-town peninsula, near my old high school, and I take him through the dilapidated schoolyard. We lean against a wall across from the yellow building that used to be a military facility before it became a school. "My classroom was where those windows and air-conditioning units are." I point to the middle of the first floor. "Though there weren't air-conditioning units back then. We had wood-fed furnaces for heating."

He laughs. "When did you go to school, in the nineteenth century?"

"Ha-ha." I elbow him with mock offense that's hard to enact. Playfulness brings out a side of him that's so tangibly personable. It's like easing myself into a hot bath after a day of hard work in the grove. "The school ordered chopped wood each fall and stored it on the ground level. We used to fight over who got to go on log duty—distributing logs throughout the school, especially if there was an exam to avoid. And this wall," I pat the cement behind our backs, "is where we spent our recesses. Having a boyfriend from another school visit you during recess was the ultimate sign of commitment on his part."

Asier reaches for my hand and pulls me between his legs. Bursts of heat flicker in my lower abdomen. "I bet you got to show off like that all the time."

"Yeah—no." I scoff. "I rarely had boyfriends, and none of them ever came to my recess."

"So, I'm the first one?"

I twirl a button on his shirt, realizing that in all the years we'd been together, I never brought Vlaho here. We passed my school many times by car and on foot, but we never stopped to admire it, to reminisce. It comes as a surprise, that there are still firsts I could have with someone else, when it felt as though all my firsts had forever been consumed with him.

I touch the scarred skin on Asier's face. "You're the first one." It's strange but comforting, this sense of familiarity sprouting so fast between us. He stands still and alert while I trace the pockmarks with my fingertips. "This happen to you in high school?"

He nods, once. "It was bad for a while. Girls weren't exactly lining up to go out with me, as you can imagine." He closes his arms around my waist. I put mine around his neck. My body burns and crackles like kindling for holding him so close.

"Did it hurt?" I ask, meaning, the acne. Meaning, the girls rejecting him. Behind my back, a whole school filled with avatars of former schoolmates, four years of festered pain.

"It was only temporary. I knew I'd outgrow it sometime soon."

The pragmatism of his answer strikes me as nothing short of brilliant.

—

After the schoolyard, I take him on a tour of the places in my town that are dear to me, instead of the usual tourist attractions. The scruffy little cafe where Tara and I hung out after school, drinking our first macchiatos. The hill in the middle of the park where Tara and I lit our first cigarette. The bench on the riva, the white stone-paved sea promenade, where I used to go when the world became too much and I needed to step off for a moment.

We stop for lunch in a restaurant where they serve seasonal food, wild asparagus and artichokes this time of year. When our plates arrive, he says, "You've told me so many things, but none of it is recent history."

Heat rushes up my neck, the kind that leaves hives. He's right. I've shown him only things from before my college years. Unwittingly, I steered us away from the city hall, where I married Vlaho, and the courthouse, where our marriage ended. And the Five Wells Square, where I introduced him to Marina, and the narrow alley where Marina and I took Italian together. His perceptiveness takes me off guard, this businessman who lets nothing slip past him. How laid bare I am to him without even realizing it. Oddly, it's not a completely uncomfortable thought.

"And meanwhile, we've spent hours talking about me, and I don't know a single thing about you." A cheap tactic to change the subject, but inside me questions about him multiply by the second.

I can't quite pin him down. He has the aura of a practical guy, but people like that usually lean toward easy, uncomplicated conversations. And all the questions he's asked so far have been of the probing kind.

Asier sits back. "Fair enough. What do you want to know?"

The things I want to know are, unsurprisingly, the very things I haven't revealed about myself. "Have you ever been married?"

He laughs. "No beating around the bush, huh? And no, I haven't."

A knot loosens in my chest. "And . . . do you have children?" The question I loathe being asked, but can't help asking, even though I don't know what I hope he'll answer. It's stupid, pretending his response has anything to do with me. We are barely anything to one another, and where can the future take us but away from each other? But if he says he wants children, whatever chance we have ends here.

He bides his time, and for the first time I feel like I've stumbled on a topic he's not comfortable with. "I do have a son," he says. "Iker. He's fifteen. He lives with his mother in Bristol."

A son. "That's wonderful."

"Yeah. He's great. I don't see him as often as I'd like."

A vulnerable thing to admit, I note, but don't say.

"I'm away a lot," he continues. "And when I'm in London, it's hard to coordinate with his schedule. There's always school, soccer practice, friends' birthday parties, camps he doesn't want to miss. It's that age, you know, when everything is more important than your parents."

I nod, thinking about it, about age. About my mom who is now gone. And about that bottomless need inside me, still present now, at thirty-eight, for her and Dad to like me, love me, acknowledge me, take pride in me.

"What about you? Do you have children?" he asks.

I put the cutlery at the sides of my plate. The question is a stage light shining down on me. I could lie. I could pretend that I didn't want kids, that I couldn't care less if I had them. Being barren defines you in a way no other medical condition does. Infertility isn't just an affliction; it's a failure. A failure to be a woman. A failure to reproduce. A nod from good old Darwin telling you that if you—your genome, your personality, your very nature—weren't so intrinsically flawed, you'd be allowed to procreate.

Asier's looking at me with his austere gray-green eyes. A smart person would weigh her words, make herself more desirable.

This, I realize, has always been my problem. That I think I have a choice in what I'll say, when in reality, it's a compulsion. I'm a valve, not a semi-permeable membrane, like most other people. I'm either open or closed. Either divulging too much, or nothing at all. "I couldn't have children."

Asier takes a napkin, presses it against his lips, allowing me the space to go on.

"I was married once," I say. "I couldn't have children and then I left my husband so that he could."

Instead of going concave, my chest expands. It's so good to lay the truth out in the open, this truth I've never told anyone. Not my mom, because she was dead by the time the decision was made. Not Tara because she wouldn't have understood. Not Marina, because we never talked about men, until we couldn't talk about the one man we both loved. And certainly not Vlaho.

"That's . . . wow," Asier says. "Having children was that important to your husband?"

Underneath his words, an implicit accusation of Vlaho. "No, he wasn't like that. As a matter of fact, he still doesn't know this is why I left him."

"Did he end up having children?"

"Two. A boy and a girl."

Asier nods, as if saying, *Touché*, and I can sense a distaste for Vlaho forming inside him, a hasty, unfair judgment of the man he doesn't know. I want to dislike him for it, but really, this sort of protectiveness only endears him to me more.

When I drop him off at the hotel, I shut off the engine. With his job of scouting done, he's going away tomorrow, and that adds a layer of urgency to how we hold each other. There's something about the way he kisses that reminds me of Beethoven symphonies, the constant change of tempo, a buildup, a release. *Adagio, andante, presto.* It's making me a little lightheaded.

"Do you want to come up?" he murmurs.

I stop, my lips pressed to the soft skin below his jawline. I know what he's really asking, I should've expected it. But finding Vlaho at nineteen means I've never done this before. I've never had a one-night, or a second-night, or a third-night stand. I've never even taken my clothes off before a man who wasn't Vlaho.

It's not only that I'm afraid I'm no match for a man as experienced as Asier must be. That I won't know how to hold him or touch him the right way. It's that if I do this, I will have erased Vlaho off me forever. His touch and taste and the way his skin felt on mine will be washed away by someone else's touch, smell, and taste. There can be more firsts with someone else, it seems, but more losses to endure as well.

"It's okay," Asier says, pulling back from our embrace, and I realize I've let the silence linger too long.

The desire that still courses through my body is going bad on the inside for being locked in, having nowhere to go. "I want to come up," I tell him, "but I didn't . . . I don't . . . I've never . . . " I run out of words.

"It's fine," he says, but I can tell he's disappointed, maybe even thinks I led him on, kissing and touching him the way I just did.

"I have to go home and make dinner for my dad," I say, my cheeks aflame.

He tilts his head, unsure if I'm telling the truth or using Dad as a pretext. He'd be right, either way.

But how can I tell him the full scope of the truth? That I need more than attraction to take this leap? Tara snorts whenever we talk about this. "It's the age of Tinder for God's sake, and you're letting cobwebs get caught down there. Most women would die to be able to hook up with random sexy men," she says, and I think of the substantial beer belly Stipe has grown over the years, while Tara, despite birthing three children, still looks like a Pilates star.

I can't help it. It's always rubbed me the wrong way, this fact that people will sooner share their bodies with one another than their thoughts or secrets.

Tara thinks I'm a prude.

But it's not a matter of morals or conviction. It's the valve thing. I'm either all in, or all out. "I need more time," I say to Asier, then struggle to meet his eyes.

A smile gets away from him. "So you don't really need to go make your dad dinner?"

"No, I do. But I'd love to come back to spend more time with you. High school style, since it seems to be today's theme."

THIRTY-TWO

LATER THAT EVENING, AFTER I've served my father dinner, I walk through the hotel lobby and climb up the stairs to Asier's room. He's waiting for me at the door, kisses my cheek as he lets me in. The room is as neat and tidy as everything about him is, a shirt folded over the back of the chair, no sign of a suitcase, no shoes scattered around. Only a laptop on the desk in the corner, and a pen resting diagonally on a notebook next to it. The smell of deodorant and shower gel wafts on the cloud of hot air flowing from the bathroom. Instead of his usual button-down, he's wearing a cotton T-shirt and a pair of jeans. The domestic edition of a man who uses business as a playground. He's barefoot, his short hair damp from the shower, and I have the urge to inhale him to the bottom of my lungs.

"Make yourself comfortable," he says, taking my raincoat. I unlace my Converse All Stars and slip them off as he opens a minibar and hands me a beer, then sits in the chair while he cracks open his bottle.

I sit on the bed, opposite him. He's stiff and awkward, like we hadn't kissed for over an hour in my car, or all around the town, under the tiramol strings with clothes drying on them, in narrow alleyways, in my old schoolyard. Funny how not having sex makes people more uncomfortable than having it. "Will you come over here?" I reach out my hand.

He gets up, walks toward me, stops between my legs.

I draw his shoulders, his face, down to me. The kiss is slow and mindful, but it gets deeper and needier fast. We start undressing each other, all the way down to our underwear. We explore each other with hands and lips, until there is no part of our skin that's not covered with fingerprints. Desire swells like a river after snowmelt, and just when it feels like the banks won't be able to hold it in, we let it agonizingly recede. The body is left heavy and impossibly alive, yearning, burning.

"You might be on to something, with this no-sex thing," he says in one of the moments when the buildup of passion makes him pull away and throw himself on his back, panting. "I can't remember the last time I wanted something this much."

It almost makes me go back on what I said. "I know," I say.

Hours pass. The night lulls us into a hush. We're bathed only in the light of the sickle-shaped moon flooding through the open balcony door, the sea rustling through the pebbles on the nearby beach. I lay my head on his chest, and he caresses me with steady, gentle strokes. It's so lovely to be held like this again, so wondrous, this closeness of his warm, breathing body. I can feel myself expanding to inhabit my own body more fully, closer to the edges of my skin, where I haven't been in a while.

He eyes the ceiling, pensive. "Can I ask you something?" His night voice is raspy, whispering like the wind.

"Sure."

"That husband of yours—"

"Ex-husband," I correct.

"Was it a cultural thing? I mean, was that expected of you, to leave him?"

I take my time filling my lungs. "No. If anything, people here are traditional, and marriages are supposed to last forever. I left him because I wanted him to have a shot at having kids of his own."

"Hmm," he whispers.

"What?" I rise to look at him.

"Don't know what to make of it. Either it's the most selfless thing anyone's ever done or . . . "

"Or?"

"An act of total cowardice." Cruel words, but he delivers them tenderly, brushing my hair behind my ear with his fingers.

Heat rushes up my face, and I'm thankful for the dark room.

He's right, of course. It was selfless and selfish at the same time. An act of altruism, rooted in fear, as so many of my decisions have been. I was so afraid of taking ownership, of taking up space. Afraid of waiting for loss so much that I did the act of cutting myself. The fact that Asier sees me with such clarity is both scary and riveting. "Tell me about your son. Iker?"

Asier's gray eyes reflect what little light they catch in near dark. "Iker was two when his mother and I split up. She took him with her back to her hometown, just outside Bristol. He likes it there."

"Does he stay with you sometimes?"

"He does, on occasion. I used to take him on weekends, odd birthdays, and Christmases. But then we stopped doing Christmases because let's face it, the point isn't to order takeout and not have a tree." He gives a brittle laugh. "We used to play soccer. Throw a Frisbee. You know, father-son stuff. But now, he'd rather spend time gaming with his friends than with his old man."

A harrumph escapes me. "You're hardly old. What are you, forty-something?"

"Forty-four. You?"

"Thirty-eight."

I lay my head back on the pillow, thinking about what he said, about his son having better things to do than spend time with him. The images rush through me, of the day I gave up on my mom. The day I closed off to her. The day I quit hoping that things could be different between us.

It seemed like such a final decision at the time, but it was anything but. In all the years after—even after she died, I still ached for a change. To think that Asier has a chance to do right by his child and is letting it slip through his fingers grips me like a muscle spasm I can't let loose.

Asier tenses up as if he's sensed my thoughts. "What?" he asks, looking at me.

"Nothing. I just . . . Nothing."

"Clearly, you have something to say."

"It's nothing," I say with finality. It's not my place to offer opinions. I don't want to ruin this evening by coming on too strong. I barely know him, let alone his son or what *he* wants. "You're not prioritizing your son." The words slip out of my mouth without permission.

Asier sits up, as if I'd whiplashed him. I sit up too and put my hand on his back to mitigate the blow. "You think he doesn't want to hang out, that he always has better things to do. But I would bet Lovorun on this—"

Asier looks back at me and smirks.

"—he just wants you to try harder."

He looks ahead, not moving, not saying anything. Steeping in my words. The atmosphere shifts. It's not that he's mad at me, I can feel as much. It's that I've mirrored back a version of him he doesn't want to see. To accept that you were wrong about something isn't only to accept the mistake itself. It's accepting each time you acted on that false belief. I can feel it inside him, this churning of all the moments when his son pushed him away and he took it at face value. The tallying of all the losses—of time, of closeness, of memories that could've been—and him coming up short.

The conversation moves on somehow, but it's not the same. Asier is heavy, sodden with my words. So after a time, the amount that allows us to pretend that what I said didn't ruin the night, I tell him I'm tired and that he too should go to bed, he's traveling to London tomorrow morning, and he doesn't fight me on it. I gather my clothes and dress, and he holds me again as I'm about to leave and says he'll call soon, but his bruised ego is dripping off him, wedging itself between us.

It's only when I get inside my car that I see several missed calls from Marina and a text message saying, "where the hell are you? i've been trying to reach you all night. call me as soon as you get this. there might be a way for you to save the olive grove."

But it's way past two a.m. and of course I can't call her back.

THIRTY-THREE

BACK HOME, I'M BRIMMING with a nervous energy that nothing seems to pacify. I'm split in two again: the Apologizer, angry with myself for ruining the night—hell, not just the night, but the beginning of something that could be beautiful—by sticking my nose where it doesn't belong; and the Observer, shaking her head, asking when has it ever worked for me to pretend to be someone I'm not? Familiar pain gnaws at me. It never goes away, and on nights like this, I'm afraid it never will.

Unable to calm down enough to go to sleep, I check on Dad. I press my ear against the door of his room to hear his loud snores before I get back into my car and drive off to the cemetery where my mother is laid to rest. It's three a.m. when I get there, and though the premises are well lit, an eeriness hovers over them. A scops owl hoots in the tall cypresses on the other side of the graveyard, tar-black against the city lights.

It pains me to admit this even to myself, but visiting my mother's grave has mostly been a mechanical thing. A rote sequence of actions that allows me to go through the motions without thinking too much about it. First, removing the bouquet of wilted flowers from the vase on the side of the tombstone, and dumping it in the garbage. Then trimming the stems of the fresh flowers and refilling the vase with water from a nearby spigot. Then, arranging the flowers. Mom liked symmetry; she would want the flowers to be arranged neatly.

Then I stand at the foot of the grave and stare at her picture in the small frame etched onto the marble surface of her tombstone. But instead of talking to her, or praying for her, my mind always goes blank, as if it were a grave of an unknown person, someone I've never met.

On a couple of occasions, I tried talking to her, the way I'd heard other people talk to their deceased at nearby graves, but I felt ridiculous speaking to a dead person, and, what stung even worse, I realized I had little to tell her. In front of her grave, I turned into a clenched fist again. I'd been shut off to her for so long before she died that I didn't know how to undo it.

When the whole charade became too uncomfortable, I mumbled a cursory prayer and walked away, feeling like I'd let both her and myself down. It takes a petty person to withhold herself from a dead mother.

But as I'd shuffle my feet along the gravel path, the words would come to me. All the things I wanted to tell her. *Dad drives me nuts. He still salts his tomatoes until they turn white. I found him frying bacon the other day and making pan-roasted potatoes as a side dish.* Or, *I saw Vlaho the other day. It would've been our wedding anniversary, but if he remembered, he didn't say anything. Instead, Tena scraped the heels of her palms when she fell, and Vlaho lifted her and pressed her onto his chest, saying, "Daddy loves you more than anything," and I wanted to dig a hole and bury myself in it.* I'd think those things walking away and realize.

It wasn't that I didn't have anything to tell her.

It was that I was afraid that if I did speak, she still wouldn't listen.

But thinking about Asier's son makes me consider all this again. It makes me think back to what I suppose was the first time I went to therapy, though I don't know if it could be considered therapy. I was only five when Mom took me there, and we only ever went that one time.

I had been wetting my bed almost every night, and Mom was flustered. She couldn't figure out why it was happening or how to stop it.

I remember only bits and pieces of the visit itself. The therapist—I don't know if she was a psychologist or a psychiatrist, though I suppose the latter must have been true, because we were in the hospital—and the massive desk she sat behind. It was afternoon and the hospital halls were empty and dark. I remember her asking what my mother did for a living, and me saying Mom was a cleaning lady, not because I didn't know that she was a store manager, but because I was pissed off at her for bringing me there in the first place. The therapist asked me what color eyes my father had, and I said, *Brown.* What color were my mother's eyes? *Brown.* Brother's? *Brown.* Mine? *Purple.*

She asked me the same question four times, and I always said, *Purple.*

I was angry. I knew my eyes were brown. The therapist looked angry too.

She fumbled through her purse for a compound mirror and shoved it into my hand. "What color are your eyes?" she repeated, and I knew the game was over, and that she had won.

I looked into my eyes, turning hazel behind the rippling of tears, and I said, "Brown."

The prescription she gave my mother: *Buy the girl a mirror, place it somewhere she can see herself. She needs a sense of identity.*

It did work, I stopped wetting the bed. And whenever she told the story to her friends, colleagues, my friends, even Vlaho, my mother always marveled at how easy the fix had been. A mirror!

But it wasn't the mirror I needed to see myself reflected in.

If I'd stopped wetting the bed, it was because I was too afraid to go back to that woman with harsh, impatient eyes who had defeated me at my own game.

And I wonder how my life would have turned out if she had told my mother what I really needed, the way I told Asier tonight. Would Mom have changed, or would it not have made a difference anyway?

I try to make myself move toward my mother's grave to tell her something, anything. That she hurt me. That I love her. That all those years that I was borderline rude and dismissive, all I wanted was for her to reach out and hold me and—*God!*—love me. As I am, for who I am. But I'm still glued to the side of my car in the parking lot, not able to take one step.

So I sit back in my car.

As I'm driving home, the road blurs.

"My eyes are hazel," I say to the empty car. They always are when I cry.

THIRTY-FOUR

I PHONE MARINA EARLY the next morning, and she doesn't pick up, and then I go to work and when she calls, I'm unable to answer, and then when I get off work, she doesn't pick up again, and so the whole day passes, until she just texts me, "Coming back from a tour. Vlaho will be making pancakes tonight. Come over and we'll talk."

So now I'm sitting at their large glossy-white dining table, Marina slumped in the chair across from me, visibly tired and already tan even though it's only the beginning of May.

Vlaho is flipping pancakes with a practiced flick of his wrist on the other side of the kitchen, and Maro is sitting next to him on the kitchen counter, "helping." No matter how many times he spills the batter onto the floor, his pants, or Vlaho's T-shirt, Vlaho never says a thing. He bows down to clean up the mess, then gives Maro the ladle again, and guides his hand as Maro pours the batter into the pan that Vlaho twirls around so that it spreads.

Tena is behind me, perched on a step stool, braiding my hair. Marina has a short bob, and my hair has recently grown under my jawline, so I'm the only person Tena can play hairdresser with. She pushes her chubby fingers into my scalp, her focus comical on her round face, and she tugs, and pulls, and jerks her comb down my tangled strands, and even though sometimes she yanks too hard, I don't protest. There's something nice about being preened this way.

"So?" I ask Marina.

She hasn't said a word yet about her text from last night. Her eyes glint with satisfaction. She's intent on ratcheting up tension before her big reveal. "You're gonna love this. After our talk on the boat, I called my cousin Tome," she finally starts. "The geodesist."

She says it as though I'm supposed to know who Tome is. Marina has cousins left and right, in every conceivable line of business. Unlike my family, who moved here only two generations ago, hers originates from a nearby village, and there is always a cousin or an acquaintance who knows someone who does something you need doing.

"Anyway, I told him about your problem with the hotel, and asked him to look into it. He didn't have trouble finding the exact plot number, given that it's the only settlement in a two-kilometer radius."

A geodesist. Looking into the plot of land the hotel is built on. I sit up, but Tena yanks my hair back.

"Did you ever talk to your dad about dividing the plot in two?" Marina leans in for more emphasis.

"We had a conversation years ago about whether it could be divided. My dad said that as per urban and spatial plans, the hotel needed at least triple the land it occupied—"

She is shaking her head before I'm even finished. "Tome consulted the maps and the urban plan, and you can divide the plot in two. Right where the small gate is." She draws her finger across the table and the lacquered surface squeaks.

All the different facets of this problem overlap as my mind tries to parse them out. That Dad lied and deliberately hid this from me. That I have already shown Asier the whole plot, including the olive grove. That to retain the grove, I would have to initiate the procedure of dividing the plot, but the bank would surely move into foreclosure before that procedure was finished.

I clench my eyes shut.

"I thought you'd be happy," Marina says.

"I am! I am." Though I'm not sure if happy is the right word. I've only just accepted the fact that I'm losing the grove, and this turns everything on its head. Worse still, it sparks a new hope, and I'm not sure if I can endure another disappointment. Sometimes new hope only makes the loss twice as hard.

Vlaho puts a plate with the first batch of pancakes on the table and squeezes my shoulder before he returns to the stove.

Marina slathers marmalade onto one and curls it into a roll, then offers it to Tena. "I'll give you Tome's number. If you give him the green light, he'll do the prep work and start the procedure with the Urbanist and Spatial Planning Office. It might take a while, but maybe you could find a way to stall the foreclosure?" She says this looking at Vlaho, asking for confirmation from the banking side of things. "Maybe ask that investor of yours for an advance on the hotel sale and then put that toward covering a couple of installments just to buy some time?"

Tossing a pancake in the air, Vlaho says, "It could be done."

Marina claps her hands in an *all-solved* fashion, and this irks me, because it's not solved, it's a set of new roadblocks in the new path that I need to figure out just when I thought I was finished figuring this out. I'm so tired I could cry.

"Where were you, by the way?"

"Huh?" I only half heard Marina's question, and when I replay the words, heat rises up my neck and cheeks, all the way up to my hair follicles. Because where I was when she called was near naked, in a hotel room, in a bed with said investor, and there's no way I can tell her that, especially not in front of Vlaho.

"Last night." She slathers marmalade onto another pancake, then rolls it and puts it on the plate next to a heap of others. "Maro," she yells. "Come get your pancakes." She looks at me, sliding the plate in his direction. "I called you like a dozen times," and somewhere in the middle of that sentence, her face, upon seeing mine, goes *Oh*.

"I was busy," I say, and don't offer more, but I can see her piecing together what she knows from before. That the investor was visiting this weekend.

That it was well past ten p.m. when she called. That I am burning like a damn blowtorch.

"I see," she says.

I worry she'll pose more questions, questions that I'll need to find sloppy answers to, because I can feel Vlaho's attention from across the room. It's one of those instinctual things, like catching a stranger staring at you from a far-up balcony as you walk down the street, even though you had no reason to look up. Vlaho pours the pancake batter into the pan, and it sizzles. I make a point of not looking at him, but Marina is casting a glance his way. The room echoes with everything that's unspoken between the three of us; between Marina and me, between Vlaho and me, between the two of them, but I can't, for the life of me, figure out what any of it is.

THIRTY-FIVE

I CALL MARINA'S COUSIN and he confirms what she said. The hotel can stand on its own, and the olive grove can become a separate plot of land. The procedure would take up to six months. My legs jitter with angst as we talk. So many things would have to align for me to pull off saving the grove while selling the hotel in time to avoid foreclosure. First but not least, my father would have to agree to this, and given how mad and disappointed he is with me, I doubt he'd let me walk away with this win for myself while I'm stubbornly letting his dream die.

Then, I'd have to convince Asier. The grove isn't a vital part of the hotel, but it does add value. When he was here, we discussed his vision for Lovorun at length. To make it a hotel that would work not only in the summer months, but all year round. A big part of that would be to offer guests a chance to work in the grove. To pick the olives in October, to trim the trees in February. "Maybe I could keep you on as a consultant," he said, and even though he meant it as a joke, I thought, *Well, maybe it's not such a bad idea.*

Before I get the chance to talk this out with either of them, I get an email from Asier with the official offer. The sum is generous. Enough to cover all our debts and leave us well-off for quite some time into the future. Enough for Dad to receive the best healthcare for as long as he has left, for Saša to invest in opening his own dental practice, and for me to buy myself a new grove if that's what I decide to do with my share.

My skin is sensitive and edgy as I stare at the numbers on the screen, contemplating how to formulate a response. The deal seems too far gone to change anything so substantial, but I would never forgive myself if I didn't try. And yet, asking puts me in the place where I most hate to be. It's like stepping onto the stage, taking my clothes off, spreading my arms, saying, *Here are my softest parts. Take your aim.*

I try typing something up, but whatever I write falls flat, so I decide to call Asier instead. The day I toured him through Lovorun, he asked me to show him the olive grove. Not because he was curious about the trees themselves, but because he wanted to know what they meant to me. Afterward, when he opened his eyes and looked into mine, I saw that he understood; that a part of him was grieving my loss too. Maybe this will make him more inclined to help me keep it.

"Hey, Gorgeous," he says when he picks up. His voice wraps around me, and for a beat, I'm poised between his legs again as he holds me against the schoolyard wall.

"Hey yourself," I say. "Do you have time to talk?"

"I'm all yours." His tone is playfully suggestive.

"About the offer—"

"I did everything I could," he says, more serious now. "Upsold it as much as possible—"

"No, no. The offer is . . . good. It's fine." It's more than fine, more than I expected, but he doesn't need to know that. It's a business transaction after all—which I'm aware is contradictory since I'm calling to ask him for a favor. "But I've been made aware the other day that . . . " I stop. How do I word this? On the other side of the line, he waits for me to continue. "That there is a way to divide the land into two plots. Where the small gate is. And we're thinking"—I use the "we" strategically—"to put only the hotel on the market and to keep the olive grove."

I stop and wait, but he doesn't say anything.

"We'd do all the prep work on our side before we draft the contract, of course," I add.

"Ivona—"

"And it goes without saying, we would expect a smaller offer."

"Ivona."

His tone is the sound of a landslide detaching. I have the urge to push against it with a wall of words, anything to keep him from calling it. "Please, Asier. At least think about it. It won't be a crucial change for the hotel. And you know how much the olives mean to me." I'm appealing to him not as the investor, but as a human being, maybe even a lover, and it feels a lot like begging.

"If I could do something, I would," he says. "But this is business, and I need to approach it in that respect. You do understand?"

"I understand you completely." I spit the words out like a hurt teenager. I'm on that stage, naked, scrambling to cover myself. I'm both devastated and angry with myself for exposing my soft parts in such a silly way.

He sighs. "I'm sorry. Our vision for the hotel includes the orchard. The thing is—" He stops, and I hold my breath, hear him puff his chest out. "They plan to build a bar and spa center there."

"What?"

"The land beside the hotel. Where the olives are. The architect says it's the perfect spot for an infinity pool, sitting as it is on that bench of land above the sea."

"And the trees?"

A pause. "I'm sorry."

The words crackle in my ears like static. An infinity pool.

They aren't buying the land because of how beautiful the grove is, or to engage their guests in local culture. They're not keeping the olives at all. They're buying it so they can bulldoze the trees to the ground and replace them with the latest fad. I've seen all those posts on Instagram, of Photoshopped, half-naked women hovering in the pool of turquoise water, their lips and breasts bloated, eyebrows ridiculously thick and combed up. Superimposing that image over my baba's land makes me sick to my stomach. *We treat our investments with respect,* he said back in Split. I have the urge to shove those words down his throat.

"But you said you would keep the grove. You said you would build branding around that." My tone is teeming with accusatory disdain. What I really want to be saying is *You asshole. Why did you ask me to show you what the grove meant to me? What sort of sick, perverse move was that?*

"I had every intention of pushing that. Seeing you there, I could envision the whole thing, the appeal of it. But the board disagreed, they thought the land would be underutilized."

I coil into myself, protecting the empty space he's punched out of me. "Could you at least try? To propose this new deal without the grove?" If I was begging before, now I'm groveling. I think about how he held me in his arms in that hotel room not even a week ago. It has to count for something. Connection—isn't that what I've been seeing my whole life, that having a connection gets things done?

"Sorry, Ivona." His tone is gentle despite the rejection. "This is our offer. It's your call, though. You can decide not to sell to us and go with another buyer."

Yeah, I think. *If I had the time*. Which I don't, as the bank has all but sold the debt off to the debt collectors. If I wait any longer, the land will go to someone else's hands anyway, and we won't even get compensated for it, let alone have a say about the olives. I've cornered myself with incredible precision. "Never mind," I say, my words clipped. "It was worth a shot." Before he has a chance to respond, I press the red button on my phone.

—

I burrow into my bed, and for the longest time don't come out. It's not just that I won't be able to keep the grove. Or that they are going to cut down the trees I've loved all my life, though that is a big part of it. It's that, for a brief while, I bought into the lie that there might be someone out there for me. That, despite all that is lost to me, there might be a full life ahead of me yet.

Dinnertime goes by, then I hear the six clanks of the spoon hitting the džezva in the morning as Dad makes his coffee. But all the energy has leaked out of me, and I can't get up. I call in sick at work, tell them I have a stomach flu. My boss doesn't doubt me because I "sure sound rough." At lunchtime, Dad comes to my room and sits on my bed. I cover my face with my blanket so he can't see my swollen eyes.

"You okay?" he asks.

He hasn't spoken a word that wasn't strictly necessary since the day I stood my ground and told him and Saša that I would sell Lovorun, but now there's genuine worry in his tone.

"No," I say.

Dad rubs my back like he used to sometimes when I was a little girl, and that makes the pain expand. For all his opinionated self-centeredness, for all his disapproval of me and my ways, for all his thinking he knows better than I do about who I should be or how I should behave, he has always had a soft spot for me. "What happened?" he says.

What happened is nothing. Everything. What happened is that every time I'm standing on solid ground, the rug gets pulled out from under me. What happened is that I'm so tired that my bones feel as though they're infused with lead. I'm petrifying, slowly, from within. I just want to lie here, give up. Why try? All the trying never got me anywhere. Everything I ever did in love, work, family, hobbies . . . ended up at zero. I am done in. I am done. It's not that I grieve not having anything, it's deeper than that. I don't even want anything anymore. And not wanting? What other proof of death is there?

PART FOUR

IVONA

THIRTY-SIX

THE MORNING COMES, AS mornings are wont to do. Light cavorts on my windowsill, and dust swirls in the sunbeams, the whole display so lively it's obnoxious. My eyes itch and throb. My heart rate is slow.

A glass of water and a full box of cookies that Dad brought me perch on my nightstand. My stomach protests. I haven't eaten a thing these two days that I've kept myself bedridden. In the back of my mind, guilt echoes: I should be feeding my ailing father, not the other way around, but I can't find it in me to care enough to get up.

But this is the thing about life—it has a way of continuing. Even past the moment when you wish it wouldn't. Even past the moment when you feel so spent you could just die. You wake up—you, with your primitive physiological needs: your digestion, your breathing, your thirst—and you subsist.

It's almost comical, that way.

I get up, because what else can I do?

I go to the living room and join my father for our morning coffee. He turns off the TV, and just sits with me. He doesn't ask any questions, maybe because this kind of weakness makes him uncomfortable, or maybe because there isn't anything to say. We sip our coffee in silence, and when we're done, we get up without a word and go about our day.

When Asier calls a few days after our clash, I let it ring. His is the face of harsh, ugly capitalism usurping my most cherished possession. His is the face of betrayal, even though I'm aware he owes me nothing, I am nothing to him.

The whole morning after the missed call, I brood in my room, more annoyed than anything else. I'm too drained to feel anything more intense at this point. Defeat presses down on me like thickened atmospheric pressure; invisible, heavy, making every movement difficult.

Despite it not making any sense, the thought that rolls on repeat in my mind: Vlaho would've never done anything like that to me. I'm comparing apples to eggplants, I know, but I'm comparing anyway.

At lunchtime, I serve chickpea stew. After that "episode" I had the other day, Dad has softened a bit, though this doesn't mean he approves of my plan to sell Lovorun any more than he did before. He slurps a bit of stew off his spoon, assesses the taste with an infuriating smacking sound, and says, "Needs more garlic."

Chickpea stew used to be one of the dishes my mom excelled at. Each bean cooked to perfection, bursting under the tooth into a blissful starchiness, the stock just the right thickness, infused with the perfect proportions of carrot, parsley, parsnip, and celery. Each spoonful a warm, comforting embrace. How she made it is one of the many things she took with her, one of many things I never asked, will never get a chance to ask.

"And it's not thick enough," Dad adds, letting the watery liquid drain from his spoon.

I pause mid-bite, all my muscles clenched in an attempt to let his criticism roll off me. My head heats up, my eyes prick, and I order myself not to engage.

I stare at him, my father with his haughty expression, and a thought pierces me, a small nail driven into the back of my head.

His incessant criticism must be why Mom perfected her chickpea stew in the first place.

Suddenly, a simple truth about my dad emerges, a graphite portrait made clear in a few strokes. You can only meet Dad where he is, not because he won't but because he *can't* meet you halfway. You can only meet him where he is, because he himself is caged, a prisoner of his own black-and-white world, the first and biggest victim of his own ways.

The thought focuses then. In many ways, am I not my father's daughter?

Have I not been just as inflexible and unmalleable as Dad?

It occurs to me that this is the exact aspect of Asier that I couldn't pin down. That he is not superficial or depthless, but he is adaptable. He takes life as it comes to him with such ease, and I keep getting pulled in the undertow with each new wave because I refuse to roll with the surf.

"What's funny?" Dad asks, looking flustered.

I realize I've hummed a laugh.

"Nothing." I put my spoon down. "I'm going to work," I say, even though my shift doesn't start for another hour and a half. I'll walk, take my time getting there.

I get up to kiss my father's bald head.

"Right now? What about your lunch?"

"Don't worry about it. I'll clean up when I come back," I say, and leave him grumbling in the background.

As I'm walking out the door, I get a text from Asier, the first since our fallout a few days ago. It's a photo message. On it, a teenage boy with the same gray-green eyes as Asier's leans over a table in his white hoodie, smiling as he bites into a burger, mayonnaise dripping down his chin. The caption below says: "You were right." And then, "Thank you." I don't respond, but I hit the like button. My heart sits a little more comfortably, a little more open in my chest.

THIRTY-SEVEN

A COUPLE OF DAYS later, Marina texts me that a friend of hers, an owner of a small restaurant-type venue downtown that offers cooking classes to tourists, will give me a call. My phone rings before I can ask Marina what her friend could possibly want with me.

The woman tells me she and Marina have been collaborating for a long time, sending tourists each other's way. They were having drinks yesterday, and Marina mentioned to her that I'm trained for sensory analysis of olive oils, which makes me an olive oil sommelier of sorts. There's been a lot of interest among tourists about locally sourced food, she says, especially the health benefits of olive oil, and she would love to have me teach in one of her classes, or even better, I could do a class on pairing food and oils of different olive varieties.

I would need to be able to issue her an invoice for my services, though, and I could handle that as a side gig or do as she did, start my own sole proprietorship, if this is something I'd like to be doing in the long run. She's heard that the European Union and the government are offering aid to people who want to become self-employed. If I make a business plan and attach her offer of collaboration, she's sure I'd qualify.

I tell her I'll think about it and get back to her shortly. When we hang up, I almost laugh, even though I'm in the middle of a crowded street. Is it possible that I could make money by educating people on the benefits and taste of olive oil? I think back to my junior year in high school, when my mom took me to a professional orientation assessment. The lady there droned on about the importance of choosing an occupation that was "sustainable in the long run." She was so emphatic about "steady," "corporate," and "safe income" careers. I have done exactly what she told me to, and here I am, decades later, selling stationery.

And all this time, I waited for the world to right itself. For the future that had been promised to me to reappear. I haven't been able to accept that the times had shifted by the time I graduated. That the future I once implicitly believed in is now locked in permafrost, gone.

But what if the times have changed again, this time for the better? There are so many people who earn money in ways that weren't imaginable before. Influencers, coaches, virtual assistants. People turning their passions into the weirdest jobs, like foraging or teaching Dalmatian cuisine to tourists. People who've not only exited the box, but punched holes in it and now wear it as a fashion detail.

It fills me with a new kind of zeal, this thought, that I might become one of them.

THIRTY-EIGHT

I'M IN THE OLIVE grove when Asier emails me the contract for the Lovorun sale, so that I can go through the details with my lawyer before he comes to sign it. He says to let him know if there are any changes I'd like made before the end of next week, so that his team has time to review them before he books his flight over. The tone of his email is professional, but I guess I deserve that for being short with him again.

I slip the phone back inside my pocket, looking up. The olives are blooming. They're casting clusters of tiny white florets, offering them up to the wind for pollination. People say the olive flowers are unimpressive—plain and unsightly—but to me they're beautiful. The trees look like upside-down ball gowns, embroidered with the most delicate lacework. It gives me a pang that these trees will be gone soon, that this is our last dance.

I was so mad at Asier because of this, but after that day with the chickpea stew, I realized my anger had been misplaced. It isn't Asier's fault. He hasn't done anything other than what we agreed on, and he doesn't have a say in what happens when the hotel is sold any more than I do. And I've villainized him for it, made him responsible for my pain.

The day is hot. I sit on the shore, take my sneakers and socks off, and dip my toes into the still-cold water. It pinches and pricks against my skin.

The small pebbles mixed with sand scrape against my soles. The sea burbles softly between the rocks.

I dial Asier's number. He isn't petty like me and picks up after two rings. Before he can say anything, I say, "I'm sorry."

He doesn't respond, and I look at the phone, afraid that the call hasn't been patched through. It has. "I'm sorry I've been like this."

"Like what?"

"Don't make me say it."

But he keeps waiting, so I push the air out of my lungs. "Difficult. Fickle. I'm just . . . This is a hard time for me." Which is only partly true. Because I'm always like this. Overthinking. Overfeeling. Overreacting. I'm an uncovered nerve and everything touches me, everything causes me pain. Even pleasure does. Even love.

"It's fine," he says. "You don't owe me explanations."

I push my legs deeper into the sand, until I'm calf-deep in water and the edges of my pant legs are getting soaked. "Funny, a moment ago, I thought something similar about you."

He laughs. And I laugh too, though disappointment staggers through me. If we expect nothing from each other, owe nothing to each other, what more is there to say? I should save face and tell him that, given the circumstances, it would be best if we proceed professionally from now on. Close the deal and go our separate ways. If I don't say that, I'm sure he will. I form the words, but they barricade themselves in the back of my mouth.

"What if I want you to owe me something?" I say instead, then shut my eyes, counting heartbeats. So. Many. Heartbeats.

"You mean businesswise or . . . ?"

"You know what I mean."

Each second of silence on his end feels like a trust exercise gone wrong. I'm falling backward, willing him to catch me, but all I hear is the woosh of air as I'm slipping through the void where his arms should be.

"You ghosted me, twice," he says.

"I know. I'm sorry."

"You called me out on being a sorry excuse for a father, even though you don't know the first thing about me or my son."

I hug my knees. The sand is grainy between my toes, it sticks to my skin, I'll never get rid of it. I want to say I'm sorry again, ask if it didn't turn out well for him that I said what I had about his son, but things feel too far gone for that.

He sighs. "You're infuriating, you know? You have these sharp little nails that scratch and dig into my skin, and then all of the sudden there's blood where I didn't expect it to be."

"I know. I'm sorry."

"I'm sorry I couldn't save your grove," he says.

I turn behind me, where three rows of upside-down lacey gowns waltz with the breeze. There is so much blood under my own skin right now, all the vessels, veins, and capillaries bursting with life. Life, as in the good and the bad. Or perhaps, the good alongside the bad. The warmth to wistful smiles, the happiness that comes with an expiration date. The exhilaration of having something, perfectly balanced with the despair of losing it. But does the loss negate the happiness that preceded it?

If I had known I'd lose the grove, would I not have groomed it anyway? If I had known I'd lose Vlaho, would I have renounced him on that first night? If there is a certainty that I will invest in this new relationship with Asier and end up disillusioned and scarred, would the journey still not be worth it?

"About the grove and the contract. I do have a small request, if you can make it work on your end," I say.

"If I can make it happen, I will," he says, and I know it's true. He's practical, and I like the fact that it also means he's dependable.

The olives' sharp leaves rustle behind my back. "The fruits will be ripe in late October. One last harvest, that's all I ask."

THIRTY-NINE

THE DAY WE'RE SUPPOSED to sign the contract happens to fall on the summer solstice, the longest and brightest day of the year. I park the car on Branimir's Coast and walk over the bridge to meet Asier on the town's main square. This is the first time we're seeing each other in person since that night in his hotel room almost two months ago.

He stands out against the ocher building behind him, in his white shirt, sleeves rolled to the elbows. As I make my way to him across the full square, he gives me a knowing smile, one that's referencing all our shared moments, texts, and touches. One that's saying, *There are so many people in this square, but you're the one I'm waiting for. The one I'm excited to see.* It strikes me, the stark difference between this image and how he looked the first time I walked toward him, all foreign and cold. He was uncharted territory then, one I felt insecure treading, but now I'm approaching him like a place I've been to dozens of times on vacation. Not quite mine, but familiar, with a bit of shared history between us.

"You okay?" he asks on approach, because he knows today will be difficult. I'm putting my signature on the contract that will take Lovorun from my family forever. It won't be my baba's place anymore, the quaint little hamlet where my roots were steadily intertwined with the rocky land. It will be someone else's hotel. An investment. A business acquisition with an infinity pool.

"I'll be fine," I say. The truth is, I'm so empty I'm almost weightless. Deciding was the hard part. Now all I want is for it to be over and done with.

The throng of tourists all but carry us in the direction of the public notary office. Bits of sentences in French, German, Italian, Polish, and English come at me like small darts from all directions, until my own town feels alien to me. Asier takes my hand as if he's sensed this disorientation. I stare at our bunched fingers as we walk. I didn't take him for the hand-holding type. Surreal, that the person I'm handing Lovorun to is the person comforting me for the loss of it.

At the public notary's office, things go so smoothly it almost feels like a letdown. In the days leading up to this, I obsessed over how the signing would go, terrified I wouldn't be able to hold it together, that I would start sobbing when they gave me the document, then rush out of there, throwing torn pieces of it in the air behind me, leaving Asier bewildered again.

But when we walk in, everything runs mechanically, a legal conveyer belt. We wait in line at the crowded reception. We chat about Asier's son visiting him last weekend as they print out the document. I tell him about my new business plan as they slide the document under my hand, and I sign it with the most basic three-kuna blue pen. The clerk takes the document to the public notary for verification while Asier asks me where I'm taking him to eat, and before we know it, we're walking out with the contract signed, verified, and enclosed in a plastic case, and Lovorun no longer belongs to my family.

FORTY

THERE'S AN ACRONYM WE use in Croatia that perfectly summarizes the absurdity of our bureaucracy: F-T-1-P. It's short for "Fali ti jedan papir," which literally means, "You're one paper short." It captures not only the nature of our bureaucratic system, but how we choose to deal with it as well. Not with anger and rage that lead to protests and change, but with ironic jokes that allow for things to stay exactly the same.

And I always seem to be one paper short as I'm trying to stack up the documentation to start my own sole proprietorship. In order to get the government support for self-employment, I first need to be unemployed. So I quit my job at the stationery shop, and after my month's notice is out, I go to various offices to regulate my status. The Public Health Insurance Office, the Employment Services Office, the Tax Government. There are forms for everything coded with indecipherable names, a strict itinerary to follow—and always that one paper missing.

Once I'm unemployed, I take the class with Employment Services, which is a requirement for applying for aid. And there, we're told we need to draft a viable business plan. I don't know the first thing about drafting business plans, viable or not, so I enlist Vlaho's help.

We meet on the terrace of the coffee shop near the bank during his break and order our macchiatos. He has a certain way of adding sugar to his cup, a ritual I've always loved observing. He pours in half a packet, and twirls the spoon around, but then he doesn't lick the spoon like I do but runs its edge along the rim of the cup. It makes one last drop form and slide into the cup, and then he puts the spoon on the saucer.

He sees me looking, and I startle, like I'm caught witnessing something deeply intimate, something I shouldn't be taking stock of anymore. "Glad to see some things are still the same," I blurt.

Vlaho doesn't smile back or concur, he only takes a sip of his coffee and gazes toward the park that lies between buildings, where some kids are at play. Two, a girl and a boy, hold balloons in their hands, but the girl's gets snatched away by the warm summer breeze. It rises until it pops in the branches of a tree overhead. The girl starts howling in dismay.

"Yeah, at least some things never change," Vlaho says. There's an emphasis in his tone I can't decipher. He isn't his usual self, and when I think this, I realize it's been a while since the energy he radiates shifted. Even the day I came over for pancakes, he had a somberness about him. I have an urge to ask him what he means by what he said, to ask him if all is well, if his parents are fine, if work is fine, if he and Marina are fine, but I can't make myself pry. It isn't my place to ask. Not anymore.

The truth is, I wasn't fine for almost a decade after we divorced, and it wasn't his job to patch me up either. This was the deal we'd had to accept in order to remain friends. A boundary we've both had to respect no matter how hard it was to maintain at times.

A bit of a vacuum forms in my chest, pulling at the rest of me as I bring my cup to my lips. I loved—still love—this man so much. I had once promised to stay with him through sickness and health, to grow old together, to stay with him until death did us part. I had a fantasy, some would say morbid, reading about all those old couples, married forever, who die on the same day, one of natural causes, the other of heartbreak. I imagined that would be us in the far future, two wrinkled silver-haired prunes, surrounded by a flock of children and grandchildren and great-grandchildren, and when one of us died, the other one would soon follow.

I hadn't been able to imagine subsisting in this world without him next to me.

In a way, what took me by surprise the most after we'd divorced was that I survived.

For a long time, I'd resented my body for this blatant treason.

But here we are, sitting together yet apart, and his face is closed where it used to be open, and I'm not allowed—or I don't allow myself—to ask why. Nine years ago, I filed for divorce, renouncing him legally. But in all those years, I realize as I'm watching that little girl hiccup her sadness, I hadn't renounced him emotionally. He was still the one, the only one, the one I would die loving. But now there is Asier, and even though Asier can never be Vlaho, in the marrow of my bones I know it means something has to change. I need to give Vlaho up on the inside too. A private, invisible loss, but a loss no less real.

So I stave off those thoughts and get the papers out of my laptop bag. He pores over them as I lay out the plan that's more a list of wishes than anything else. Short courses on best olive-growing practices for busy professionals who grow olives as a hobby. Olive oil tasting and food pairings. I add two letters of reference for teaching classes and running workshops, one from Marina's friend and one from the owner of the oil mill where I usually take the harvest for milling.

Vlaho annotates some of the pages, explains how to make a spreadsheet to show the potential revenue versus the potential expenses. He fills in some of the expected expenditures, taxes, social security, and all the other things that my mind doesn't like to dwell on. He gives me some pointers on how to frame my "comparative advantages" and target audience by highlighting my occupation and training.

Once we're done and I put the papers away, he says, "You might have something here." He looks surprised by what he just said.

His approval gives me a boost of much needed confidence. "My expectations are low," I say. "But if I manage to match what I made at the stationery shop by doing what I love, I'll consider it a success. Not a bar set high, really."

"Yeah, I talked to Damir the other day." Damir being his high school best friend. The last I heard about him was that he was specializing in endocrinology. "He's moving to Germany because he can't afford rent anymore. He decided to call it quits when he learned his cousin the plumber earns five times as much as he does, all by working in the gray economy. The guy's officially unemployed, but drives the most expensive BMW to collect his unemployment aid each month while hiding his triple-figure business from the Tax Government."

I should be repulsed, but stories like these don't shock me anymore. The last census revealed Croatia has lost over 10 percent of the population in the last decade, and it's only the young and educated who are leaving. Brain drain, they call it. My gut twinges. If it's only the brains getting drained, does that mean that mine got caught in the strainer?

We watch the children on the playground, the sound of raucous cheer ominous now. Like that balloon, the higher they aspire to go, the sooner they'll burst. In moments like this, I'm almost grateful I don't have children. Perhaps evolution threw me out of the game for a reason. Maybe I don't have it in me to withstand the type of pain that being a parent requires, the kind I can sense in Vlaho.

"We should've just packed up and left for Tarifa back when we had a chance," he says, and his words put me on edge. Another hard rule that formed after the divorce is that we never, ever talk about the times we were together. We can mention people we both know or reference situations we both witnessed, but we never talk about us as a couple.

"Tarifa was a bad idea, even then." I keep my tone playful, but I'm struck by the image of him, sitting across from me in that bar all those years ago, the way he got up and held me by my arms, the fierce warmth of his love nourishing me, infusing me with gratitude for him, for the life that I foolishly thought awaited us. "Can you imagine me at forty, selling seashells?"

He meets my gaze, and I know he too is thinking about that long-ago moment. The way we made love that night, so fervently, with abandon, with so much tender hope for the future.

The sounds around us dissipate, he feels impossibly close. His eyes flick between my eyes and my lips, once. Twice. "Yeah, I guess not," he says, and looks toward the playground, toward those children again.

FORTY-ONE

ASIER HAS SOME VACATION days saved up, so he says he would like to come and stay for a couple of weeks. He needs to sign off on some of the Lovorun renovation work and interview a few people for the hotel's managerial positions, but he should be done with that in a matter of days. "And then," he tells me, "I'd love to spend some time with you."

When he arrives, it's the middle of August, the days already shorter, beckoning for slower movements and reflection. Unlike July with its never-ending merry-go-round of brightness, heightened colors, scorching sun, and hustle and bustle of tourists, August has a melancholy to it, like a party that's dying down, and you're torn between wanting it to last a bit longer and itching to go home and curl up under a blanket.

Asier and I spend our mornings sipping coffee in the shade of the town's piazzas, and our afternoons at the beach. I take him to the solitary beaches only the locals know about, and most days we're alone. We lie on our towels talking, and then chase each other into the surf like a couple of teenagers when the sun becomes too blistering. Kissing Asier in the sea is my new favorite thing, the salt on his lips perfectly punctuating the sweetness of his mouth. His skin is sleek under my hands that slip everywhere, and the restraint that is necessary is the best kind of agony.

The thing I love most about Asier is that he's nothing like Vlaho.

They're not opposite exactly either. They don't even occupy the same spectrum.

There's a pragmatism to Asier, a levity that brings out the most uncomplicated part of me. I feel simpler even to myself when I'm around him, my thoughts easy to follow, my emotions a traversable path.

Sometimes, we stay at the beach long after the night has fallen, and the stars spark up the black sky above us. He's reluctant to go into the water when he can't see the bottom, but I talk him into it, because this isn't the Pacific or Indian Ocean, there's nothing dangerous lurking within. The Adriatic is tame, a deep cove in an already closed Mediterranean, the Croatian coastline protected by its thousand islands. Even the tides are docile here, I tell him, the difference between high and low barely more than the length of his foot.

He trusts me enough to follow me in, and when we're waist-deep he eases himself in, starts floating on his back like a buoy.

"Look." I wave my arm through the water. Plankton bursts in fluorescent light wherever my hand goes. I dive in next to him.

He moves his arms and legs, the pitch-black sea around us exploding with bright neon dots, until it's hard to say if the sky is above us, or if we're swimming in it.

"It's like we're in the belly of the universe," he says, and I feel a surge of pride for my beautiful country. I think of my mom for some reason, how easy it is for love to live right next door to resentment.

When we get out and towel ourselves off, we lie next to each other, watching the sky for the meteor shower. I open the container with what's left of the cantaloupe cubes and grapes I brought with us today. The cantaloupe smells even sweeter now that it's been mellowed by the afternoon heat. He pops a cube into his mouth then offers me one, and I lick the salt from his fingers as I take it into my mouth. I love how hard it is for him to keep his composure when I do this.

I ask him about his childhood, where he had lived growing up, and the list is impressive. French Polynesia, Brazil, Kenya, Australia, Indonesia, South

Africa. I ask if he liked moving around. He says that sometimes he did, depending on where it landed him. But there were also places he didn't like.

"How did you endure those?" I ask.

He huffs, smiles. "As with the places I did like, I knew it had an expiration date. When it was good, I would think, *wait for it*. When it was bad, I would also think, *wait for it*."

"That's either totally cynical or superbly Zen," I tell him.

He says nothing for a moment. Then, a shrug. "Heraclitus, you know? The only constant in life is change, and all that. Nothing is truly permanent."

I nod but wonder if Heraclitus, or Asier for that matter, had a need for safety amid all that acceptance of constant change.

"Tell me one thing I don't know about you," I ask.

He tells me he's never learned how to drive a car.

"What? You don't drive?"

He grins. "That a problem?"

"No, but that's the first thing any male in Croatia does when they turn eighteen. Driving school." I take him by his forearms, trying to discern the muscles and tendons in the starlight. "You've got such handsome arms. You'd look amazing behind the wheel."

"I guess I didn't get around to it while I still lived with my dad back in French Polynesia, and later when I got into college, and even later when I started doing what I'm doing now, living in London, traveling around, I had no need for it."

I tell him I can't imagine how he does that, traveling around. The constant coming and going, living out of a suitcase. Figuring out airports. "I've never been on a plane in my life," I say.

"What?" He raises himself on an elbow to look at me, his turn to be perplexed. "You've never flown?"

"Didn't have anywhere to go," I say, the simplified version, but I think about the flight Professor Tomašek's team took to New York and how I was supposed to be on it. Why I wasn't. "Besides, I can't imagine. Landing in places I don't know, obsessing over where I'll find a cab or if there'll even be cabs to catch. And what if the hotel messes up my reservation, and there're no other rooms available—"

"That hardly ever happens," he says. I widen my eyes, and he says, "Relax, it never happens. I've never not had somewhere to stay the night."

We stay silent for a while, lie back down looking for the Perseids, the sky tears. My life seems to me suddenly the same as the Adriatic. Tame and shielded.

"Risk-averse, much?" Asier teases, pulling me closer. In the distance, an old wooden boat tack-tack-tacks across the channel.

"You think I'm kind of neurotic, don't you?"

"Absolutely you are." He grins and leans in to give me a kiss. "I also think I'm kind of in love with you."

FORTY-TWO

A FEW DAYS INTO Asier's two-week stay, Marina calls to invite me over for dinner. It's her forty-first birthday, but she doesn't want to make a thing out of it; it would only be the three of us, some food, some beer. I tell her I'd love to come, but that I'm busy that day, and when she offers other days in the same week, I decide I'm done hiding. "You know that investor I told you about?"

"Yes?" she says, cautious.

"Well, we're kind of seeing each other, and he's, um, here. For another week. He took time off work to be with me, so it wouldn't be fair to him if I blew him off for a night." There, I said it. I told her what she'd wanted to know since the first time she'd heard about him.

Marina falls silent for a moment. "Why don't you bring him with you then?"

My head goes woozy. Taking Asier to meet Vlaho, in Vlaho's home? The image alone threatens to undo me. "Are you sure?"

"I'm sure," Marina says. "If you're truly moving on, then we all need to get used to it." She says this fast, and it sounds logical at first, but when we hang up, I repeat the words in my head, and they leave me bewildered.

—

On our way to their apartment, Asier keeps teasing me. "I'm not going to get my lights punched out, right?" He's amused to no end by what he calls our "triangle."

I pretend to be game, but it irks me that we're turning this into a joke. It shouldn't be a big deal, I'm pretending it's not, but my every nerve is on high alert. My lungs are cemented into two bricks sitting in my chest, I can only breathe in a few molecules at a time. Having Asier meet Vlaho feels dangerous, like in one of those time-travel movies when the past shouldn't meet the present, because it would make the future collapse.

"I didn't punch Marina's lights out back in the day. You'll be fine." I try to sound casual. Whatever Marina meant to say the other day, she was right. If we're going to stay friends, the way we stayed friends when the two of them got together, we need to get past this. It's like ripping a bandage off, and I'm readying myself for the stinging pain of it being yanked back.

The elevator stops on the fourth floor. When we exit, Marina is already opening the apartment door. She's wearing a boho-style sundress. I don't often see her wearing anything feminine, so this adds to the effect—she looks like a tanned goddess. I'm struck with angst: What if Asier too finds her more attractive than me? But I push the thought aside.

"Hey, lovely." She kisses my cheeks.

"Happy birthday." I hand her a bouquet of sunflowers and a bottle of wine, and she hugs them to her chest so that she can shake hands with Asier.

"Welcome," she says, then moves to the side to let us in.

We find Vlaho in the kitchen, preparing the fish for the grill. Asier reaches out for a shake, but Vlaho lifts to show his slimed hands. "Sorry," he says, but doesn't look it. Something tells me it wasn't a coincidence he plunged his hands into the fish just as Marina was opening the door.

The table is set with a white-gray tablecloth and fine china. They never use tablecloths except for special occasions. On their big balcony, a fire is burning in the grill area. A faint smell of smoke lingers in the air. Vlaho washes up and opens a beer for me. "Are you up for beer or wine?" he asks Asier. I've never heard Vlaho string more than two words of English together; we never went anywhere where he'd need to use it, and it surprises me that even his English is doused in his southern accent.

"Wine would be nice."

Vlaho nods, as if this tells him more than just Asier's drinking preferences, and pours him a glass of red. We walk out to the balcony, overlooking the old town. The sun droops on the horizon, heavy and red like a zit about to burst, and the stone walls of the town glisten beneath.

"This view is spectacular," Asier says.

"Where are the kids?" I ask.

"My mom took them for a few days." Marina stands next to me, opening a beer for herself. "Since this is going to be such a wild party, and all." She nudges me, grimacing toward the men, standing rigid next to one another. I'm transported back to those early days when I first started spending time with Vlaho and Marina after they'd gotten married. It took some getting used to, knowing that the two of them made a couple, that I no longer had any claim over him. Being territorial comes naturally; it's an impulse I had to learn to let go of, that I'm sometimes still letting go of, and a bout of compassion fills me for Vlaho, who'll now have to do the same. An awkward beginning is all this is. The birthing pains of a triangle turning into a square.

—

Over the third glass of wine for Asier, and as many beers for the rest of us, the atmosphere starts to coalesce. Marina's tales of tourists' antics make Asier laugh so hard he produces a series of throaty sounds I've never heard him create. Marina has that effect on people, lifting the mood, making everything breezy, and as I watch her host—in the real sense of the word because she is seamlessly corralling the rest of us together—it becomes clear to me what a gift it is. What a gift *she* is. We wouldn't be here if it weren't for her. I wouldn't have been here for the last six years, and that would've been a massive loss for us all.

She puts a bowl of tuna pâté on the table, nudging Asier to take some, she's made it herself, but when Asier politely declines, Vlaho asks if it's a matter of taste or conviction.

"I was in Japan once," Asier says, "and the business partners took me to see tuna fishing." His face contorts. "Let's just say I'm not eating tuna again."

Vlaho doesn't say anything, but his softening is obvious. For similar reasons, he stopped eating octopus a few years ago. They're intelligent creatures, it's cruel, he said, and asked Marina not to bring them home when she caught them on her tours. For a while, she gave her spearfished octopuses away, but then she stopped catching them altogether, and Vlaho declared a victory for the oppressed octopi.

From there, they launch into a half-hour conversation about the fish industry and how much it's polluting the oceans. Vlaho tells Asier that the Adriatic sardines have become smaller. They used to come fifteen in a kilo, and now there can be up to fifty. Asier shares a few stories about the fishing trips he took with his friends while he was growing up in Indonesia.

It's already midnight when Asier and I get up to go. Marina leans in to whisper in my ear, "Total success." Her cheeks are flushed with alcohol and the visible relief and happiness that the night has gone so well. "Maybe we could all go to Noć Punog Miseca the day after tomorrow?"

"Night of the Full Moon," I translate for Asier. "It's a fešta, a traditional celebration downtown. I guess we—"

"Great!" Marina claps her hands, and we all move down the hallway. Asier and Vlaho shake hands, and Marina kisses me, then we change places, and as Marina hugs Asier goodbye, Vlaho hugs me, and says in Croatian, not lowering his voice, "He's okay, I guess, but not good enough for you." I hug him close and say, equally loud, in Croatian, "You liar. You loved him." There's an air of finality, like we're saying goodbye and not just for the night. He breathes me in, his arms tight around me. The feelings I have for him burble up, and the only reason I let him go is because Marina and Asier are standing there, watching us, waiting.

FORTY-THREE

ON THE NIGHT OF the Full Moon, the town is so full it could burst at its bulwark walls. The evening is sweating through its pores, the faint smell of alcohol evaporating from the throngs of people that move no faster than a sailing ship in a dead sea. Sardines are grilled on various corners near konobas and cafes, the sizzling sound of their flesh against flame igniting a savory hunger.

Asier and I settle in Varoš, where we're supposed to meet Marina and Vlaho. Varoš is the quaintest part of the old town, where streets are the narrowest and the buildings huddle together like gossiping old nanas. It's the most authentic part too, and I have the need to show it to Asier, to make him a part of it.

Everywhere, there's music and chatter. Older men with round bellies and ruddy cheeks stand next to cauldrons of fish brudet and seafood risotto. In their hands, glasses of bevanda—half water, half red wine—are drained slowly, sip by sip.

They talk and laugh, and then without warning, one of them hums the beginning of an elegiac Dalmatian klapa song. The other men stop talking, their gazes softening into the distance, and they join their voices a cappella. They sing about long-ago times, the solace of drinking wine in konobas with friends, the haunting sadness of olive groves no one tends since Pape fell asleep. It's tender, and beautiful, and as I imagine what it might evoke in Asier, exposed to it for the first time, I feel another surge of pride in my country.

The men's song reaches full volume, and the whole street full of people start singing along, the words that have been sewn into us from before we can remember, a silent identity that works its way from the inside out.

The song ends. Asier is barely breathing. We're pressed together, and he watches me as if I'm making more sense to him now.

"For a moment there, I thought it was a flash mob," he says, and I laugh, lightened by his wit.

"Hey, you two." Marina tugs at our connecting arms. "Had anything to eat yet?"

We turn to face her. Vlaho is standing behind her, hands deep in his pockets. He's wearing a military-green T-shirt, knee-length beige combat pants, and Converse All Stars, and it touches a place inside me no bigger than the tip of a needle, to see him like this, looking young, looking so much like Kurt Cobain, which is why I bought him that T-shirt almost fifteen years ago, and then ripped it off him as soon as he'd tried it on. Asier's torso against mine now feels scalding hot, and I step back. "No, the line for the sardines is insane."

Drinks flow in abundance, and no matter how many sardines on bread we eat, the alcohol gets to our heads. We talk, but yelling is the only way to do it, the street pulsing around us, and that makes me tired fast, so I sip my beer while Marina does her thing, animating everybody, especially Asier, who's taking it all in wide-eyed. Before I know it, she's got him to promise to come back to Zadar at the end of September, so she can take all four of us out to Kornati National Park with her sailboat. A prick of alarm goes off in my body when I picture the four of us in such a confined space, half-naked in our swimwear for a whole day. Hanging out with Marina and Vlaho with Asier has turned out better than I'd expected, but a full day on a sailboat might be pushing it.

I glance at Vlaho as she announces this. He seems disinterested, more focused on the crowd around us.

Marina notices his aloofness too, and she tousles his hair, the way she sometimes does their son's, and then she plants a kiss on his shoulder. She's tipsy, sure, but her gesture still gives me pause. She has never been very affectionate with Vlaho, and neither has he with her, at least not in front of me. They probably didn't want to make me feel awkward. But now that Asier is in the picture, she's obviously becoming freer herself. As we continue to stand there, drinking and chatting, I notice more of it. Her hand on Vlaho's forearm. A brush of her fingers down his back. Something protective about it, but also tender, and it pierces me despite Asier's arm hanging heavily over my shoulder.

There's a concert on the Five Wells Square that Marina wants to attend, so we push our way through the crowd to get there, what should be a five-minute walk turning into a half-hour-long exercise in swimming upstream.

The square is packed, and we squeeze ourselves into a spot only a couple of steps away from the place where I introduced Vlaho to Marina all those years ago. I wonder if either of them thinks about it now, how unlikely it is that the four of us are standing here, in this exact constellation of relationships.

A cover band is playing the best of Dalmatian pop oldies. It's eleven, and the crowd is drunk by now, they sing along in not always flattering tones and voices. Marina is standing on Vlaho's other side, and I'm squeezed between my ex-husband and current lover. The irony of this is its own beast. My eyes are glued to the stage, but all my attention is on the fact that I can feel both men's arms grazing my own. The music is too loud to do anything but stand there, and as people sway around us, the simultaneous brushes of Vlaho's and Asier's skin against mine ignite a pleasurable panic.

I know I should turn so that I move away from Vlaho's arm, but I can't make myself do that. The warmth of his body, the familiar velveteen feel of his skin magnetizes me. A thought bolts through me, that he must be as aware as I am of our arms touching, and he's not pulling away either. The anticipation—of what, I can't say, because what could possibly happen in this crowded place, with his wife and my lover next to us?—but it flares inside me like a mighty bird flapping its wings between the inhales.

The song changes to an old love ballad from the eighties, a woman singing about a lover long lost to her, who remains her deepest desire and her most harrowing sadness; she still belongs to him, and he to her; he makes her hurt everywhere, everywhere. The words I always thought were too melodramatic now seep into my soul, and it's not my imagination that Vlaho's knuckles graze mine during the refrain.

Then, all of the sudden, his fingers twist aside and his hand is grasping mine, and mine is clasping his back, as if they're creatures with their own volition. Hard, hard, hard, with so much need, all the years we've been apart sutured into this moment. The rest of our bodies unmoving, our eyes locked to the stage, his wife and my lover flanking us in an unknowing silence.

The song ends but our hands stay together, a betrayal of our partners hidden by the mass surrounding us. It's a sumptuous secret; I'm unable, unwilling to break the bond. My head swims, with alcohol and the risk of whatever it is we're doing, my breath a shallow trickle filling merely the top of my lungs, but I can't—won't—let go. Instead, I am squeezing, and brushing my thumb against his knuckles, conveying what can never be spoken through words. *I'm still here. You're mine. I feel you. I love you.*

As the evening draws to an end, the crowd dissolves and we stop to say goodbye on the main town square. The moonlit sky is covered with plump clouds that travel fast on the wings of an oncoming thunderstorm. The wind rushes through the emptied streets, and it won't be long before the first fat droplets fall. Vlaho's eyes bore into mine, challenging me to acknowledge what we've done. Holding his hand was wrong, immoral even, and no one will ever find out about it, it serves neither of us. But for the first time since I let him go, a small piece of him has been handed back, and God forgive me, I feel entitled to it.

"You should leave your car in town overnight," Marina says because she knows how much I've had to drink. She links her arm through Vlaho's to support her own unsteady legs, and rests her head on his shoulder. "You want us to walk you to a cab?"

The cab station is on Branimir's Coast, on the other side of the town bridge, which is on their way home. I should do just that, go home, sleep it off. I'm tipsy and tired, and hungover from feeling too much holding Vlaho's hand, but I'm not ready to go home yet. I want to stay with Asier, go to his apartment. Vlaho's clandestine touch—the forbiddenness of it—has me buzzing with a sensual energy I'm aching to expend. A mere touch could set me off. All these years of harboring quiet yearnings are firing up, setting me aflame.

"No thanks," I tell her. "I think I'll stay with Asier for a while."

Asier pulls me closer by my waist.

Vlaho's eyes dim. I'd be lying if I said a part of me doesn't enjoy his discomfort. I've been exposed to this exact type of agony so many times, leaving their home to go to my father, images of them falling into bed together and making love bombarding me as I went. But he can't do anything about it but accept Marina's nudge to go.

When they leave, I turn to Asier.

His face is a smirk. "I'm guessing you want to come up this time."

Asier has been patient, and whenever I asked him if he minded my needing time, he said it was a part of my neurotic charm. But I've noticed how increasingly difficult it was becoming for him to stop when things got heated. The relief he radiates now confirms it.

I press my body to his, slide my hands into his back pockets, and pull him so close he laughs. I'm a ball of pulsating desire. I'm not thinking straight. I've never thought straighter. "Let's go," I say, with my back to Vlaho, walking away from us with his wife.

FORTY-FOUR

THE NIGHT IS ALWAYS the darkest before dawn, they say, but tonight it's lit up, with the moon ablaze after the thunderstorm. I stayed at Asier's longer than I'd expected, waiting out the rain, and as I'm driving back home, slowly and carefully, I feel myself loosen, relaxed in a way I haven't been in years.

Images rush back to me, of us arriving at his apartment, sticky with sweat and smelling of grilled sardines and wine and beer. We took each other's clothes off and took a shower together. We left the lights off, allowing only the lightning to illuminate us through the small bathroom window, revealing us to one another in thunderous flashes. He soaped me up with the shower gel that smelled of him, and I closed my eyes, letting myself be infused with his touch. The whole night was a long foreplay and I ached for him so badly that we didn't even get to bed. We reached for each other in that confined space, the tiles cold against my back as he pressed me against them, his shoulders looking so beautifully defined as he held me up, as he pushed into me.

The water ran over us the whole time, washing away the smells and soot of the night while he was erasing Vlaho off me, until we came completely clean, smelling fresh, like laundered clothes.

I pull into the driveway and turn the key. The car exhales into silence. I sit for one minute, my hands on the wheel, allowing the sensory overload of this night to settle before I insert myself back into reality.

The air is humid and smells of wet lavender and rosemary from our garden as I exit the car. The remnants of stormy winds rustle through the hedge, and this is why I don't hear him until he speaks. "What does he have that I don't?"

Vlaho stands against the gutter that still trickles tiny rivulets of rain from the roof. He is soaked, his hair slicked against the side of his face, the olive-green T-shirt looking almost black. "God, Vlaho, you scared me. What are you doing here?"

He doesn't answer, doesn't move. The rain stopped at least half an hour ago; he must have been standing there for a long time. Waiting for me. I see in his eyes that he knows, he knows what I've done, why I haven't come home until now. He knows and his face is broken, a mere mosaic of his beautiful features.

"You didn't answer me."

The accusation trills up my body. He has no right to call me out on anything. He, who's been sleeping with another woman for years now. He, who's made wonderful, beautiful babies with her. Babies even I can't help but love. A feeling I've never felt for him arises, something rotten that I can identify only as contempt. A disdain for his hurt ego that can't stand being dethroned, even after all this time, even after the horrible display of pining I've been offering him for years.

"You should go home," I say. "To your wife." I spit the last word out, the lack of sleep thinning my usual tact. I regret it at once, because it reveals that I am still angry with him for marrying her. For not choosing me and my flawed body over having children with someone else. Which I know is not entirely fair; I'd left him years before he met her. But right now, I don't care about the order in which things happened, or my share of responsibility for it.

He walks over to me, pushes himself close until his chest is right in my face. "You don't know the first thing about my *wife*." His breathing is both loud and shallow, and for a moment I'm not sure if he'll kiss me or hit me—which of course he'd never do, but his towering presence feels threatening enough for the thought to cross my mind. He steps back and launches down the street, and all I see is his retreating back in the moonlight.

"What do you mean by that?" I yell after him, a shrill sound slashing through the sleepy street, but he doesn't turn back. I should let him go, but before I can be reasonable about it, I'm running after him. I need to know what he wanted to say, what he meant by it, what he meant by holding my hand this evening. I reach him and turn him to me.

When he flips around, my heart folds in on itself, like origami.

He wipes his face and nose on the back of his hand and looks to the side. I want to turn his face to me and yell at him that I am his place, I'm where he can be his most vulnerable, but I know it's a lie, it hasn't been like that for a long time.

His hiding from me is the worst kind of punishment. It hollows me out, and I reach for him to fill in the missing pieces. He huffs as I wrap my arms around him, pulling him into me. His arms, lifeless at his sides, slowly encircle me, then hold me closer, tighter, then so hard I can't breathe. But that's okay, I don't really need air.

The stale monotony of my room is weirdly stirred as Vlaho and I sit side by side on my bed. After I'd held him to me outside my house, we stood in the middle of the road, suspended in a mute slow dance. Until a car came careening down the street, casting its angry lights at us, and we moved to the sidewalk to avoid getting hit. I pulled him inside the house and told him to wait for me in my room while I checked on Dad. He touched the leaves of the weeping fig he hadn't seen in nine years, now taller than him, and then he disappeared down the hall. I went to press my ear against my father's bedroom door, relieved to hear his loud snores.

When I came to my room, Vlaho stood by the shelves, holding the babuška. I told him once that I'd lost the two smaller dolls inside. Babies, I called them. Like me, the babuška is now an amalgam of only three women—a grandmother, a mother, and a daughter—held within each other. For her too, the future generations are lost. Vlaho cast me a somber glance, and it was as though he had struck a match, a flicker of light illuminating me from within. I'd forgotten how it was with him, being seen without saying a word.

I sat on my bed, and he put the babuška down and sat next to me, and here we are, minutes later, disoriented. A delicate soap bubble is enveloping us, and neither of us wants to burst it with words.

He shudders in his wet clothes, and I get up to fetch him a towel from the bathroom. He catches it when I throw it to him, and haphazardly wipes his face, his arms, his hair. Outside, the birds are starting up with their banter. Soon, a strip of blue will form above the rooftops, and broaden, until it overtakes the darkness. Cicadas will start shaking their rattles, slowly at first, sleepily, then faster and more cheerful the higher the sun rises.

"The room smells like you," he says. "I thought I forgot your scent because I can never willingly recall it. It always floats just beyond my reach. But here . . . it's everywhere."

"Why are you here, Vlaho?" I ask more softly than I did the first time, when we were outside.

It occurs to me that we might have set in motion a horrible streak of events when I first allowed his hand to rest against mine, and then accepted his grip. That indefinite future looms above us, holding everything in balance. His marriage, his kids' childhood, my own new beginning with Asier.

He lets a lungful of air out, looking away from me. His back is curved, as though his arms, rested against his thighs, are weighing him down. "Two days ago, I wanted to go along with it. I mean, I knew this day would come, that you'd find someone new. I thought I could handle it, and two days ago, at dinner, I did. A part of me was even glad that you're not alone anymore, I'd felt guilty that the ground wasn't even between us. But tonight, when—" He takes my hand in his, intertwines our fingers. "You squeezed back. And I thought—" A sharp inhale. "But then you *stayed* with him. And we went home, and all the while these images kept churning in my head. Images of our hands. Of his arm around you. And when Marina and I reached our building, the sky opened above us, and something . . . something . . . " He swallows, lets go of my hand. "I couldn't go inside with her."

He looks at me, his face a collage of soft shadows and the type of pain I know so intimately. "I had to find you. To ask you, why?"

"Why I stayed with him tonight?"

"Why you stopped loving me."

The secret I've kept for so long pounds inside my spleen. What to disclose? What to withhold? Long ago, we sat in our kitchen, in our bedroom, in our car, in the courtroom as I slowly chipped away at both his heart and his confidence, telling him I didn't love him anymore. I never admitted to the truth, that I was leaving him because of the weight his mother had put on me. Because of my own weight that I had been putting on him. Because I was so tired of pulling him down like a boulder, making his life miserable. Because I was so tired of waiting for him to get tired of me, of waiting for that guillotine above my neck to snap.

Tonight, my hand admitted to the lie. And if I put the truth in words too, where will that lead us? I can't think. Being rational after a night of alcohol, emotional turmoil, and lovemaking is proving impossible. I'm hungover in more ways than one, weakly aware of this lack of usual prowess, of my mind's inability to play out a million different scenarios at the same time, so that I can choose the one that's safest for everyone. "I think we shouldn't go there," I say. "What happened tonight between you and me . . . It was—"

He takes my hand again, traces the lines on the inside of my palm. "Everything."

"A mistake," I say at the same time, pulling my hand back.

He smiles. His shape against the dark is so familiar it hurts. Outside, the birds warble, reminding me of that nest of swallows above our window back in Zagreb, how we would sometimes lean out to watch them fly in and out, feeding their hatchlings.

"Does Marina know where you are?" I ask, getting up because being close to him feels dangerous.

"No," he says. "But I'm sure she wouldn't need to guess twice."

"What do you mean?" The bond of our hands earlier this evening was invisible to anyone but us.

"Marina knows."

My pulse rises to my throat. "Knows what?"

He looks at me then. Straight into my eyes. "That I love you. That I'm in love with you."

The room sways. This can't be real. Vlaho seems colorless in the dusky room, an apparition. I'm either dreaming or recalling the past. But he gets up and nears me, and his warmth centers me back inside my body.

I can feel the full power of blood rushing through his veins as he puts his hands on my waist, the strength of his breath, the life inside him vibrant and pulsing. My thoughts branch out in a myriad directions. Is this really happening? If he loves me, what does that mean? For our future, for his marriage? For my life? If he loves me, why did he marry her? How come she knows? What exactly does she know? Does she hate me? Do I love—

But I don't even finish that question because my whole body is the answer, powering up, burning in his presence. I love him with the kind of ludicrous love that won't let itself be extinguished. The kind that digs its nails under your skin and stays. The kind that acts like an X-ray, seeing inside your deepest layers.

Which is what makes it so infuriating.

He, who could see it all, who knew how to see to the very bottom of me, did not see why I pulled away. He asked me so many whys during those months when our marriage was falling apart. So many whys, except the one that really mattered. *Why now?*

I break away from him, sit on the bed, and cradle my head in my hands. It is heavy, a steel ball. After almost a decade of stagnation, everything is pummeling me all at once. "So by coming here, you've put your marriage in danger?" It's a weight I don't want to shoulder. I don't want to be made responsible for other people anymore. For what they do or don't do. I did that with us, with Vlaho, all those years ago. Took it onto myself to set him free. But that was another version of Ivona. The Ivona sitting here is not ready to shoulder anyone else's responsibilities but her own.

"Not exactly," he says, easing himself next to me. "Marina and I . . . We're not together-together. Like, *involved.* We've never been."

His words, barely a whisper, sweep across the room. I sneak a glance at him to catch any sign of bullshit, but there is none. He has said this with such composure that I have no doubt he's telling the truth. But how? Because there are two children between them that didn't make themselves.

With the day alighting outside, he tells me what happened in those early months after they'd met. She taught him sailing, and when there wasn't enough wind, they talked. At first it was small talk. But the sea is primal and reflective, it has a way of drawing secrets out of you. Masks fall easily when you're left to its devices. He told her he still loved me, and this must have been such a powerful confession that she felt like she needed to confess something in return.

So she told him what she'd never told anyone else. What he has never repeated to anyone until now. That she'd never been in love, never had a crush, never felt like she needed a relationship to feel whole. That she'd sensed early on she was different that way from her friends, who were always fantasizing about guys, relationships, and marriage, while she was always the happiest on her own. She thought something was seriously wrong with her, for not being able to produce the emotions that came so naturally to everyone else. Years later, they read somewhere on the internet that it was an actual thing, being aromantic. That there are more people like her.

But back then, while she was teaching him sailing, Marina often complained that her mother was pressuring her into settling down, and his own mother was getting more depressed the longer he refused to move on after our divorce. His dad called one day, and said, *Son, you're killing your mother.* And when he told Marina that, she repeated her mother's similar words, professed the same day. *You'll be the end of me, Marina*, her mother had said.

"It dawned on us then," he says. "We got along great as friends, liked each other well enough. So we figured we could have children together and make a happy home for them even if we weren't in love." He presses his eyes with the heels of his palms, as if his own words are making him incredulous. "It seemed like a good idea at the time. If I'd gotten together with any other woman, still feeling the way I did about you, I would have made her—both of us—miserable. But Marina didn't need me to love her that way, and I didn't need her to love me that way either."

I sit back, stunned.

All the hard truths I believed, facts, waft above me, like smoke tendrils. All these years of wondering why. Why she welcomed me into their lives so readily, without an ounce of jealousy. What she was thinking, inviting me for coffee, then over for dinner the first time, to their son's birthday, or scandalizing everyone, even myself, by asking me to be Tena's godmother. By then, I was too starved for Vlaho to really care about her motives, but if I'd ever concluded anything, it was that she had always liked me, and straightforward and confident as she was, she didn't see a problem in having me there. And this I thought could only mean she was sure he was over me, sure of his feelings for *her*.

I filter all that against what Vlaho just said.

The truth of his words drills even deeper when I bring back the early days of my own friendship with Marina, when I thought she might be gay because she wasn't showing any interest in men. A thought I ended up dismissing, because I didn't see her showing any interest in women either.

"She tried to tell you once, the first time you talked after we got married. Only you wouldn't listen. We both thought it was because you'd moved on and had no interest in looking back."

"I was not . . . She never said . . . ," I start, but then remember that she did try, the day I first held Maro. She tried to talk about what had happened on that sailboat, but I stopped her, unable to hear how or why they'd gotten together because I thought hearing it would have downright killed me.

The stack of photos on his socials that I stalked so many times crystallizes before my eyes in mesmerizing detail, the one where they're sharing *the look* reigning over them all. I cried myself to sleep so many times with that photo open on my phone. I reassess it now, the angle of his lips, the warmth in his eyes, her casual smile, and see what he's saying. He loves her, but he's not in love with her.

FORTY-FIVE

THE FIRST RAYS OF sun sneak in, dust motes lighting up like fireflies. Vlaho shivers against the cooling air. His T-shirt is sleek against his torso, still fully soaked.

"You should take that off, you'll catch a cold," I say. "I'll find you one of my dad's T-shirts." As I'm getting up, I remember that all my father's clothes are in his wardrobe, in his room. He sleeps lightly and my going in might wake him.

But before I voice this, Vlaho gets up too, takes his shirt off in one swift move, and stands there looking at me. All of him—his eyes, his skin, his intentions—is an invitation. I take the wet T-shirt from his hand and spread it over the back of the chair to dry. My body drums as I turn to face him. This new Vlaho is bolder than he used to be, a satisfying change. This new version might not have let me go back then.

We were both such children, I think, and for a moment a profound sadness makes my heart ache for those two young people who first healed each other, only to rub coarse salt into each other's deepest wounds.

I walk over to him and put my hand on his chest, the way I did all those years ago, at the Cavtat cemetery. His heartbeat is strong and fast, pushing into my palm. I close my eyes and trace his shoulders and back with my fingertips, willing the muscle memory to show him to me as he was then.

That way no time would be lost, other people wouldn't stand between us. It would be just him and me. But his body has changed, it's grown sturdier, more concrete with the years.

I put my palms on his cheeks, and it's like the world is slipping back to its axis from whence it long ago fell off. I breathe him in, just below his jaw. He smiles as he rests his forehead against mine, and when our lips touch for the first time in a decade, I'm exploding inwardly. I'm everything all at once, the invisible girl seen for the first time, a young woman in love, a broken thirty-year-old, and this new woman holding the man she loves.

—

My bed is too small for us, but the proximity is rapturous. Our elbows scrape against the wall as we move our hands over each other. In the back of my mind, a thought: I lived in self-inflicted celibacy for nine years and now I'm making love for the second time in one night. It's upsetting. Asier deserves better, Marina deserves better. I chase the thought away. Vlaho is inside me and all around me, and that's all that matters. He's always been this, a universe unto himself, the only space I wanted to exist in. Pain, lodged in the depths of me, starts evaporating. Slowly, like seawater in the sun, leaving only salt crystals behind.

Six clanks of a spoon against the džezva.

Vlaho looks at me but doesn't stop moving. In his eyes, a homesickness and homecoming all at once. I'm suffused with them too; they gather behind my sternum like hunger that's finally being sated.

—

After we make love, a fatigue so dense settles in every muscle and bone. I'm fighting sleep with all I have. There's no way of knowing where tomorrow will lead us, and I want to hold on to these moments for as long as I can. But Vlaho's warm body is enveloping mine, and it's hard to keep my eyes open.

We're, once again, hunkering down.

"Guess this means you still have feelings for me," he says, quieter now, because the thump-and-drag of my father's feet sounds somewhere out in the hallway. Dad isn't in the habit of coming into my room, but his presence behind the door is making us more cautious. Vlaho pulls himself up on his elbow. "Which brings me back to my original question. Why?"

The one conversation we haven't had yet. I wish we wouldn't today; it's too much on top of everything else we've said and done, all the truths that have crept out from their hiding places. It's the one conversation that can corrode everything beautiful between us, vaulting us in opposite directions.

Because I did lie to him about the reasons why I was leaving. I *am* much more to blame for our breakup than he is. I retreated from him without asking what he thought or wanted, turned myself into water and slipped through his hands.

But he failed to cup them.

A part of me always believed that deep down he must have known it was because of my infertility. He must have sensed it in that way we know things even if we don't give them words. In the way we choose to not know the things we're unable to confront. But for all the bargaining, anger, and convincing he did, he never once addressed it head-on. As if it didn't compute at all, this mountain of a problem wedged between us.

Not that I'm blaming him; I never allowed myself to dwell on that either. It was easier to shoulder all the blame myself, shroud myself in guilt for breaking his heart, for leaving him. Because otherwise I would've had to accept that maybe, just maybe, he didn't love me enough. That maybe, just maybe, it came easier to him to let me decimate him, to let me decimate myself, than to cause more pain to his mother.

"I think you know why," I say. "I think deep down you've always known."

He winces. "I'm not sure I do."

"Did you never wonder why I stopped loving you so soon after the diagnosis?"

He ponders this for a moment. "No," he says. "I told you a thousand times I was fine with us not having children."

"You did. And maybe you were," I say, though I still see his hand on that toddler's ankle. "But we weren't the only ones affected by that decision, were we?"

I don't need to mention his mother because she's practically in the room with us. Vlaho has always felt indebted to her. As if it were his fault that his sister had died, and he survived her. As if it were up to him to do whatever it took to make his mother happy. Back when we were together, I accepted this as a fact, and this riles me up now, because I should've challenged it, challenged *him*, instead of just offering solace. He didn't owe his mother anything. It was she who'd, in her grief, wronged him. In the essence of things, we'd both missed that point. If I'd only pushed him, way before infertility became a problem, to face it and claim his life as his own, and not an extension of hers, maybe we would've been here, in each other's arms, all along.

Vlaho rakes his hand through his hair. The turbulence inside him is a physical thing.

Maybe it's cruel to say the words that are kind of obvious by now. But I need to say it to his face. "I never stopped loving you. Never, not for a second. I only did for you what you had done for her."

The wrongness of both our sacrifices is a thorn slipping between his shoulder blades. He presses his forehead against mine and mutters, "Goddamn it."

—

The atmosphere shifts, depleted after our exchange, and now we're once again standing on the opposite sides of the fault line as we're readying ourselves to go back to our lives. On his phone, three texts from Marina, asking where he is, if he's okay. "Just walking it off. I'll be home soon," he texts her back, and seeing him type both the lie and the word *home* slams into me with doubled force.

Maybe she isn't in love with him, but Marina loves him. It was obvious tonight, when she tousled his hair, when she rested her head on his shoulder. It's been obvious in so many ways all along; the way she listens when he talks, the way she gleams when he plays with Maro or reads fairy tales to Tena. The way she prides herself on the beautiful home they've built. Not the apartment itself, but the harmonious, cheerful space they've created within, where even I feel at ease.

And now her husband is standing in my room, naked, after making love to me. My head churns. I always felt that by marrying him, Marina had wronged me. He was the love of *my* life. *I* am his *home*. But now I have wronged her, and bitter heat spreads in my stomach because of it.

"What now?" I ask him. Meaning, now that we've made love. Meaning, now that we've admitted we still love each other. What with his marriage and my relationship with Asier? What with *us*?

"I don't know," he says. "I really don't know." And even though it pains me, I understand that this is the only answer we can give each other right now. A multitude of relationships and people hang in the balance, and what happens next isn't a decision either of us can make at six a.m. after a sleepless night.

Vlaho takes his wet T-shirt from the chair and starts to put it on.

"Wait," I say, and slide the big plastic box from under my bed, where I've stored trinkets from my youth. High school diaries, some photos from our life in Zagreb, when photos were still developed. My old herbarium. A few Post-it notes he used to leave for me around the apartment that I've saved over the years. *I feel you all the time, in my lungs, in between breaths.* An old T-shirt of his that I sneaked into my suitcase as I was moving out of our home. I unfold it and give it to him.

"You still have this?" he says, incredulous.

"It smelled of you. For a while."

He smiles but looks like he'd rather cry.

"I'll have to keep this one in its place." I snatch the wet T-shirt from him. It's intended as a joke but my voice breaks, and I know there's no way I'm giving it back. This one still carries his scent.

He laughs, and rummages through the things in the box, pulling out a couple of photos of us in Zagreb's botanical garden, when he studied for an exam, and I was working on my herbarium. We were so young, it's impossible to imagine we considered ourselves grown-up. He unfolds a couple of his notes, then puts them back in. Then he pulls at another piece of fabric and takes out the baby-girl onesie I'd put there years before we broke up. The one I had bought for Tara when she got pregnant, but then couldn't make myself give her, and kept for our own future daughter instead. It's so small in his hands, a delicate pink thing. He handles it with care, like it's alive. The image develops between us, a shared vision of a baby girl we should've had. She would've been our entire world. She would've saved us. He brings it to his face, drives it across his cheek. My heart numbs. "Oh, Ivona," he says.

FORTY-SIX

WHEN VLAHO LEAVES, THE absence that stays behind pulls me into its vacuum. It feels as though everything inside me is shattered, has been shattered for a long time, only now it's been acknowledged. And what's seen can't be ignored anymore.

For the longest time, I was arranging my life around the fact I still loved him, a truth I couldn't confront but couldn't exactly avoid either. So I relegated it to the corners of my mind until it became a background hum that played while I ate, slept, worked, even while I was falling in love with someone else.

But now it's materialized into something tangible, something requiring attention.

Because what is spoken cannot be unspoken. I love Vlaho. Vlaho loves me. Vlaho is also married to someone else. Even if their marriage is platonic, in many ways it's more real than many of those "normal" marriages that had once been rooted in love, and then turned apathetic. He is the father of two small children who need him, who need the stability of their family like we once needed the stability in ours. And I have a man in my life who makes me laugh, and lifts me up, and lightens me. Gambling that away on the off chance that things might work out with Vlaho despite all that stands against and between us is both precarious and plain foolish.

And yet, and yet! All I can think about when I close my eyes is Vlaho's skin against mine, his fingertips raining over me like tears slipping down sleek cheeks. The way he sees me, the way I am around him, my deepest, truest self, with impossibly big feelings, so enormous they scare me, so enormous they're all I want.

—

I fall asleep, and this is the dream I have. I'm with Asier taking a nighttime swim. A million plankton and stars fire all around us. I'm peaceful, the way the sea is calm. Asier looks sated, smiling, but as I approach him, his face morphs into Vlaho's. A twinge of excitement, I'm a child receiving a gift. I reach out to him, to cup his face with my hands, seawater spilling between my fingers. Vlaho angles his body away from me. I try to walk around him. I wade through the water, it weighs a ton, but I can never reach him. I'm calling out to him. I can feel, clearly, my mouth forming the two syllables of his name. His name, which sounds like the drum of my heartbeat. But nothing comes out. There is a gap in my throat. A black hole, endless, gravity pulling. Panic surges. Vlaho's head morphs into a mirror. The same ornamented mirror my mother bought on the day she took me to the hospital all those years ago. I finally get to it, look into it. What it reflects back is nothing. Only an absence, and behind it, the wall of stars.

FORTY-SEVEN

OVER THE COURSE OF the next few days, I focus on my chores because sitting with what happened is too hard. It only makes me obsess over what Vlaho and I did, what it meant, and what it could mean going forward. The pain of leaving things as they are, the pain it might cause if we don't.

Different scenarios play on repeat in my head. The one where Vlaho leaves his family for me and we ride off into the sunset. The one where I discourage him from leaving his family, because I'm *that* good and self-sacrificing. The one where he tells me that his children come first and I either concede or make a scene. The one where what happened never gets mentioned again, and is instead swallowed by the oblivion of the coming years, until neither of us can be sure if it happened at all.

To spare myself these ruminations, early every morning I go swimming. I swim so hard and so far from shore that sometimes I wonder if I'll be able to return. I need it, the exertion, the cleansing. On my way back, I let go of motion and just float there, allowing the sea to even the pressure between my body and the world.

When I come home, I make phone calls to try to get my dad into physical therapy. The right side of his body has drooped further lately and he's been complaining of more pain. Getting help is, as always, a task of climbing up a rotten ladder with no stronghold.

I spend the afternoons and evenings with Asier. He's here for only a couple more days. I'm easy around him, a version of myself that isn't entirely true, but that I wouldn't mind being true. If he sees a change in me after that night, he doesn't mention it. Or maybe, he ascribes it to the fact that we—the two of us—had sex that night, and so of course the dynamic has changed.

We take endless strolls around the old town, or go to dinner, or make love in his apartment. It seems to me in those moments that I could go on like nothing happened. That I could be the person I'd started out to be just half an hour before Vlaho dove into my life again. There are glimmers of that person. If only I could hold on to them.

By the time I get home at night, I am exhausted and can only crash into bed. But sleep won't come. Not until I take Vlaho's T-shirt and hold it to my nose, to my chest.

FORTY-EIGHT

IT ALWAYS HAPPENS IN a single day. A storm sweeps in, seemingly like any other summer shower, but afterward, the temperature doesn't quite bounce back, and the sea nibbles at your skin when you go for a swim. The colors dull, even the falling sun's orange and pinks are filtered through a thin layer of gray. The cicadas sing without the usual ardor, each day fewer of them in the choir, as they die one by one after mating.

The subtle signs of the world sputtering to a stop.

Dad's not been well. On bad days, he barely gets up, and refuses to eat anything other than oatmeal. When he gets like that, I would gladly fry him some bacon and French fries, and salt his tomatoes until they turn white if it meant he'd eat something. But whatever I make, he just pushes the plate away and goes back to his room. It's scary how small and depthless his eyes are, like a very old person's at the end of their life. He is stoic about his agony, but when he goes to his room some of it lingers in his wake, and I just sit there basting in it, unable to cry.

The administrative work of closing Dad's company is almost a full-time job. Everyone I know advises me not to pay off some of the debts and let the company go bankrupt, as liquidating it is a more complex, costly, and time-consuming process. But I would go against everything I believe, everything my father stands for, if I didn't do things the proper way, so I make sure I attend meetings with attorneys and court dates, and pay fees, and submit all the documents needed to shut the company down.

Asier finds this hilarious. One more of Croatia's quirks. He calls me most evenings from his apartment in London, or a hotel room in Greece, or Portugal. We talk for hours. When I'm done droning on about the horrors of Croatian bureaucracy, he tells me that he bought a couple of mini olive and lemon trees for his apartment and asked his neighbor, the older woman who has that dog he always sees when he's on his balcony, to water them when he's gone. "She'd do that?" I ask. I can't even make my brother come and take care of our dad so that I can visit Asier in London. But Asier is so good at connecting with people. He does it with such ease. "She was happy to do it." A warmth wraps around me, because I ribbed him for not committing to anything, not even to a houseplant, and this is his way of showing me he's doing just that.

But then I feel like I'm cheating, because I'm in a relationship with this man—that's what this is, a relationship, even if we haven't called it that—and it might be going somewhere, and I like where it's going, but I'm withholding a crucial part of myself from him, I'm not in this completely, the way I ought to be.

"Guess where I am?" he asks me when he video-calls one day. It looks like he's in a gym. He has some sort of harness over his T-shirt, and his forehead is beaded in sweat.

"No idea, but I'm sure you'll tell me."

"I'm in Bristol." He turns the camera toward a gray wall peppered with colorful handholds. "Taking my son and his friends rock climbing. They made me do it too."

"I didn't know you were susceptible to peer pressure," I taunt, but my lungs tingle with warmth. Asier told me heights make him uneasy. We were on Zadar's bedem, the city wall, overlooking the entry to the old town, with only a thigh-high barrier protecting us from a ten-meter drop, and I told him drunk tourists have been known to take a plunge. He couldn't go near and look down. It wasn't a phobia, he said, but being high up made his hands sweat and his vision swim. And here he is rock climbing to get closer with his son, all because I made that comment in his hotel room months ago.

"I'd love to introduce you to him," he says.

"What? Right now?"

He nods. He's naughty that way, likes to keep me on my toes.

"Are you sure?" My pulse beats in my temples. Meeting his son would level us up to a type of seriousness we haven't acknowledged yet. That I'm not sure I want to acknowledge, given the circumstances.

"I've met his friends. It's only fair to let him meet one of mine."

I swallow, steady myself inside my body. "So, is that what I am, a friend?"

Asier focuses his gaze on the screen, the look of a man who knows what he wants, and I'm it. "A very good friend. The best." He calls Iker over. My palms sweat as if I've climbed the rock myself. Iker appears on the screen, his dark hair swept onto one side, his eyes the same pallid green as his father's.

"Hi, Iker," I say, too aware of my accent. "Your dad told me a lot about you." A cliché if there ever was one, but also the truth.

"Hiya," he says. "Nice to meet you." Despite having dark hair, he has the typical British complexion, fair and prone to blushing. His cheeks are pitted with acne, and I have the urge to tell him, *I know it looks bad now, but I promise one day some girl will find it very sexy.*

"So I see you got your dad to climb up the wall," I say.

"Yeah, suppose I did." His British accent is nothing like his dad's untraceable one. "It took a while to talk him into it."

"I'll bet. He told me he was afraid of heights."

"Not afraid," Asier intervenes from behind. "Just . . . not a fan."

Iker and I laugh. A couple of Iker's friends yell for him to come over, and he excuses himself.

"He's nice," I say. "And handsome, like his father."

"He's a good boy," Asier says, looking after him. "His mother did a good job." He focuses back on me. "Thank you, Ivona. I know I sort of sprang this on you. But I don't only want to insert myself into his life. I want to make him a part of mine as well, you know?"

"I know," I say.

After we hang up, these are the words that stay with me. I am a part of Asier's life. Important enough to be introduced to his son. A month ago, this would've made me happy. Proud to have the attention—affection—of a man like him. But now, I'm not sure what I want, and that seems unfair to Asier, even if he's in the dark about it.

As if on cue, a text fires on my phone. It's from Vlaho. The first one since we made love three weeks ago. It says, "Fališ mi."

I miss you too, I think. But I don't get to type it before the next text arrives. "Can I see you tonight?"

FORTY-NINE

THAT EVENING, AFTER MY dad goes to sleep, I meet Vlaho in Borik. It's the westernmost part of the town, where the hotels are. Where the hotel Asier stayed in the first time he was here is. It's the beginning of September, and the evenings are not as hot anymore. There are fewer tourists milling about, and no locals come here this time of night, which is why we agreed to meet here. The air smells of pine resin and salt. We sit on the small boardwalk overlooking the deep cove.

It's only when I'm sitting next to him that I become aware of how visceral my missing him has been. There's an opening in my chest, as if I'm about to cry, but it has nothing to do with sorrow. It's more like famine, an unmet need. I run my cheek along Vlaho's shoulder. He weaves his fingers through my hair. The pain of wanting so much stretches my chest to impossible lengths. I wonder why he called me, what he's about to tell me.

"I went to Cavtat last week," he says.

I snap back to look at him, and there it is in his eyes. Among the many truths we said that night, I spared him one—the one about his mother. That she had asked me to leave him. I saw no need in causing him one more loss. But there it is. The hurt, riled. He knows.

"She told you."

He fills me in on what's been happening in the weeks since we last saw each other. Marina had been asleep when he came back home that night, so she didn't know how late, or rather, how early it was when he'd arrived, and she didn't see him wearing another shirt, a shirt she'd never seen before. Next morning, she made him iced ginger tea for the hangover, and rubbed his back as he drank it. Her acts of kindness made him feel even worse, and he didn't know how to tell her what had happened, where he'd really been. So he told her he just had a moment. A weird jealous spell, probably alcohol-induced. Nothing to worry about. He put his hand on her hand, resting on his shoulder. "I'm fine now."

"It'll get better," she told him. "She was bound to move on sometime, and we're lucky it's with a guy we both like." Marina, always wanting to corral us all together, always keen on keeping us in each other's life.

He nodded, reinforcing her misunderstanding. How could he tell her what had really happened, what he was thinking of doing next? They'd built a good life together. She was his closest friend, mother of his children, the only person who knew him almost as well as I did. *Almost.* So he allowed the lie to fall between them.

Last weekend there was a fešta in the village where Marina's family is from, and she took the kids and went to stay with her mother, and he said he would go visit his mother in Cavtat. For some reason he felt it was critical he saw her, though he couldn't pinpoint why.

He hadn't been alone with his mother since he and Marina had gotten together. There were always children around, a birthday, a Christmas Eve, Easter. Now the house was empty but for the two of them, and he sat for the longest time on the couch, staring at his sister's photo surrounded by its sentinels, the forever-lit candles.

It didn't take long for his mother to sense something was wrong. She'd been used to an obliging son, always looking for particles of sorrow on her face, always trying to dissolve them. But this Vlaho was rigid, unmoving. He only sat there and stared at his sister's photo, the girl he barely remembered, but who had shaped his life in such unforgiving ways.

"What is it, Vlaho?" his mother asked.

He faced her and said, "Did you ever say anything to Ivona? About our marriage? About her infertility?" He said it on instinct, because I hadn't told him what his mother had done, what she'd asked of me on the day of my mother's funeral. But he intuited it somehow—perhaps the crumbs that were left lying there after it had happened simply started making more sense after I told him the rest of the truth.

His mother sat next to him on the couch. For a while she wrung her hands. "I didn't do anything," she said. He waited, because silence has a way of making people speak. "I didn't do anything," she repeated, "I only told Ivona she shouldn't keep you hostage of her situation."

"When?" he rasped, struggling to keep himself in check. "When did you tell her this?" He couldn't think of one moment when his mother and I had been alone after the diagnosis. He had made sure of that, and only now was it becoming clear to him why.

Turning to her daughter's photo, as if it gave her entitlement or offered protection, she said, "At her mother's funeral."

He shot up. "For Christ's sake, Mom!"

She got up too. "It wasn't right. It wasn't right for her to keep you tethered to her."

"Who gave you the right to decide that?" he hissed. He had never hissed or cursed at his mother before.

"You were unhappy, Vlaho."

He laughed, a broken, ironic sneer. "No, Mom," he said. "*You* were unhappy. There's a difference. Or did it never occur to you that I am capable of feelings of my own?"

His mother looked chastised, pained, but he could tell from her stoic expression that it wasn't because she was sorry for what she'd done. It was more that she was inconvenienced by being found out. She was waiting his anger out as if it were a child's tantrum.

She hadn't understood what he'd said, not really.

But for the first time, *he* understood. The choices he'd been making his entire life unfurled before him. How he didn't take sailing lessons when he was a child because she was afraid he'd drown. How he chose economics over nautical engineering because she thought seafaring was dangerous. How he absorbed her sad soliloquies after the diagnosis because he didn't know how to ask her to stop. She had held herself on the pedestal of pain for so long it had made it impossible for him to imagine anyone could hurt more than she did, and he never wanted to be the one adding to her suffering.

But now *he* was hurting. He had been hurting for over ten years.

Suddenly, he felt queasy, disoriented, and he had to sit down. It had been more than just this, an occasional concession he'd made for his mother, however big or small. It had been that he had formed his identity around appeasing her. Who was he, without that? What was his true nature if not to pacify, placate, acquiesce? Who would he be had it not been for her influence? He had no idea.

This loss of true north was dizzying. Everything felt up in the air. Even the most essential parts of him were now up for debate.

His mother approached him. Her aquatic eyes filled with tears but even so, she retained some of that confidence, the conviction that he would ultimately yield to her. It had been that way his whole life, after all, she had no reason to doubt it even through this upheaval.

"Son," she said, "whatever happened back then, it was for the best. Look at you now! You have two beautiful children. A wonderful wife. You lead a full and happy life. Tell me, would you go back, even if you could?"

It caught him off guard. Saying yes would be as good as saying he didn't want or love his children.

She took his hesitation for confirmation, and pressed on. "It was for the best. And what's the point of looking back anyway? It was all so long ago."

"The point is, I love her," he sputtered. He felt such rage at his mother's righteousness that he had to clench his fists against it. "I will never not love her. The point is, I already had a wife. I was complete."

He couldn't stand sharing a room with his mother for one more second. He pushed toward the door, shoving her to the side, not hard but with intent. "It was you who've kept me hostage all these years," he said, grabbing his jacket and car keys.

On his way out, he did something he'd never thought himself capable of. He walked up to his sister's photo on the credenza, and blew the candles out.

—

He breaks down, telling me this. His shoulders shudder, the pain quaking him from within. "What sort of person does that?"

"Oh, Vlaho." I pull him into my arms. I kiss every part of him that's available to me, but I will never hold him close enough, I will never be able to erase this pain.

He curls up in my lap. "I'm sorry. I'm so sorry for not doing a better job of protecting you."

I hold him tighter. The weight of him makes my arms tremble, but I can't let go. I don't know if I will ever be able to let go.

"What are we going to do?" he asks, his voice hoarse and desperate.

I shut my eyes against the mess we've made. Against these sacrifices—choices, decisions—that we let braid into this reality, where we owe more to other people than to each other, than to ourselves. The tension of it, the weight of our past, the elusiveness of our future threatens to undo me. *Call it*, I want to plead. *Say you're coming back to me.* But I can't say it, it needs to be his choice. I need him to choose me this time.

FIFTY

THE NIGHT IS THICK when I come back home, but I can't sleep.

The longing is back.

If I hungered for Vlaho all these years, if there was a thirst I thought I could quench by stalking his social media posts, by seeing him on random Tuesdays or Saturdays, by savoring an accidental touch of his T-shirt against my skin when I pressed my hand against his shoulder as we kissed goodbye, it's proved itself insufficient.

A mere sustentation.

It's not enough anymore. Now that I've had a full-sized bite, now that the juices of that love have trickled down my throat and mouth as I bit into its tender flesh, my fingers sticky with it, my palate dancing with its taste, my heart thundering to the joy of it, I am ravenous. I want more. I cannot subsist on crumbs anymore. I need it all. I need all of him, or I'll die.

FIFTY-ONE

WITH THE WEATHER TURNING moodier, I head to the Supernova mall to do some shopping, because I'm short on long-sleeved clothes. What I need more than clothes, though, is a distraction. To take my mind off what Vlaho said, how he wept in my arms only a few days ago. It's agony to know all the ways he's hurting, and not be able to offer solace.

I'm exiting one of the stores when a tiny voice calls from behind, "Hey, there's Aunt Ivona!" I turn around, and sure enough, Maro is pointing a finger at me. Marina is standing behind him, smiling, holding Tena's hand. I squat as Maro runs over to hug me, and when I release him, I open my arms to Tena, the more cautious of the two children, but whose hug is therefore more worth the earning. She chews on her lower lip as she walks into my embrace, and I lift her in my arms, kiss her glossy cheeks. They reward me with the most satisfying popping sound. When she surrenders herself, it's with her full heft.

I try to ignore the tear in my chest, the guilt for having slept with her father, for wanting him for myself the way I do. I bury my nose into her scalp, stinking faintly of baby sweat, and work hard to purge myself of those thoughts.

"Fancy seeing you here." Marina approaches to kiss me with the same ease she always does. She's oblivious, then. Vlaho hasn't told her a thing.

"Even people who hate shopping as much as I do need a new pair of socks now and then."

"We've come to buy new bathing trunks for our little fellow here," she says, then whispers with a hand over her mouth, but her strained cheekbones betray a grin, "He tore his last ones on a rock. Straight across his butt."

I laugh with her, but the sound comes out all wrong.

"There's a sale over at Calzedonia, by the way, if you're thinking about getting a bathing suit for yourself. Something nice and sexy to dazzle your new boyfriend, perhaps?" She wiggles her eyebrows. "Won't be long till that Kornati trip."

My throat closes in on itself.

Vlaho emerges from down the mall, jiggling car keys in one hand, rummaging through his pocket with the other. When he looks up and sees me standing next to his wife, holding his daughter, his face does something painful that twinges in my own stomach.

"Hey," he says, leaning in to kiss my cheek, because not kissing me would cause more suspicion.

Tena reaches for his neck, and he takes her from me, props her on his hip.

Without her in my arms, I feel exposed. I don't know what to do with my hands.

"Oh shit," Marina says. "Maro, come back!" She hurries down the mall, chasing after their son, who's taken off running. It's painfully hard to turn back to face Vlaho.

"She doesn't know," I say, in a cheerful tone that doesn't quite match the accusation, because he is still holding Tena, and I don't want to alarm her.

"No, not yet," he says. "Things were busy. Tena had a stomach bug last week." But I don't know if it's just a pretext and he doesn't plan on telling Marina at all. Maybe he shouldn't, not if he decides that that night was a mistake.

"We shouldn't be taking that trip," I say. It was never a good idea to begin with.

"Yeah. But Marina is looking forward, and I—" He doesn't finish, but he doesn't have to. If he wants her to cancel the trip, he has to tell her. If he tells her, it changes everything, and we will never get to do this again. We will never stop to catch up when we run into each other, much less meet on purpose. It feels like we're teetering on the edge of a cliff, all of us.

Tena is watching me with her big eyes. I tuck a strand of hair behind her ear. It's so wispy, her hair. As delicate as she is.

"Vlaho, we need to get going," Marina calls to him. She gives me an apologetic shrug, then turns to chase after Maro again, who giggles, running away from her. Vlaho and I look at each other. So many unspoken words in his eyes. He is tormented, I see. Pained. But why? Why? Because of me, or because of them? *Which one of us are you planning to hurt?* I almost ask.

"Daddy, I'm tired," Tena says with her caramel voice, and tucks her head in the crook of his neck. As I rub her back, I feel her heft again, even though I'm not the one carrying her.

But I am.

I am.

FIFTY-TWO

WITH THE END OF September nearing, Marina creates a WhatsApp group for the four of us. "it will be simpler to share info about the trip this way," she writes. She dubs the group The Square after I told her that Asier jokingly calls the three of us The Triangle. She and Asier exchange a smattering of texts about the weather forecast, what clothes, props, food, and drinks we should bring, all peppered with a hefty dose of Captain Jack Sparrow gifs. I interject with an occasional remark, not wanting to make my reservations about the trip obvious, but Vlaho's complete silence feels like a statement.

It's a scary prospect, this open channel of communication between the four of us, and the fact that soon we'll be sequestered together in a space as confined as a sailboat.

Every day, I expect either Vlaho or Marina to notify us that the trip is off. But the days pass, and it doesn't happen. I imagine being inside their home and wonder what Vlaho is thinking, how he's bearing our secret, being so close to her all the time. He is not a liar or a cheat. He has the purest of souls. Even across town, I can feel this eating away at him, a relentless dog gnawing on a bone.

In a moment of panic, I almost back out myself. After picking Asier up at the airport and helping him get settled in a rental apartment in the old town, I come home and open the group text to type, "guys, i'm not feeling well. i think i'm coming down with something. could we postpone?" Which of course we can't. The weather won't hold forever, and Asier is here only for the long weekend.

My finger hovers over the send button, but then I can't go through with it.

Because I need it to happen.

It has been six weeks since that night. Things are weirdly settling, and I don't want them to settle. If the only way to figure out what's next is to put the four of us in close proximity, so be it. Turn the heat up and let the water boil. Let the whole thing blow up if it must, even if it takes me out with it.

—

The day of the trip is one of those beautiful, mellow late-September days, the weather so still that the horizon resembles a painting. When Asier and I arrive at the sailboat, Marina is already there, transferring coolers and a case of beer from the pier onto the aft deck. The engine is puttering quietly, letting out a thin tendril of exhaust fumes and seawater.

"Let's go, lovebirds. This trip won't take itself," Marina yells like the true sailor she is. She ushers us in over the wooden plank connecting the aft deck to the pier, hugging Asier, then me. For a moment, I'm overcome with the need to apologize, to beg for her forgiveness. The urge is so powerful, my whole skin pricks with it. She's been such a good friend to me. She's trying so hard to make it work for the four of us.

"Can I help with that?" Asier points to the case of beer Marina is lifting up.

"Could you get it down into the cabin? They're still cold."

"Let's keep 'em that way then." Asier takes the case from her. Marina hops down into the cabin to show him the way, and I'm left alone on the aft deck. I glance around. There's not a hint of a breeze. The sky is open and high above, spacious, the sea so calm it could be made of oil. One could easily mistake it for the height of summer, except the colors are less saturated, like fruit past its prime, and there's no feverish pitch of cicadas coming from the trees in Vruljica Park, just across the street. The mating season cost them their lives.

I don't see Vlaho anywhere. For a moment I think he came up with a last-minute excuse not to come, but then there he is, carrying a bag of snorkeling equipment from the car.

In the slanted light of the morning sun, he looks almost haggard. He puts the bags down, his T-shirt damp with sweat. There's a pulling in at his chest when he straightens up, like he can't quite make his shoulders stand back. He gives me a "hey" and a smile, but neither is fully inhabited. It makes me uneasy. His face has never been unreadable to me before.

"It doesn't look like we'll do much sailing, but it'll be a beautiful day," Marina says, coming up from the cabin.

As Vlaho passes me, he presses his palm against the small of my back. Not hard, but with purpose. The touch lingers long after it's gone.

—

The sea is a silvery mirror stretching between the islands, and the boat cuts through it, leaving a wake that ripples behind it like outstretched, foamy arms. We sail to Kornati National Park, an archipelago of rocky islands that more resemble the surface of the moon than Earth, bare as they are, dappled only with patches of low, sun-scorched grass.

Asier's excitement has a childlike quality to it, his gaze running over the horizon with reverie. I'm still in shock that this is his first time sailing, a man who's circumnavigated the world hundreds of times, and lived on four different continents. All this time I feared I was missing out on so many things, and maybe that's true, but what's also true is that there are a million tiny miracles right here, within the fifty-mile radius of my front door.

Asier's elation is making him more tactile too. He keeps reaching for me, intertwining our fingers, touching my hair when the breeze blows it over my face. When Marina brings out a bowl of fresh fruit, he peels the green skin off a fig, bites half of it off, then feeds the rest to me, the way he used to, at the beach. Only now, the whole display feels lascivious, and I push his hand away. Playfully, so that he can't see my discomfort. If Vlaho is watching from behind the helm, I don't know. I don't want to know.

On our port side, we pass an island with a small cove. A single stone-built house is snuggled in the crook of it, surrounded by a verdant olive grove that grows straight from the rocks. Asier notices it, nudges me. "Looks like Lovorun," he says, with too much levity. I avert my eyes. Inside me, a wave builds up, crests.

—

We anchor in a breathtaking cove, the sea so lucid that the sailboat looks suspended midair. Save for the four of us, there's not a living soul around. In this otherworldly setting, it's easy to imagine we're the only four people alive.

I slip off my oversized linen shirt, which leaves me only in a bikini. I make a point of avoiding the men's eyes, self-conscious about being half-naked with both of them so close to me, to one another. I jump into the water and swim ashore. There, I collect turbinate monodonts from the rocks, allow them to latch onto the skin of my palm.

Back on the boat, Vlaho takes his shirt off, and stands at the top of the prow. I can feel how hard he's trying not to look my way. He bends, then straightens into a clean line as he enters the water headfirst.

Asier stands on the aft deck. Unlike Vlaho, who wears board shorts, he's only in briefs, and even though he's a whole head shorter than Vlaho, he looks impressive with his well-defined torso and that innate confidence that wafts off him.

Marina claps when he jumps in, then yells "Bombs away!" and drops into the sea with both her legs bent and held to her chest. I can't help but laugh. Maybe this is the third door I've been looking for, the solution for surviving today. Marina, with her magnetic force, with her invitation to not take ourselves too seriously.

I join them in the water, and we splash each other, swim and dive and climb back on the sailboat, then launch ourselves off it again. We chase and push each other underwater, then towel ourselves off only to jump in again, and for a moment, all is forgotten, all the hidden agendas, all the secretive yearnings, are tamed and washed away by the sea.

———

For lunch, Marina makes pasta. On the tiny hob in the cabin, she sautés onions in olive oil, adds a bit of garlic and basil, stirs in peeled shrimp tails, then adds the thick šalša sauce made from tomatoes her mother grows in their village. It's a whole different dish than the one I make from canned plum tomatoes I buy at the store. It's sweet and sticky and savory, and you can't get enough even when you're full. When we're done eating, Vlaho takes the dishes to the platform to rinse them in seawater, and the three of us remain on the aft deck seats, Marina alone on the port-side one, Asier and I snuggled together on the starboard. The sun has moved past the zenith, and I'm sleepy, pleasantly drained by the sun and the sea, buzzed by the after-lunch beer still sweating in my hand.

"Who's up for snorkeling?" Marina says, tireless as always. "There's a shipwreck just outside the cove."

"I'm game," Asier says.

"You go." I push him off, and burrow deeper into the seat. "I'll watch the boat."

Marina brings out three pairs of fins, masks, and snorkels, and I close my eyes, doze off to the sounds of their voices as they're getting ready to leave. There's a loud splash when they drop from the platform into the sea. I hear them mumble and giggle through their snorkels, the splash of their arms as they're swimming away.

A cold hand on my thigh, and his voice. "Hey."

I open my eyes to Vlaho.

"I thought you went with them," I say, scooting up so he can sit.

He looks like he wants something. To say something, to set things straight between us. *What? What? What?* I want to ask. *Tell me now, waiting is agony.* Everything about him is heavy, like he's saddled with more than he can carry. I think, unflatteringly, of the donkeys that passed near Lovorun when I was a child, the way they bore the heft of full bags of pumpkins or watermelons from the fields beyond the estate. How their eyes, when I offered them an apple or a carrot, looked sad and also gone.

We hold our bodies unnaturally still as we wait for the sounds of swimming to fade. A thought pierces me, *This could be the moment Vlaho tells me we're done, forever.*

As soon as I think that, I'm reaching for him, running my hands up his arms, through his hair, pulling him closer, willing him to come back to his body. He looks surprised, but soon the surprise morphs into a different kind of need as I straddle him, cupping his face in my hands, kissing him like I can find him in his mouth. My heart pulses in my ears and toes as our tongues touch. He smells like the sea, like heaven, like the sun itself. He slips his hand between the edges of my towel, pushing it aside, pulling me closer. Reaching for the bikini tie on my left hip. Undoing it.

"What if they see us?" I ask, but I'm untying the drawstring on his board shorts beneath me, my fingers clumsy with fear, with desire. It feels like he is slipping from me, and I need to center him back to myself.

"They're far away," he says, catching my lips with his. The taste of tangerines and watermelons, and all things verdant and blooming. The taste of all these years of being apart, of silent misery without him.

"God" is all I can say as he enters me. I clutch his head to my breasts as we move, curled around him like a cat, a creature of instinct. Around us, the sea, the rocky, bare island, the endless skies, sounds of nothing. We are alone in the universe. I close my eyes to keep the world out. There's only us, this feeling of coming back home.

"I love you," he says. "I love you so much."

I hook my palms behind his ears, make him look at me. If I had reservations about us getting back together, about him leaving his family, his children, for me, those reservations are gone. This is what I want, this is what I've always wanted. To find my way back to him. *I love you too,* I want to say but the release comes from my lower abdomen in waves and pulses, rendering me mute.

Afterward, I tie my bikini at my hip, and Vlaho pulls his shorts on, and we sit side by side. A seagull screeches, careening into the sea. I'm emptied when I should feel full, as if having sex has robbed us of something. He's back to how he's been the whole day, something about him cumbrous, but he works through whatever makes him that way to open his arm to me. "Come here."

I crawl into his embrace, overcome with the sudden urge to cry. To push my sadness out of my chest like garlic through a press. I know it makes me a horrible person, but at this point, I don't even care if Marina and Asier find us this way. All I want is for Vlaho to acknowledge what this means. That he's done his thinking. That he chooses me. But I can sense this is the one thing he can't or won't give me, at least not today.

"Vlaho, talk to me," I tell him. "What is going on with you?" I touch his face and he winces, like my father recoils when I brush against his right side. This act of dismissal no less painful because it's involuntary.

"I made such a mess of things, haven't I?" he says.

"What do you mean?"

"I opened a can of worms that night. With you, with my mother, Marina. And now everything is up in the air. For everyone." He turns to face me. "I love you, you know I do." His tone is that of someone delivering a consolation prize. "But I need time to figure things out. How to move forward. Tena and Maro—"

My body stiffens at the mention of his children. I don't want to know how hard it is for him to do what comes so easily to me.

He deflates a little, feeling this shift in me. "But I can't do this either," he continues, nodding to where Asier and Marina have swum. "Watching you with him, it's too much."

I get up. "What the hell, Vlaho? I spent six years watching you with someone else."

"That's different. Marina and I, we weren't—"

"Yeah, well, I didn't know that back then, did I?"

He gets up too. My breaths come in rapid bursts.

"Yeah, but I never had feelings for her. Not that way. You're sleeping with that guy, Ivona. He's been all over you all day long."

"Are you telling me you never slept with Marina?" I give an ironic laugh.

He wipes his face. The patch on his cheekbone turns bright red. "I never betrayed you, is what I'm saying. I didn't sleep with her for the same reasons you are sleeping with him. I never wanted anyone but you."

"You fucking got her pregnant," I burst out. The mother of all betrayals. I catch myself, look out to the entrance of the cove, but there isn't anyone there. "You did betray me. You let me go."

"That's not exactly how it happened, and you know it."

We stare at each other, two bulls refusing to budge.

There's a wildness in his eyes, a fire consuming him from within. "It's not just . . . You really broke me when you left, you know that?" His voice is heavy, dark.

I sit down. I'm stripped of all my weapons, defenseless. The days and months before I left him open themselves before me in mesmerizing detail. How cruel I had been to him. How much I had made him suffer. My breath goes shallow, it coils at the top of my throat. Vlaho is staring past me. I pull him nearer, draw the hem of his board shorts up, exposing the skin on his thigh that was once punctured with blue dots. I drive my fingers over it. Kiss it. The scars can't be seen anymore. But they are still there.

"What are you saying? That you're afraid?" I ask. I want to tell him that I'm not that person anymore. I was green. Insecure. Broken in seven hundred different ways. The world had put too much on me and I didn't know how to carry it. I didn't know how to occupy space, to ask for what I needed any more than he did. But that was a long time ago. I've changed. I've grown. I'm asking now, I want to tell him. I'm asking now.

He shakes his head. "It's just that . . . I gave it my all. I loved you through all those dark moments. The unemployment, the infertility, the grief. And still you left me. Still it wasn't enough."

I let his words ripple through me. But as I search myself for compassion, I find annoyance instead. "I didn't choose to be barren or jobless. I didn't inflict those things on *you*."

"That's not what I implied, Ivona."

"That's exactly what you implied. And I know those things affected you, Vlaho, but they happened to *me*. They were inflicted on *me*." Old pain rises within me, and I rise to my feet with it. "You gave it a lot, yes, but you didn't give it your all."

Not just because he had given in to his mother, if subconsciously. It was all those silent days, when he failed to find the words to reach me. How he waited for a way out of our agony, but never offered one. Not really. If there even was a solution other than breaking us apart. It was that I could sense his relief when he'd go to work. The strain in his step when he returned home. How wary he was of asking the painful questions, starting the difficult conversations. How thankful he was when I played along, and told him my day was "fine" and I was "doing okay." Because he didn't know how to handle it, because it was too overwhelming. Because I'd become too much for him.

I think of Asier and his son; of my mother after the boot incident. Maybe he didn't want to, but Vlaho washed his hands of me too.

"So what do you suggest we do now?" I challenge him. Meaning, show me. Cup your hands.

He opens his mouth, but nothing comes out. He lowers his gaze.

And for the first time, I recognize a truth I've been trying to ignore. Back in the era of hunkering down we were the same kind of broken. But we've taken different roads since. Mine, fraught with challenges, swimming upstream and against the current to carve a place for myself in the world. The change the only constant, like Heraclitus said, like Asier said.

Vlaho's—a chrysalis.

He is still that man, I realize. The one who was too afraid to admit his needs even to himself, let alone to rise in defense of them, to stand up for the one he loved. Still a boy allowing others to pull his strings. It spikes in me, this frustration for having come all this way only to hit the same old wall.

"You know what, Vlaho? Grow the fuck up." I snatch my towel from the seat and wrap myself in it as I turn my back to him.

There behind the transom, Marina is standing on the platform watching us, her wet body glistening in the sun, mask hanging in her hand.

FIFTY-THREE

THE ATMOSPHERE IS SCINTILLATING as we sail back. Vlaho is at the helm, tight-lipped, wrought. Marina is winding up the winches. It's impossible to say how much she heard apart from that last sentence, but she is as tense as the ropes she is tightening.

Asier is the only one appearing to be unknowing of, and unaffected by, the sour mood. He's taking in the view from his perch on the prow as the ship hurtles toward the Zadar Channel, port-bound. Only, I can't look at him, having had sex with Vlaho for the second time behind his back. I can't even explain to myself how I became a person who does such things.

My bikini bottoms are still moist between my legs, proof of what Vlaho and I did. After Marina caught us fighting, things sort of happened through a haze. Marina stored the snorkeling equipment, and announced we should be heading back. Vlaho tossed beer bottles into the case, swiping what was left of snacks into a trash can, clearing the deck. I wrapped myself in my shirt, but I was too frozen to do anything else but sit there.

Halfway back, I muster up enough coherence between my mind and body to go to the cabin and change into a dry bathing suit. I lock myself inside the small toilet. Tears catch in my throat as I'm wiping myself clean, washing what's left of Vlaho off me. The day was so beautiful, and now it's ruined, and not just the day, but the triangle we have worked so hard to maintain all these years. All those moments come to me. Marina tossing her head back in laughter when she tells me and Vlaho about tourists' shenanigans. Tena's sudden hug from behind as she braids my hair. Maro's incessant running. Vlaho's peck on the cheek at the end of the evening, when they're seeing me out, how it infuses me with warmth that sustains me for days. Gone, all gone.

I splash some water on my face, then rinse my bikini bottoms in the miniature sink. When I exit, I hear Asier on the outside, saying something to Vlaho. I wonder what he's saying, and if Vlaho is responsive at all.

"I don't mind, you know."

Marina's voice comes at me from behind, her tone not nearly matching her words.

She minds, she minds a lot.

I turn to her. She is the most serious I've ever seen her. "If you guys sleep together. Vlaho and I, we're not . . . " Her voice falters.

"I know," I say, my mouth arid. "He told me."

"I've always known he still has feelings for you. He never kept that a secret. And I suspected you do too. In a way, it didn't feel right for me to stand between you two. But—"

With this, she exits from the shadow of the doorway, and nears me. "Leave him where he is, Ivona. I told you a long time ago how I felt about divorce. What it does to children. Our kids are at a sensitive age, they need both of us, together." Her blue eyes darken, her voice is waterlogged. "We have a good home. We make a great team. Besides, you live with your dad anyway. It's not like you could—" She crosses her arms at her chest. She is imposing, frightening, tall as she is. A mama bear protecting her cubs. "You two can fuck all you want for all I care, just leave him where he is."

The crass word detonates between us. It's not fucking. It was never fucking. If there was fucking, it was done when she and Vlaho made those babies she now wants me to back off for. I did have feelings for him, and she just said she always suspected it, and still she fucked him and made a family with him. "You know what, Marina?" I say. "Screw you."

When we dock, I can't get off the boat fast enough. I mutter quick, perfunctory thank-yous and goodbyes, squeezing my beach bag to my chest and jumping off before the boat is even properly moored. Vlaho's and Marina's faces are both hard, their goodbyes equally caustic.

"What was that all about?" Asier asks me as I stride toward Branimir's Coast, where I'll catch a cab and he'll go over the bridge to his rented apartment.

"Nothing," I say, my whole body rigid. I can't get it to coordinate itself.

Asier catches my hand, stopping me mid-stride. For the first time this afternoon, I'm forced to look at him. Back when I first saw him, I thought his face austere. I've learned its curves and arches since, like one would understand an abstract painting better if they knew the artist's intention behind it. It's softer-looking now, affable where it seemed stern, and it pains me to look at it after what I did today.

"Whatever it is, you can tell me."

The way he says it, with deliberation, gives me pause. He may not understand Croatian, he may not have overheard the strained conversation between Vlaho and me, or Marina and me, but Asier is great at reading people. That's his job, after all, to read people. Of course he knows much more than he lets on, than I'm ready to reveal. I want to cry for how I've mistreated him. I squeeze his hand that's holding mine. "I'm sorry. I wasn't—I'm not . . . I'm so sorry." I touch his face, those craters on his cheeks that always make me feel closer to him. What do I say, how do I explain? If I tell him what I did, it will be as good as letting go, but I don't want to let go yet, and that's one more thing confusing me, because I should be doing just that.

He smiles, pulling me closer. "It's okay, Gorgeous. Take your time."

FIFTY-FOUR

THE INSIDE OF THE cab reeks of spring onions, the taxi driver burping silently, exuding new invisible clouds every few minutes. The streets blur together as we go. When we pull up in front of my house, I notice with slight annoyance that the windows are all dark. Even though it's dusk, Dad has not turned the lights on, and is likely sitting in the living room in front of the gleaming TV screen in an eye-hurting darkness. I pay the taxi driver and thank him for the ride.

The house is not only dark when I enter, there's no sound of the TV either. Dad must have gone to bed early. It was probably one of his bad days. I should've called to check on him, asked him how he was doing. Not that it would've helped him, but it might've made him feel less alone. I make a pact with myself to get up early tomorrow and have coffee with him, maybe even talk about politics, let him vent a little. I go to the utility room, put my towel and wet bathing suits inside the washing machine to rinse.

"Dad?" I say, entering the living room, in case he's awake. "I'm home."

Everything is as I left it this morning.

Exactly as I left it.

The food container with schnitzels in gravy I left to defrost on the kitchen counter now sits in a pool of water, untouched. The sink is empty, not even the cup he eats his oatmeal in every morning is inside. No džezva on the burner. The curtains unopened, the air unstirred, slightly stale.

An eerie feeling rises up my back. "Dad?"

The door to his room is half open. "Dad?" I move fast, but it feels as though I'm extra slow, like wading through oil. I see his leg before I see the rest of him, lying on the floor in the doorway of his bathroom. "No." I'm running now, both wanting to look and not to see.

He is lying on his side, facing away from me, in his pajamas. I fall to my knees, turn him over slowly. I can't look. I have to look. His skin is cold, but I can't tell if that's because he's been lying on the tiles for so long, or because he's dead. "Daddy?" My voice transmutes to that of a little girl.

The sharp smell of urine. His pajama pants wet, the floor below my knees wet.

I press my fingers against his jugular, feeling for a pulse. I can't sense anything, but I don't know if that's because I'm not looking in the right place, or because it's not there. A series of indistinguishable grunts and gurgles mix in my throat as the panic builds. I press harder. A faint flutter of his pulse against my fingertips. The relief is transient, replaced with more panic.

"Hang in there, I'm calling for help," I tell him as if he can hear me. I scramble up, run for my phone. I struggle to steady it in one hand as I'm punching in 112 with the other.

"Emergency center," a dispassionate male voice says.

"Hi, yes, hello. My father's unconscious. I think he had a stroke."

The man asks for details—what I know about the patient's condition, current status, brief medical history, our address. It sounds as though someone else is responding as I'm filling him in. "The ambulance is dispatched," he says. "They should be there within minutes. Ma'am?"

"Yes?"

"Are we within the golden hour?"

My stomach drops. I know enough about stroke to know what he's asking, that any reasonable means of therapy, as well as recovery, depends on bringing the patient to the hospital within that first hour. I bend and press my forehead into my father's unmoving side. In all likelihood, he's been lying here since early this morning. While I was away sailing, swimming, making love, fighting, he lay here, unconscious, half dead. "We're way past the golden hour."

FIFTY-FIVE

MY FATHER IS IN the intensive care unit in Neurology, ironically in the same bed he lay in four years ago, after his first stroke. They tell me I can stay with him for only a few minutes. Not that he's aware of my presence.

There are a dozen beds along the walls, patients lying in different states of decline, no screens dividing them. I try to not let my gaze skate over them. How undignifying it must be, being displayed in such a vulnerable state to the eyes of every stranger who enters the room. The furniture is from the eighties, not a dime spent since the building was first erected. A knob dangles off the nightstand next to Dad's bed like a comma in an unfinished sentence. The blanket he's covered with is frayed, evoking the refugee era of the Homeland War. I worry a hole in it with my fingers. Machines beep and there's always a nurse rushing around, and yet there is a hush that lies atop of it all, as clinical as the smell of bleach permeating the air.

I focus on my father. I wish we could have some privacy. An apology sits in my throat, for not being there, for not checking up on him, but before I muster up the strength to speak, a nurse comes over to usher me out. "The doctor should come by shortly if you have any questions."

It's hard to let go of his hand.

I sit on an orange plastic chair in the hall, a cold draft licking my bare legs and feet. I'm still in my flip-flops, in my bathing suit covered only with an oversized shirt. It's a bad joke to look like this at such a defining moment in my life.

This is the second time my life has been defined by sitting on these orange chairs. Ten years ago, it was Mom lying in the intensive care unit. It was a different kind of intensive care, though, her room was off-limits to visitors. The doctors floated around, godlike. Nobody was giving us any information.

I had been at the peškarija buying a skate fish for lunch when I first received the call. I held the mucousy handles of a plastic bag in one hand, handing the fisherman money with the other, before I managed to wipe my fingers against my jeans to grab my phone. When I picked up, no words came from my dad. Just a coughy whimper, sounding like a *huh*.

"Dad, is everything all right?"

"Your mother. She's in the hospital."

I dropped the bag. The skate slid out on the dirty floor.

When I arrived at the hospital, Dad said that Mom had pulled out the ladder to clean the stained-glass window above the front door. He found her when he was going out for work. She had fallen on the back of her head. "There was bird shit on the glass, and she just couldn't ignore it," he said, and that was the last thing he said that whole day.

He couldn't—or wouldn't—talk, so it fell on me to break the news to Saša. Saša went mute at first too, but then he started crying. I hadn't heard my brother cry since he was a teenager. "But I just talked with her last night," he said, as if I were lying about her condition. "Silvija is pregnant," he said next. "We didn't want to tell anyone before she was at least three months along, but I guess this changes things. Will you tell Mom? If she wakes? If I don't make it there in time?"

"I will," I said, though it was unlikely that would happen. "And congratulations."

I hung up, gutted for the second time that morning.

The doctor finally met us in the hallway at two p.m., after rounds. It struck me as odd that he didn't have an office to receive us in. Or maybe that was on purpose so the meeting wouldn't last as long. Other patients' family members hovered around us, waiting for information on their loved ones, inevitably eavesdropping on ours. The doctor barraged us with words. Trauma to the back of the head, a break in the skull, brain swollen, bleeding in her brainstem, coma. "If she wakes up, she'll be an invalid," he said, as if implying we should pray that she doesn't.

At four-thirty, my phone rang. Vlaho. He had come home from work to an empty apartment. It wasn't that I hadn't thought of him at all since that morning, but every time I did, I made a small excuse to postpone the call for a minute longer, then a minute longer, then another minute, until I'd managed to push him into the corners of my mind. "When did this happen?" he asked after I'd given him a brief breakdown of what was going on.

"This morning."

"This morning!" An accusation. Hurt. A silence that acknowledged the rift between us. "Where do I need to come?"

"Hospital. Intensive care unit."

I should've been relieved he was on his way. But the honest-to-God truth was, I didn't want him there. My pain had worn his face for so long I couldn't disentangle him from it. And yet he came, and he held me, and he cried with me when they told us Mom had passed away.

And here I am on these orange chairs again. Ten years ago, when Mom was dying, I didn't call Vlaho because I needed the space. But now, I need the vanquishing of space. There's nothing I want more than for him to come and hold me again, for his gentle murmur in my ear, for his warmth to unlatch the valves that are keeping my tears locked, and this horror suspended painfully inside me. But my last words to him still ring in my ears, their foulness. *Grow the fuck up.*

Funny how I could address myself the same way.

When I'm coherent and poised enough, I call Saša to break the news to him.

"Ivona," he says by way of hello.

"Saša," I say. "Dad's had another stroke. I'm not sure he'll make it this time."

Saša doesn't answer. In the background, Silvija is giving instructions to the kids, trying to get them dressed for bed. Then, her worried voice, closer to the phone. "What is it, Saša? Everything okay?"

"You sure you're not exaggerating? He made it out okay last time."

I cringe against his words. Only Saša could say that Dad came out of his last stroke okay, but that's a privilege of someone who hasn't been here, who doesn't know Dad's limitations as well as I do.

"He's unconscious," I say, clutching my throat.

"When did this happen?"

"I'm not sure. I wasn't at home. I didn't get him to the hospital in time."

"Where were you?" His question comes out sounding like an accusation.

"What does it matter where I was? I wasn't home."

Saša falls silent, his judgment louder than if he put it into words. I have failed as my father's caretaker. I wasn't there when he needed me most. The pungent smell of Dad's urine still attacks my nostrils. Dad cares so much about being clean, scrubs himself with meticulous rigor every night before bed, his hygiene another way to show the distance he's come from his underprivileged childhood, so all I can think about is how mortified he must have been if he'd been conscious when his bladder hadn't held.

Saša can spare me his indignation, I have plenty of my own.

"I think you should come," I say.

"I'll—" A sharp exhalation as the reality of what I've said to him is slipping inside him, finding a place to release its poisonous roots. "I'll come first thing tomorrow morning." I can imagine my brother's eyes watering, the lump in his throat growing. I know his pain well. Ten years ago, I was the one losing the parent I still hoped I would please someday. A loss of a mother but also of potential is what it was, and now my brother is going through the same thing.

Silvija murmurs something. In my mind's eye, I can see her putting her arms around my brother, stroking his back, comforting him the way I wish Vlaho were consoling me.

We say goodbye and hang up, because we don't have anything else to say to one another.

The only thing connecting my brother and me are our parents. Our mother is gone, and now our father is hanging by a thread, so where does that leave us?

It seems to me we've always been, and always will be, two islands bathing in the same sea with our backs to each other—him facing the sun, me facing the moon, both of us resenting the light the other got. But one of those lights has gone out already, and now the other one is fading too. I guess where it leaves us, then, is in the dark.

The sounds are hushed, lights turned off in most of the rooms, all the doors open so that the nurses can check on the patients as they walk by. Machines bleep, punctuated by soft moans of those who can't sleep, can't tolerate the pain. It's close to midnight. I turn the phone in my hand. The loneliness feels like an affliction, a chronic ailment. I open the group text, The Square, that's now turned into four disconnected, stand-alone points. The last messages are from last night when we were preparing for the trip. Cheerful exchanges between Asier and Marina, about the coves we'd visit, and how much sailing time we could expect.

I put the phone away. In the darkened room down the hall, death looms over my father. I can feel it, licking him, tasting, hovering. I realize, with a hefty dose of irony, that Dad is the only person who was always around, even if his presence was insupportable at times.

I wait longer, until the plastic seat numbs my butt. Until the neon lights of the hallway dim behind my eyelids. Until sleep pulls me under.

"Miss?" Someone's hand nudges my shoulder. It's that nurse from before. Her eyes are tired, but also compassionate. "Would you come with me?"

My legs are paralyzed. I cannot get up.

The knowledge is instant.

Dad is gone.

FIFTY-SIX

HAVING TO ARRANGE A funeral is a ploy to take the mourners' minds off their grief. The thought first occurred to me when Mom died, but it feels even truer now that I'm getting everything ready for my father's burial. Last time, Dad and I split the duties between us. Now there's no one but me. So much to do in such a short period of time.

Saša hasn't arrived yet. He was supposed to drive down in the morning, but Dad died in the meantime, so Saša concluded there was no reason for him to rush. He needed to pack better, and of course, now that it wouldn't be a hospital visit but a funeral, he had to arrange for the kids to stay with Silvija's parents so she could come with him, which also means she'll have to buy some black outfits, because all her wardrobe is eye-smackingly bright-colored.

I arrange for the date of the funeral—a few days out because "everyone hurried to die over the weekend," according to the gruff guy at the cemetery. I guess one needs a connection for a timely burial too.

I call the funeral company and send them Dad's photo and basic information so they can arrange for the death announcement to be printed in the local newspaper. "The mourners?" the woman asks me, and I read her the names: son Saša with wife Silvija, and children Leon, Noa, and Eva; daughter Ivona. It's not lost on me that my name comes both last and unaccompanied.

They will also put up a printed death announcement on the noticeboards scattered around the town: on Branimir's Coast near the town bridge, at the town entrance, on the main square, near the market. News travels fast through the grapevine here, and I wonder how many people will show up to see Dad off. It wouldn't matter to him, he never cared much about tradition. But if there is a heaven, I'm sure my mother is watching from up there, keeping tabs.

A horrifying thought nags at me. When we buried Mom, the grave was empty. But now, Mom is already in there. Will her coffin still be inside? Or have they moved her bones to the part of the grave they call the bone deposit? The whole thing unnerves me, and I wish we had individual graves here in Croatia, rather than family graves with shelves inside, as if they were a fridge to put pork halves in.

Sometimes I wonder if Mom and Dad will bicker in there.

Sometimes, I play out a five-minute argument before I catch myself.

Close to noon, I make some coffee and sit on the terrace. The absence of Dad and the droning of his news is conspicuous and makes my eyes sting.

I put together a list of people to call. Dad's cousins, the few friends he had left. I imagine Vlaho or Marina going into town and seeing my father's photo on the noticeboard. Or someone calling them—everyone knows Marina after all—and asking, *Did you know Ivona's father died? Isn't she Vlaho's ex?* The discomfort of it churns in my gut. For ten years, my father was Vlaho's father-in-law. And even though they were never close, and haven't sustained a relationship after our divorce, it feels wrong that Vlaho should find out about his death from someone else. But the thought of talking to him is equally unbearable. Not just because of our fight. But because if I call him, if I so much as hear his voice, I'm not sure I'll be able to hold it together. It might be the final crack that undoes me, and I can't allow that. There's still so much to do.

So I open the group text and type the message:

"my dad died last night"

The phone starts ringing before I even put it down. It's Marina. Her tone is deferential as she asks me the basics of what, how, and when. After we go over the funeral information, a sense of finality frames the silence between us. I'm thinking how there's nothing more to be said. I want to apologize for my harsh words and everything else I've done, and yet what good would that do when I want her husband?

"Have you arranged for the music yet?" Marina asks. "One of my father's friends plays a violin at funerals. I could get in touch with him if you'd like."

Her tone is calm, resigned, as if she too is accepting the fact that after what happened on the sailboat, we won't be able to remain friends. Recognizing also, perhaps, that in that foul word she used—fucking—she showed more emotion, more protectiveness of the life she's built with Vlaho than even she might have expected.

She must have thought she could control it. Bring us together so that we could quench our thirst for one another with mist instead of mouthfuls. But maybe she's realizing, as I am right now, how naïve that had been. How vastly she underestimated the power of this kind of love, having never experienced it herself.

"I haven't had the chance yet," I say, touched. "Thank you, that would be nice."

—

When Vlaho and then Asier call soon after, I don't answer. I cut the calls and type a message instead. "sorry, can't talk, talking to the cemetery," even though that's a lie.

"I'm so sorry for your loss," Asier types back. "I've postponed my flight. I'm here if you need anything."

Despite all that's happened, I smile and press the phone against my chest, as if his energy could enter me from there.

Vlaho's text says, "are you home? can i come over?"

To him, I type, "running some errands. i'll call you later." I know there'll be a point when I won't be able to avoid an actual conversation. Vlaho is the only one of the three who knew not just my father but all the facets of our complicated relationship. All the convoluted ways I loved my father and resented him and sometimes hated him at the same time. All the ways my father loved me, but failed to understand me. But I'm not ready to go there yet. I have no filter, I might ask more of him than he's willing to give right now, and I can't bear to hear him say no.

FIFTY-SEVEN

IT'S A FEAT, BUT in a couple of days I manage to get everything ready. I order the platters of prosciutto and cheese to be served in our home at the wake, give instructions to the florist for the farewell wreath with Saša's and my name on it, and another one with Saša's, Silvija's, and the kids' names. I arrange for the funeral car to take Dad's body from the morgue to the chapel; change the sheets on Saša's bed to prepare for his and Silvija's arrival tomorrow morning; successfully avoid both Asier's and Vlaho's calls and limit our communication to texts. "busy, busy," I say each time. "so much to do, so little time."

Between the delirium of fresh grief, all the texts, calls, and the telegram condolence cards that fall out in heaps whenever I open our mailbox, I almost miss the two emails that arrive in my inbox. The first one is from the Croatian Employment Services. It's mercifully succinct.

> *We are sorry to inform you that your application for self-employment aid has been declined. Unfortunately, the Committee didn't find that you have the relevant work experience in the field you want to start the business in, or that you have successfully demonstrated that there are enough potential business partners to make your business plan viable.*

As soon as I read those words, I want to scream at the screen, at those fools who wrote this nonsense. Of course, I don't have the relevant work experience. If I did, I wouldn't be needing self-employment aid. The urge to crumple my phone and hurl it into a wall is overwhelming. But what's the point of getting upset? Absurdities like these are the air we breathe here, so I push it down to where I store all my defeats, my legs leaden with them.

I mindlessly move a dozen newsletters and spam emails that got through the filter into the trash folder, and almost miss it, the subject line being as spammy as they get: *Financing just came through from the EU*, but then just as I'm about to hit delete I recognize the Italian scientist's name as the sender. If I'm still interested, she'd like me to send a CV and a cover letter, and we can do an interview via Zoom. It's a formality, she says, she already knows she wants me for the job. She discloses what they'll be able to offer if I'm interested. It's not a hefty amount of money, and I wouldn't be eligible for a relocation package. But she offers to help me navigate the difficult Florentine apartment market herself, which I assume is more than what she does for other people, a nod to the way we hit it off seven months ago in Split.

I turn around in my excitement, almost yelling "Hey, Dad!" but then I catch myself, the words on the brink of coming out, in the place where they're the most difficult to contain.

In the garden in front of me, the grass glistens with morning dew, the rusty leaves of hibiscus peppering the ground. A strange sensation comes over me, like I'm detached from this place I've called home my entire life, like I don't belong here now that everyone else is gone. But then I realize, it's not just this house, it's this town, this country. Croatia has been rejecting me all my life, and I refused to accept it. She's made every step of my life difficult. A climate where the favored succeed over the capable. A place where adoptions take decades and sometimes never happen. A place that offers a chance of free education but no work in your field of expertise, and then denies aid for self-employment as if it's your fault that you couldn't obtain the required work experience. And yet, I've kept binding myself to it. But it's over. I'm done. I'm ready to set myself free, cut the last thread holding me here.

FIFTY-EIGHT

EARLY THE NEXT MORNING, I park at the Lovorun main gate. There are people milling about, construction workers building additional walls. I have to hand it to Asier, the place looks good. He's honoring the traditional aesthetic with the drystone walls, instead of concrete ones that would have come cheaper.

I open my trunk and lift out a chain saw. The workers shoot me a wary look as I walk through the smaller gate and into the olive grove. The trees are lush and green, basking in the morning sun. Olive fruits hang in clusters, like constellations in the night sky. The yield would've been good this year, I think, and for a moment, I almost backtrack, change my mind.

I take the chain saw and approach the first tree. I pull the cord and the saw roars to life. One by one, I saw the branches off the old trunk, this act of maiming cutting into my own soul. My vision blurs. My shoulders burn with exertion. After each branch falls, I feel so exhausted, like I won't be able to lift my arms anymore, but then I do, over and over again down the three rows of trees.

The workers gather along the small iron gate, watching with indignation. What I'm doing is sacrilege. Olive trees have earned an almost mythical status in these parts, and seeing healthy trees get castrated like this is no better than seeing someone desecrate a church by pissing in it. Their murmurs of disapproval travel through the short intervals of chain saw silence. But I know what I'm doing. Early fall isn't the best time to transplant olive trees, but if I cut the foliage way back, it will reduce the shock and give the trees a fighting chance when they're transplanted.

Once I'm done sawing, I call out to the excavator operator standing with the other workers by the gate and ask him to dig out the root balls with caution. The excavator is jerky and imprecise. I shout instructions over the loud roar of the engine.

The truck comes at two p.m., along with the owner of the mill where I used to take the yield. The two men cover the root balls in burlap and pile the trees onto the trailer. When the trees are loaded, the mill owner gives me a wad of cash, and I put the money into my back pocket without counting. "Thanks for thinking of me," he says. "There's a big demand for old trees like these."

I ask him if he knows where they'll end up, and he says, "A friend of mine is renovating his estate on Dugi Otok."

I'm ashamed for not being able to hold back tears. For the first time since I found my father on the floor, they come, hot and fat. Stringed like pearls.

The man looks at me with the type of understanding only another olive lover can have. "They'll have a good home there. They're in good hands."

I nod. He leaves. The workers disperse. The money in my pocket burns like Judas's thirty pieces of silver. I could've refused it, but what difference would that have made, except to make me look even more pathetic, even less in control. I turn to the land.

Its emptiness is shocking. The holes in the ground are like gunshot wounds, bleeding red dirt, gaping in the yellowed grass. The piles of cut branches lie scattered around. I'm tired but I can't leave it like this, Baba's land. It deserves more. I pile the branches into big heaps, then take the chain saw again to cut the thickest ones into smaller pieces.

I start a fire in the center of the field so that it cannot spread. Slowly, I feed it the remnants of the boughs, of my dreams, of myself.

"Hey, Gorgeous!" Asier's voice comes from behind me.

I turn to face him.

"The workers called," he says. "Said a madwoman came out here with a chain saw and cut down the olives."

I can't speak, so I shrug. Seeing him here is making all my emotions burn closer to my throat. If I say anything, I might fall apart completely. He opens his arms to me. I want nothing more than the containment of those arms, but he is wearing a blindingly white shirt, and I'm covered with sweat and dirt and ashes. "I can't. I'll get you dirty."

He smiles. "You can get me dirty anytime you want."

I start laughing, but when he folds me in an embrace, the relief is so instant that the laughs turn into hiccups turn into sobs. "It's okay. Let it all out," he says, kissing my sooty hair, but instead of enticing my tears to come more freely, it makes them retreat. I don't deserve this. I don't deserve him after all I've done.

"Come with me to London," he says. We're sitting in the dry grass, the flames devouring the last of the twigs and branches. The sun is hanging low between the islands in the distance. A round bug with an emerald exoskeleton weaves its way through the blades, and it strikes me that it has never seen its own beauty, the gemlike glint of its dress.

Asier is looking at me with his slate eyes. I can imagine an entire life with him, free from the constraints of everything I've ever known. A chance to reinvent myself. Enough time to see where I fit into this world, a thing I should have determined long ago, but that continues to elude me. But that means giving up on Vlaho. I've been plenty unfair to Asier already—to both of them. And even though I don't know if Vlaho will choose me yet, I can't drag Asier through my own muck anymore. "I'm not sure that's such a good idea," I say.

"I think it's a great idea." He turns his gaze to the flames in front of us. "Look, I'm not proposing that you marry me or move in with me or anything.

But a change of scenery might be good for you. Stay with me for a while. I can show you around town. We have the best gardens and parks. And you could water my plants while I'm away." He nudges me with his shoulder. "Or you can come travel with me." He looks around the empty plot of land, and adds, more quietly, "There's nothing left holding you here anyway."

His words coalesce between us like mercury. I think of my dad, lying in a cold morgue. Of the olives, on the ferryboat somewhere toward Dugi Otok, shocked into silence after what I've done to them. Of Marina, and the painful acknowledgment between us the last time we talked, that our friendship has come to an end. And Vlaho. How I already bet all I had on him and lost, but all of me wants to bet on him again. Again and again for as long as it takes.

Asier puts his arm around me. His embrace is a mirror, reflecting the least flattering version of me. Someone who cheats, who does stuff behind other people's backs. Someone who inflicts the kind of pain I always resented others inflicting on me. For the cool businessman I initially took him for, Asier's been nothing but wonderful to me, and I've not paid him in kind.

"There is something you should know." I reach for the last few branches and toss them into the flame, unable to look at him. "Vlaho and I . . . Something happened. We . . . Something happened, and we haven't resolved it yet."

Asier lets his arm slide off my shoulder. "I see."

"I'm sorry," I say. I'm always apologizing to him, it seems, then ending up doing more stuff worth apologizing for.

He picks up a stick and draws infinity signs in the dirt, then erases them. "We never spoke about being exclusive."

"That's such an American concept," I say. "Or foreign. I wouldn't know."

"Oh?" He grins. "How so?"

"Here, you're either with someone or not." I feel hot in my toes and fingers for saying this, because this means that, at least by my standards, I've cheated on him. By the sound of his silence, it must be what he's thinking too.

I rub my face with my dirty, ashen hands. "You really got to see me at my worst," I say. First with the ghosting, now with sleeping with Vlaho behind his back. "This is not who I am." But even as I'm saying it, I wonder if that's true. I wonder if, given the chance, I wouldn't have done it all over again, because this is what happens when you want something so badly, the way I want Vlaho. "You deserve better."

"I've seen some good parts of you too," he teases, but then adds more seriously, "And don't we all?"

I remember what he said to me when we were watching the Perseids, when he quoted Heraclitus. That there is an impermanence to all things, both good and bad. I thought it sounded either cynical or superbly Zen then. How he shrugged off the pain of being rejected over his acne, or denied the ache of living his uprooted life, his mother dying while he was still so young. Now I can't help but think there's a sort of defeatism to it. That it's a coping mechanism. A way to keep the pain in check.

The sun has dipped into the sea, the fire has turned to embers.

"It's late, we should head back," I say.

He gets up, and I know this is it, this is goodbye.

I run my gaze along the terrain. It is pockmarked where the olives were, and are now gone. Imperfect, like the skin along Asier's cheeks.

We face each other.

"I'm sorry about your shirt," I say, the greasy motor oil stains and ash a mirror reflection of the filthy composition on my own T-shirt.

"This old thing?" He smiles, though knowing him, it's probably an Armani. He waves the stains off, but I can sense his hurt for this parting of ways. Perhaps he's thinking, as I am, about our bodies together, our laughs over coffee, the way we fed each other ripe fruit at the beach, and how all that is over.

I kiss him on the lips for the last time, taste the ash and salt gathered on them.

FIFTY-NINE

WHEN I GET BACK home, Vlaho's car is in my driveway. I close my eyes for a moment. I'd hoped for a long, hot shower, a quick snack, the oblivion of sleep. Time to process what happened with the olives, with Asier. I'm not ready for another earthquake.

As I exit the car, Vlaho comes from around the house, carrying an empty tote. "You're back," he says. "I tried to call you, but you weren't answering." He stands in front of me. "I'm sorry." Then more quietly, more intimately, "I'm sorry about your dad."

I nod, a hollowness creeping up my throat. It would be so easy to fool myself that he's here because he's choosing me. But I know that's not true. He's here because my father's death devastated me, and he can't bear not to offer comfort.

"I figured you wouldn't have time to cook, so I brought you some food," he says. "Put it on your terrace because you weren't answering the door, or your phone."

"My phone died," I say. "I forgot to recharge it last night, and this morning it just—" Words leave me at the overwhelming thought of where I was this morning, managing the whole olive operation. This morning, when those olives still stood there, gnarly and vibrant. It seems so two lifetimes ago.

He walks over to me opening his arms, and caught in the space between us is all my sorrow with nowhere to go, like a shoal of frantic minnows about to be caught in a net. He closes the distance, and the minnows are now pressed between our chests, thrashing, fighting for air.

He pulls back a little bit. “You smell like smoke.”

“I had some work to do at Lovorun.”

He stiffens, but doesn’t ask the obvious question, what sort of work could be so important that I had to do it the day before the burial, and on a piece of land that doesn’t belong to me anymore. Perhaps he’s afraid that if he asks, the answer will involve Asier.

“I made you some chicken soup, and polpete with mashed potatoes. It’s all on the table down on the terrace. The polpete and mashed potatoes should still be warm, but you’ll need to reheat the soup.”

“Thank you,” I say, even though I don’t have any appetite.

Worry forms two sharp lines between his eyebrows. “You know what? Why don’t you go take a shower, and I’ll reheat it for you.”

I can’t make myself tell him to go away, so I nod.

I unlock the door and let us both in. He goes to fetch the food from the terrace while I retreat to my bathroom. My skin pinks at the hot water, the pain in my arms releasing under heat. The relief is only temporary. When the muscles cool overnight, the pain will be unbearable. That chain saw weighed a ton, it seems impossible I’d wielded it for as long as I did. It was like I was possessed.

I turn the shower off, wrap my hair in a towel. I put on shorts and a T-shirt and go into the kitchen. The fumes of the rich chicken broth bring me back to those long-ago days when Mom would feed spoonfuls of chicken soup to me while I was sick, and I would deem being sick not such a horrible thing after all.

“It smells divine,” I say.

“I can’t find any noodles,” he says at the same time.

I open the drawer where we usually keep them. “It looks like we’re out.”

We.

I correct myself inwardly.

"Do you have any semolina? I could make gnocchi."

He takes out a ceramic dish, cracks two eggs in it, and whisks them. I pass him the semolina. He pours the grains inside and whisks some more. I take the salt container and drop a pinch over the dish. He adds a drizzle of olive oil. I marvel at the familiarity with which our bodies occupy the same space. Our minds might have forgotten how to be together, but our bodies still remember the choreography.

In those early days after we moved from Zagreb to Zadar, when we lived in that shabby little apartment in the suburb, this was the dance of the day. He would come home from work, and unbutton his shirt, and I would slide it off his back and wedge a kiss between his shoulder blades, in the very center of him, and he would release an unwinding hum. He would put on a sweatshirt, and move around me in our miniature kitchen, taking out plates and forks and knives, two of everything, and I would finish up whatever was on the stove, some version of vegetable stew usually, because that's all we could afford back then, and we'd sit down to eat in silence, not because we didn't have anything to say to each other, but because we didn't need words to begin with. Happiness is like grief that way, often silent.

I lean against the counter as he brings the soup to a boil and drops teaspoonfuls of the batter inside. The gnocchi sink first, then pop back up. He turns the hob off, ladles the soup into a bowl, and puts it on the table for me. "Eat," he orders, softly, and turns to the sink. On my way to the table, I stop behind him, and I can't help it, I place a kiss between his shoulder blades.

When I'm done eating, he orders me to the living room while he takes care of the dishes. I remove the towel from my head and, with my hair still moist, curl up on the couch. Too tired to keep my eyes open, I listen to him rustling through the kitchen. It's such a comforting sound after these few lonely days, the clatter of something as mundane as tidying up proof enough that life really does go on. I settle into it, and the next thing, all is black.

Then, his hand on my shoulder. A gentle stir.

I open my eyes. I'm covered with a blanket that wasn't there before.

He's kneeling by the couch, in front of me.

"Sorry," I say, "I dozed off."

"It's okay. You've had quite a day . . . quite a few days." He's so close I can smell the scent of his laundry soap, warmed by the humid, nutty scent of his skin. It's hard to believe it's been just three days since we made love. Since I said those harsh words to him.

I wish I could take them back. Not because I don't believe they're true. He's handled everything, *everything* so poorly. Seeking me out before he figured things out on his own, just because he couldn't bear seeing me with someone else. Marrying someone he didn't love in the first place, only to have children. Choosing to stay married all these years, leading some sort of a half life, not unhappy, but not fulfilled either. But so did I. I handled everything so poorly too.

The need to turn back time, to play it all out differently, is so powerful it makes my lungs burn.

"I'm gonna go now," he says. In the background, the soft purr of the dishwasher. His warm hand wraps around mine. His face is so close my lips become eager. Around us, the house is big, ballooning into something larger and scarier the deeper the night gets.

I take his hand in both of mine. I can feel it, in my bones, his reticence, but I don't want to acknowledge it. It's too painful to even think that this new chance is slipping through my fingers. I had promised myself I wouldn't ask, that he needs to choose me this time, but I am hanging by a thread and I don't have the luxury of waiting anymore.

"Come back to me, Vlaho," I say. My voice is full and hollow at the same time, it's hard to keep it steady.

He winces, as if each of my words is its own razor. I know I should stop, I've already said too much, asked for too much, but the words start coming as if the dam has broken, letting the deluge out. "We screwed up, both of us did, but we can still make it work. We're not even forty. We still have so much life ahead. So much life. Please."

I might have martyred myself back then, but I'm not that person anymore. His children are here, aren't they? They are alive and well, and it wouldn't be such a disaster if Vlaho lived with me instead of with their mother. They'd have two homes instead of one, but they'd be loved in both. "It will be fine," I say. "Your kids will be fine."

Vlaho is looking at me through damp eyes. "We shouldn't be talking about this today, you need to rest before—"

"No." I snatch my hand from his grasp. "I don't care how raw I am. This," I point between us, "this is what's making me raw, and it won't go away until you decide."

Vlaho sits next to me on the couch.

"I want to," he says. "I want to so much."

His whole body is invested in each word he is saying, lumbered with the truth, and the longing, and the pain. "But I can't."

He puts his head in his hands, and I can feel the full horrible breadth of his want and his impotence at the same time. "Someone thought we would be fine too, whatever they threw at us," he says. "Because we were kids, and kids look so sturdy and resilient because they don't understand their needs the way grown-ups do. They don't know how to put them into words. But kids *feel* what they can't understand, Ivona. They're anything but resilient. I mean, look at us, look where it got us."

The misery in his eyes imprints itself on me, and I can see what he's saying, how the seed of insecurity planted in both our childhoods is exactly what got us here today. Making us both so starved to be seen while shying away from it at the same time, relegating ourselves to the shadows because we didn't know how to claim the spotlight. How, because of this, we shone light onto each other in all the wrong moments, only to leave each other in the dark at precisely the wrong times too.

But above his need to be seen, there will always be this—his need to see his children. For his children to feel seen when he wasn't. This is the difference between us, I realize. I will never know how that feels, I will always ever long for myself to be seen.

"I need to do better as a father," he says.

His decision is gravity itself, and I let it draw me in, maul me, reduce me to nothing.

I'm undone. Obliterated.

But even as I'm sitting in the debilitating silence of it, there is this. The smallest flicker of satisfaction for seeing Vlaho draw the line.

For he may not have chosen me, but he has chosen himself for the first time.

I've never seen him set a boundary, with me or anyone else. In a way, it was what cost us our marriage. His entire life is a sum of his countless concessions to others. Built on him giving up on himself, betraying himself, time after time.

And here he is now, drawing a line, with me of all people.

I should feel hurt, but I'm strangely elated. Because, what better proof of our love?

Because, we don't set boundaries most easily with strangers or those who mistreat us. We set them with those who make us feel loved and safe, who hold space for us to admit our needs and limits, even when they're the ones paying the price for it.

Despite the pain it's causing me, his rejection is the greatest gift he's ever given me. I made him feel safe. I made him feel loved. I made it necessary for him to choose himself. To hold fast by his convictions, to be true to who he is, even when it hurts someone else, someone he loves. Because, otherwise, what would be the point of having him? I only ever wanted the whole of him, the truest of him, or nothing.

"I get it," I tell him. "I do." If I had children, there's no doubt this is exactly what I'd do too.

He untenses a little, pulls his hand through my damp hair. It knots around his fingers, it too unwilling to let go of him. "Maybe one day, when the kids are grown, we'll find our way back to each other. Because I can't imagine this ever ending, what you and I have."

It's an absurd hope, but I nod nonetheless.

"How did we manage to squander it all so spectacularly?" I ask, gathering all our moments as if they're scattered grains of sugar and salt, sweet and biting at the same time. All that love. All that pain we inflicted on one another. All this insatiable yearning.

He says nothing because there's nothing there to say.

"I don't think you and Marina should come to the funeral tomorrow," I say. My voice is calm enough that it's clear I'm not asking this from a place of anger. It's just unimaginable, seeing him there, inaccessible. One more thing for me to mourn.

"Okay," he says.

I reach to touch his hair, his face. He nestles his cheek in my palm, closes his eyes, releases a breath. All the love I have for him gathers in my center, and I will for him to feel the full extent of it, for my aura to become so infused with it that it envelops us both. "Stay with me tonight," I say.

He scoots closer, kisses my hair. "Okay."

—

We go to my bed, curl up against each other, fully clothed. I try to keep my eyes open, stay awake to absorb and memorize the feel of him against me, the specific smell of him, the way my head fits just under his jaw. The drumming of his heart. But I'm so tired. So damn tired, I close my eyes.

—

When I open them again, he is gone. One blink is all it took for the night to turn into dawn, and for Vlaho to vanish from my arms, this time forever.

SIXTY

I MANAGE TO HARDEN myself for the funeral. At the chapel, I stand beside my dad's casket with Saša and Silvija. The river of people snakes around the coffin as they offer their condolences. *I'm sorry for your loss*, they say. *Your father was a good man.* I look at the casket that seems too small to contain a man of Dad's size, and think, he wasn't particularly good. Not that he was bad either. He was the way he was—honorable, strict, decisive, but flawed as we all are. He was human, I want to tell them, and so the loss of him is as unique as his fingerprint was.

Mom would've been happy with the turnout. So many people, many of whom I've never met or heard of. *I worked with your father*, they say. *I knew him from the army*, they say. *I knew him from his village.* All knowing who he was at different points in his life. So many versions of my dad that are unfamiliar to me.

There are a few of Saša's friends from high school. When they approach us to pay their respects, the absence of my own friends is even more conspicuous. I look outside and wonder if Vlaho is respecting my wishes that he and Marina not come. I wonder if that was really my wish in the first place. But he is not there.

Someone's arms close around me. Tara. I'd texted her but didn't expect her to come all the way from Split. "I'm so sorry, Ivona," she says, and this almost destabilizes me, almost makes me cry.

I receive hands, and shake them, and murmur the required thank-yous, and think about my dad. How separate he is, lying inside that coffin, from all of us. How none of this matters to him, how none of this matters anyway.

This thought follows me as the pallbearers put the coffin on the funeral gurney. The people carrying the wreaths line up before the gurney, and the rest of us line up behind, first my brother and his wife and I, and then everyone else. Over the open grave, the priest gives a brief speech about passage of life, and how my father—whom he didn't know—left a big mark on all of us who've gathered here today, and I think about the one mark he wanted to leave, the Lovorun hotel, and how I was the one to deny him this wish. I also think about the marks we all leave on one another, willingly or not. Gentle touches we offer. Scars we inflict.

When his coffin has been lowered into the grave and shoved onto one of the concrete shelves, I throw one white rose in for him, and another for my mom. I don't wait for Saša and Silvija to do the same as I retreat toward my car. At home, everything is ready for the wake, but I won't be there to see it through. There's nothing left for me there, all the ties already neatly cut. It is just a place, a house, not a home.

A single suitcase in the back seat of my crappy little car. A car that's not meant to travel far, that I bought for my very contained life in a very contained town of this small country and my curtailed place in it. A car that's no more made or destined for big adventures than I am, but that's going to get one just the same.

Inside the suitcase, some underwear, socks, a few trusted T-shirts, an old hoodie. A couple of pairs of jeans, one blue, one black, so I'm set for any occasion. A couple of towels, one big, one small. The T-shirt Vlaho left on the night we laid all our cards open after a decade of hiding our hands. A journal with rich golden intarsia that Asier brought me from London, with a couple of olive twigs from Lovorun pressed between the pages. An ordinary blue pen. An old, tattered wallet with a note folded inside, a perceptive teacher once responding to a girl in pain, a girl who remained in pain, but who is now tired of pain. A printed email from the Italian scientist, saying to get in touch if I need anything. Need is all I have right now.

And perhaps a little potential.

PART FIVE

BEARINGS

SIXTY-ONE

FLORENCE. RHYTHMS AND CADENCES of a new town, of a new self. Beauty that is similar to the one I know from my hometown, but bolder, grander, more imposing. No sea. Hard to get my bearings without the ground always sloping toward the sea.

New old habits. Drinking coffee every morning in a cafe at Piazza Santo Spirito. The sound of Italian all around me, memories of Šime, the Italian teacher, and of Marina. A question unanswered: Where is she, what is she doing? Are she and Vlaho still sleeping in the same bed, waking up together? I'm sure they still live together, that was the whole point of Vlaho renouncing me—us—but I can't imagine that after everything that happened, things between them stayed exactly as they'd been.

In a paper bag next to my feet, a dry-cleaned, ironed white lab coat. I inhabit it intimately now, six months after I first received it. I know its coarseness and hardiness the way the skin of a woman knows the touch of her lover. Tighter across the breasts and hips, looser around the stomach and arms.

Pasta. So much pasta that I might need a new lab coat soon. It's not that it's so delicious, it's that it tastes of home.

Homesickness. A nostalgia that catches me by surprise at the craziest, most unexpected times. At dawn on Sunday when I'm between sleep and wakefulness, and the church's tower bell starts clanking, inviting people to Mass. When the sun filters through windows a certain way, the motes dancing in the same circles I watched so many times in my room back home. The sight of the babuška when I open the drawer where I keep my documents. In a restaurant, the taste of fennel soup bringing me back to the dry summery scent of its wild cousin at Lovorun.

Asier. Who sometimes passes through town and takes me out for coffee or dinner. Whom I sometimes invite back to my apartment for a night spent next to the warm body of someone I hold so dear. Asier, showing me photos of Lovorun. "The infinity pool looks good," I say, though it pains me to admit it. The olives, at least, have been salvaged, or I'd like to believe that they were. That they managed to take root somewhere on Dugi Otok, maybe the part of it that overlooks Kornati National Park, the place where Vlaho and I made love the last time.

Vlaho. Opening Instagram religiously with my morning coffee at Piazza Santo Spirito. Looking for a green circle around his profile photo. "Only close friends can view this story," the green circle implies, but I believe it is intended for one person alone. This, the only means of communication between us since we last talked.

In his stories, sometimes a photo. Of an olive tree. Of the sea, blue like forget-me-nots. Of the town bridge. Of my family home, shutters closed over my room window. Of a chestnut husk in his hand, tips of his fingers charred with ash, looking like an offering.

Other times, a photo of a note, scribbled in his slanted handwriting. The same handwriting I remember from the Post-its he used to leave all over our home. A note that talks of longing. Of homesickness too, for home is not a place, it's a person. A story intended for one, viewed only by one.

My world tipping ever so slightly in his direction, as it always does.

ACKNOWLEDGMENTS

MY MOST HEARTFELT THANKS to my agent, Abby Walters at CAA. My life keeps changing in ways I never could have imagined because of that first email you sent me. I didn't know it at the time, but the way you worded it was so quintessentially you—enthusiastic and warm, efficient, and professional. That combination, of course, makes you the perfect advocate for me. Thank you for having the courage to take on a Croatian writer writing in her second language, and for moving mountains to carve out a place for my book in the world.

I'm also indebted to the rest of the team at CAA, especially my amazing UK rights agent, John Ash, for making sure that *Slanting Towards the Sea* finds the perfect home in the UK, and my fabulous foreign rights agent, Gabby Fetters. My gratitude also to Berni Vann and Lauren Holland.

My deepest thanks to Hana Park, my editor at Simon & Schuster. I knew you were the perfect editor for this book the moment you told me how you saw Ivona. Your brilliant editorial vision made this book the best version of itself, without compromising any of its essence. I'm forever grateful for your astute guidance and incisive line edits, as well as your openness to collaboration. Thank you for believing so wholeheartedly in this book and me, and for making this journey possible.

My effusive gratitude to the entire Simon & Schuster team; the inimitable and keen-eyed editor Carina Guiterman for her support; Amanda Mulholland, Samantha Hoback, Jonathan Evans, Rick Willett, and everyone else whose combined efforts turned *Slanting Towards the Sea* from a manuscript into a real-life book. Special thanks to Jackie Seow and Maddy Angstreich for creating the cover of my dreams, and to Wendy Blum for the incredible interior design. Also to Shannon Hennessey and Tyanni Niles, for their tireless efforts in connecting *Slanting* with readers.

To my wonderful UK editor, Dredhëza Maloku, and Marigold Atkey, the extraordinary publisher at Daunt Books Publishing—it is such an honor to be a part of a list as outstanding as Daunt's. I'm indebted to the whole Daunt team for the remarkable care and attention they've brought to *Slanting*. Special thanks also to my publicist, Jimena Gorraez Belmar.

To Nita Collins, my fellow book coach, thank you for being the best writing partner I could've wished for. Writing this book would have taken years longer if not for our biweekly sessions and your encouragement. Our conversations gave me the space to define and fortify what I wanted to achieve, and your edits pushed me to express myself in the clearest way possible.

Thank you to Barbara Boyd, another one of my book coaching colleagues. That one session we had early on in my writing process forever changed the trajectory of this novel.

To Mary Incontro. Our friendship has given me more soul food than you will ever know. Your belief in me, first as your book coach, then as your friend, and ultimately as a writer, changed me in ways I will never be able to define, but I feel their effects daily.

Thank you, Mary, and also Ariane Elizabeth Scholl, and Mate Marin, for reading the early draft of this novel, and giving me the confidence I needed to start querying. I'm also deeply grateful to the luminous Reema Zaman, for all the support and friendship.

To my writing group, Rubies, I so appreciate your encouragement over the years. Special thanks to Kitty Johnson, whose proposal that we share a paragraph of our new work on one of our calls prompted me to write what is now the first scene in *Slanting*; and to Natalie Dale, MD, whose medical expertise helped me depict Ivona's infertility with more accuracy.

To my family of book coaches at Author Accelerator, and its founder Jennie Nash, thank you for the wealth of knowledge, and your unwavering support throughout the years. I'm also indebted to the Women's Fiction Writers Association—being a part of this incredible community shaped me into the writer I am today. Enormous thanks to members of my Writers' Book Club as well. I've learned so much from and alongside you.

The painting featured on the cover is a work of a Croatian painter Hana Tischler. The synchronicities that had to occur to connect us—two Croatian artists establishing our careers abroad—are nothing short of astounding. Hana, your talent is dazzling, but what moves me every time I see this cover is that you captured Ivona so accurately—both physically and emotionally—before you even knew she existed.

This novel is a work of fiction, but one aspect of it is inspired by my own life. Nine years ago, my father suffered a massive stroke, with consequences even more dire than the ones Ivona's father struggles with in the book. My father's limitations are many, but the one that hurts us all the most is his impaired speech. The part of his brain that connects words with their meanings was burnt in the stroke, rendering even the most basic communication difficult. My mother is my father's sole caregiver. The stroke happened on the eve of my parents' retirement, and it pains me that they didn't get the chance to enjoy their golden years. To my parents, I am in awe of the grace and the stamina with which you are enduring this situation.

To you, my reader. Time is, alongside health, our most valuable commodity, and I'm grateful beyond words that you chose to read *Slanting Towards the Sea* among so many other books. What a privilege to enter your life, if briefly, with my words.

Finally, to my daughters, Jasna and Iris, and my husband, Juraj, thank you for the haven we've created. It made it possible (and necessary) to become the truest version of myself. Here's to always choosing ourselves, and each other.

ABOUT THE AUTHOR

LIDIJA HILJE is a Croatian writer and certified book coach. After earning a law degree, she spent a decade practicing in Croatian courts before transitioning to book coaching and writing in English as her second language. She lives in Zadar, Croatia, with her husband and two daughters. *Slanting Towards the Sea* is her first novel.